Refugees
Among the Lines

by

Roger Johnson

The principal characters in this novel are fictional.
Major historical figures are real.

ISBN   9979-8-9872510-2-7

Email: rogerj47@gmail.com
Website: Roger-Johnson.com

To three great friends who read all my books, either in manuscript or book form and support my efforts.

Bob Harr

Elizabeth Scrimgeour

Kal Fallon

And to all those who have read most of my books. Thank you!

Acknowledgements

Lionel Rosenblatt for answering my questions about the Indochinese refugee crises in the 1970s and 1980s. Lionel is a true humanitarian and a lifelong advocate for refugees. He represents those unselfish men and women who devote their lives to improving others.

Joe DesGeorges for formatting and cover design help on this and my previous novels.

Books in Print

Historical Fiction

Laments for the Dead

Layers of Darkness

America's Soul

Refugees Among the Lines

Girls'/Women's Basketball Novels (Cheetah Basketball Series)

On Point

Gifts: The Return

Coach Izzy

Hoops and Seeds: A Pause in the Harvest

Other novels in the queue

The Why Station

The Hill, '67: A Love Affair

Refugees Among the Lines

by
Roger Johnson

IngramSpark

2023

Refugees Among the Lines

Joining hands, the "criminals" said a prayer, which seemed
to be equal parts grace, entreaty, and confession.

"Whenever you find yourself on the side of the majority, it is time to pause and reflect."

Mark Twain

SEGMENT I
TRANSITION
1975-1977

1

Paul Garrity jerked awake and then shivered, a whisper from a not too distance past. Reestablishing where he was, he shook his head and grinned slightly. He leaned over to massage his ankle. Sitting in his truck parked outside Frontera, the state prison for women in Corona, California, Paul thought about the last time he had seen Abby, sometime around 1968, at a late-night gathering in his apartment at the University of Colorado. Seven years ago. She had been screaming at her date, Paul's friend Jonas Cullen, about his nonaction regarding the war, and then struck him on the shoulder—hard—and Jonas had recoiled. Every conversation with Abby was a rant about Vietnam or civil rights. She was always the most committed person in the room, always the angriest. *The Explosive Abby Archer!* Some months after that, she left Boulder, disappearing for a semester or so. Paul wondered what six years in jail had done to her, living in an eight-by-six-foot cell among women whose main concerns did not coincide with hers. He knew what incarceration had done to him. Different situation, but desperate and damaging, nonetheless.

Paul looked out over the prison fences and guard towers to the hills beyond. A deceptively peaceful setting for a prison, for a compound designed ostensibly for reform but simply to house the offensive and undesirable of society; women who had been abandoned for the most part. He wanted desperately to walk inside the compound to see and feel the conditions of those like Abby who had their freedoms stripped away. He had experienced that feeling of abandonment once. He shivered again.

Paul had arrived at the prison before sunrise, driving two hours in the dark from Oxnard to avoid the massive traffic flows on the 101 and 134. He wasn't going to be late even if it meant arriving early and delaying a work project another day. Abby's parents informed him that she would be released precisely at 8:00 a.m. in front of receiving—now releasing. Besides her six years behind the fences, Abby was to serve 30 months of parole. Abby's father, a Unitarian minister in Chicago, negotiated the residence arrangement: a private home instead of public housing, an advantage many parolees don't have, especially poor felons. Paul remembered his one meeting with Abby's parents four months earlier when they flew out to visit and set up arrangements for her reentry into society. He met them at Ontario Airport and drove them to this facility. Prior to this, they had talked on the phone several times after he suggested Abby serve her parole in California. They had been preparing to take her back to Chicago for parole. Nice people. Gentle on the surface but committed to service in the Chicago area, union organizers once, who now ran a soup kitchen on the east side of the Pilsen neighborhood. Mrs. Archer had hugged Paul, grateful for the months of letters he and Abby were exchanging, part of the lifeline that had been thrown to her when she was drowning. Reverend Archer wanted to know what Paul's intentions were. All Paul promised was that he and Mose and Sally Robinson would provide a safe environment for Abby where she could fulfill her parole requirements: no drugs, no contact with other parolees, close to colleges so she could complete her degree, free room and board. Reverend Archer rejected that last part. He would send a check each month until Abby started earning a paycheck, and then she would be required to pay her fair share. Paul understood Reverend Archer's purpose immediately. The Archers came to Oxnard the next day in a rental car to inspect the Robinsons' house. Modest but with three bedrooms, within walking distance of the docks where Abby might be able to get a job.

A Black woman exited the prison compound at 7:45. She was met by what appeared to be her parents who hugged her and led her to a station wagon parked just a few yards from Paul. The middle-aged man gave Paul the thumbs up sign. When they drove away, Paul stepped out of his truck and walked to the front gate to be visible to Abby. He recalled his return to The World in '73. Seeing his parents and Mose and Sally when he stepped off the plane meant everything. A Chicano man about Paul's age sat on a concrete bench outside the prison's chain link fence, a barrier topped with concertina wire. Jails come in many forms, he thought. His fence was sharpened bamboo sticks and a hemp tether on the other side of the world.

"Girlfriend?" the man asked stubbing out his cigarette.

Paul turned. "No, an acquaintance from college. I haven't seen her in seven years. Her family asked me to meet her. They're back in Illinois." He and Abby had exchanged letters for nearly a year, letters that were formal early, but more personal recently about the experiences of being a prisoner, about surviving, about hope and moving forward. "You?"

"My lady . . . once. It's been two years. This will be her second release. Didn't make it the first time. Maybe that's what she is to me now, an acquaintance. Driving her to the half-way house."

The metal door opened with a female guard exiting first. Abby followed wearing a yellow and green pants suit, an outfit sent by her mother for this day. Colorful, but too Midwest-winterish for a California summer day, like something Mrs. Cunningham might wear on Happy Days. Abby stood without expression at the first chain-link fence. She appeared heavier than he remembered, and her hair was short. She held a laundry bag in one hand and a manila folder in the other. The female guard followed the release format, asking Abby several questions, with Abby responding "yes" to each one.

"Pretty lady," said the man on the bench. "Probably made it harder."

"I don't know about that, but I imagine it's hard for everyone," said Paul.

The gates opened one at a time, that moment of last physical confinement. An older female guard said firmly, but with the slightest hint of concern, "Don't come back, Archer," and Abby's head nodded ever so slightly, but her eyes never deviated. She walked cautiously toward Paul as if inspecting him. He had promised himself that he would step forward and hug her. Mose hugged him in San Francisco after both his mother and dad had let go and taken Paul's duffle bag. It had meant the end of his solitary existence and signaled a beginning. Paul gently placed an arm around Abby's shoulders and whispered, "Hey." She accepted his hug, surrendering to the moment. She wrapped her right arm around his waist as if for support, and her head bumped against his shoulder.

"Come on, let's get out of here," said Paul. He pivoted, taking the bag from Abby while leaving his arm around her shoulders.

Abby turned to the man on the bench, "Jada will be out next. She showed me your picture. She's excited to see you, but be gentle, they were tough on her."

At his truck Paul placed the bag in the bed next to an ice cooler. He opened the door for Abby, removed a JCPenney's sack, and held it while she climbed in. He didn't start the truck immediately when he was seated, a deliberate pause. He intentionally did not ask her if she was okay, because he knew the answer was infinitely complex. "Hungry?"

Abby's mouth was open as if taking in new air or measuring her first words. "I will be, but right now I just want to get as far away from this place and these hills as the law will allow." She closed her mouth and dipped her head. With her fingertips, she rubbed her forehead hard.

Paul nodded and handed Abby the sack. "From Sally. She has a way of knowing just what's needed at any moment. I can pull off the interstate when we get down a ways." He turned the key and pulled out of the lot, noticing that Abby did not turn her head one last time. A dozen questions swirled in his mind, but he held them back. There would be time. Let Abby talk when she wanted, tell what she wanted, what she was comfortable with. "I ordered up this nice weather."

Abby nodded. "My mom says the room at the house is nice."

"It is. The window faces the backyard and gets the morning sun. You'll have to share the bathroom with me though, but I have pretty good habits. I'll put the seat back down."

"I didn't have a separate toilet seat, but I guess at a women's prison, it's not really necessary, is it?" They rode in silence for a few miles while Paul navigated the freeway system at rush hour, first onto the 91, then north onto 71, the Chino Valley highway, for the drive to the 10. Without turning to Paul, Abby said, "Thirty months will be December 11, 1977. That's a Sunday, so I'll probably have to wait until

Monday to get processed, but on that day, I'm leaving California. I don't know where I'll go yet, but I'm leaving here. If there's a futuristic bridge that will carry me to Timbuktu or any faraway place, I'm on it. For these next 30 months, I'm going to be the most law-abiding person on the face of the earth. I'll take no chances about who I'm with, where I shouldn't be, getting to work on time and being a good worker, meeting with my parole officer, and doing whatever it takes to never come back to this place. These next few years are not going to be about parole. It's the start of my next life, not the tail end of my childhood. Prison ended that." She gnawed on the inside of her lower lip and turned toward Paul. "I owe you big time, and I will be forever grateful." Paul started to respond, but she cut him off. "Jonas's letters about his teaching and his students kept me afloat for those first years, those years when you were in Vietnam, but when you started writing, I began to see an end. I felt hope. The staff read them all, you know, and that bothered me at first, but I got over it and focused just on what you were saying." She wiped her nose with the sleeve on her blouse. "We hear the stories of the women who get released and ride a bus to a halfway house or tenement and the things they're forced to do to survive." She paused and turned her eyes back to the freeway. "When I leave California, if I need to live in a tent or under a tarp in a rain forest on the other side of the world, it will be better than going back to Frontera."

Paul nodded but remained silent contemplating her mood. After a few minutes and more miles away from Frontera, he motioned to Abby to open the store bag that was on her lap. Sunglasses. Flip-flops. A sunhat. Shorts with a draw string. A tie-died tee-shirt. A sundress. Abby smiled for the first time.

"One of the things that I forgot because of my ordeal," said Paul, "was the kindness of friends. I came home and lived with my parents in the house where I grew up. Parents are different than friends in how they treat you. Parents hurt along with you and try to share your hurt, not consciously, but they do, which reminded me each day of that ordeal, as if I needed more remembering. Mose and Sally and I weren't your best friends in Boulder, but we did hang out some, and I thought living with us would work out better than having you go back to Chicago so your parents would monitor you. They wanted to, expected to, but we talked and decided on this. I know that moving here to live with Mose freed me to start over. He still gives me shit, as does Sally a little, but I know. Maybe this arrangement won't work out but give it a chance. Sally is the easiest person to be around. If you need a shoulder, she'll be there. If you need space, we'll give it to you. Just know that this isn't an imposition on any of us."

"My parents didn't pawn me off on you guys, did they?"

"No. Chicago was their first choice. I think they wanted to have you work at the soup kitchen."

Abby slipped on the sunglasses. "I haven't worn a pair of these in six years. When we stop for breakfast, I'm changing clothes."

Paul pulled off the interstate in Covina where they ate breakfast. Abby changed clothes, commenting that she wished Sally had included underwear in the sack. "She probably doesn't know my size." Twice she caught herself comparing the food to that in prison, but stopped herself, not wanting to get into that habit. She finished quickly. "I worried that I wouldn't recognize you when I got out, that your physical appearance might have changed. I'm relieved that it hasn't. Then I worried that maybe you wouldn't recognize me, or you'd be disappointed. I've added a few pounds."

Paul shook his head softly and joked, "They wouldn't let you wear those giant hoop earrings and dark eyeshadow?"

Afterward, they strolled through a residential neighborhood just to the north of the shopping area without saying much. Paul had walked the neighborhoods in Lakewood, Colorado, after returning from Vietnam, but he walked alone. At various intervals Abby paused to look at a house or a yard, especially those with roses. "Someday." She would admire a yellow rose bush, point it out to Paul, and they would move on. Wearing the sundress, flip-flops, sunglasses, and hat, she looked nothing like a felon on parole.

Traffic on the 10 was heavy and the drive to Santa Monica took a little longer than it should have, but Abby didn't seem to mind. She stayed mostly quiet, and Paul sensed he needed to do the same. When they finally parked at the beach, she didn't immediately move to leave the truck, but just stared at the ocean. The waves were gentle.

Eventually, they got out, took the cooler, two beach chairs, a mesh bag with towels, a blanket, and a beach umbrella from the truck bed and walked onto the sand.

"You can swim if you'd like. I'm kind of afraid of the ocean; not much of a swimmer," said Paul. "Grew up near mountains."

"Not yet," answered Abby. "I didn't sleep last night; maybe I'll just lie down and take a nap. You don't mind, do you?"

Paul handed her a tube of sunscreen, warning her about this first day at the beach and what she would look like if she didn't lather up. He unfolded one chair, pulled a paperback from the mesh bag, and sat. Abby applied lotion to her arms, legs, face, and neck, and then laid face down on the blanket under the umbrella. She was asleep before Paul turned a page. It had been nearly five hours since her release, and other than her diatribe about her plans after parole, he did not have a clue as to what she was thinking. He tried not to compare an over-crowded American prison with his solitary captivity in Vietnam, but he couldn't help it. Nearly six years versus just over one year. He had told Mose that Abby committed a crime while he hadn't, but Mose said that maybe by going to Indochina, he too had committed a crime. America's Crime. It was the conclusion they had reached when they were safe college students 10,000 miles from the scene, years earlier. Paul participated in the anti-war demonstrations in Boulder, walked the talk, but when his draft number was called, he acquiesced. He could have fled to Canada or spent his jail time in America like Abby instead of jail time in Vietnam. Did it matter in the long run? Either avenue led to purgatory. Paul got up and walked a few times while she slept, never wandering far away in case she awoke. He listened to the music from a nearby couple's radio, rock & roll, and most of the songs carried a meaning that seemed to apply to this moment. He didn't read his book. Mostly, he watched Abby.

She spoke before she stirred. "How long did I sleep?"

"About two hours. How do you feel?"

"I don't know yet." Abby sat up and pivoted to Paul. "What's the book?"

"*Fire in the Lake.*" He handed it to her. "It's the first thing I've read about our little war, the first time I've looked critically at it since I got back. Couldn't do it until now. The war has ended, for America anyway, and hopefully for all that region. But I doubt it. We can't seem to find the right path, the pathway to doing the right thing over there. It's a helpless feeling since I can't do anything about it."

Abby scanned the back cover. "Looks like an intellectual treatise, unlike my visceral response. Seems he could have been smoking dope with me and yelling at all of you back at CU."

"She. Frances Fitzgerald is a she."

"Who does she say was the enemy?"

Paul shook his head. "Not who, but what. Ignorance. America failed to understand Vietnam's history, and our lack of imagination doomed the people caught in the middle. There's always that segment of the population caught in the middle." His eyes looked out onto the water for a moment before refocusing on Abby. "I imagine the two of you would've had a go at Jonas and me and Mose."

"Not so much you; you were on my side. That's what I remember; you were angry too. It disappointed me when Jonas wrote that you had gone, when you let yourself be inducted, and my first reaction when he told me you were missing was that you got what you deserved." She stared at Paul as if she was about to cry. "I'm sorry for those thoughts. I was so angry and stupid." Paul made a face and shook his head as if to say no big deal. After a moment of silence, Abby asked, "What are they like now? Mose and Sally."

"They're the best people." Paul pursed his lips, smiled, and nodded. "You'll see, the best people."

Abby scooted over to the cooler, opened it, and took out the two beers. "Haven't had one of these in a while, not sure I'm supposed to, but I'll find out tomorrow, I guess." She reached into the ice for a key and opened each bottle, handing one to Paul. "What shall we toast?"

"It's your day, you decide." Paul leaned forward, holding his bottle at an angle, waiting for Abby to say something.

"Well . . . I've been pretty serious all day, and that's not good, so how about something silly. To . . ." she paused and smiled, "to no underwear," and they laughed. She clinked Paul's bottle and they both took hearty swigs. "Left it back in Covina in the restroom. The last piece of prison clothing."

Leaving the beach around 4:00, Paul drove up the Pacific Coast Highway to Oxnard. He had called Sally from a beach pay phone, telling her to expect them around 6:30, asking her if she needed him to stop and bring anything for dinner. Summer was moving closer to its longest day, California into its driest season. The highway shadowed the Pacific Ocean, a truly scenic drive. "June gloom" avoided this day, but the evening fog was beginning to roll over the offshore islands. The day for both Paul and Abby had been unlike their letters, letters that exposed their deepest fears and regrets. They both wondered about their future paths. For ten hours, two people who had lost much of their twenties to war and imprisonment sought a connection like a ham radio operator spinning the dial, searching for another ham who communicated on the same frequency.

"Will I get in the way at their house?"

Paul shook his head before he answered. He had worried about the same thing when he moved in with Mose and Sally ten months earlier, but they were insistent that he do so, and it had worked out well. Never did he feel as though he was intruding. Mose and Sally came and went as needed, as their jobs and social life dictated. Paul had arrived in the summer just like Abby was about to, was shown to his room, the room Abby would now occupy, the larger spare bedroom closer to the second bathroom, and their lives didn't seem to skip a beat. Still, Paul knew there was a difference here. Where once he had been roommates and best friends, Abby was an outsider whose private life was unknown to them, as were theirs to her. "No," he answered extending the o in a gentle way, hopefully a reassuring way. "None of us are complicated people. We barbecue hamburgers a lot and eat the local fish and produce, and when I cook, it's often Italian. If you don't like jazz, you'll have to hide out in your room with earplugs, because Mose loves his jazz and Sally loves Mose. They're pretty affectionate with each other."

"It only occurred to me this week that I never asked what they do for a living. I always assumed I would be serving my parole in Chicago."

"Mose teaches at the junior high, so he's off now. He just finished his first-year last week, so he's off for the summer. He'll be taking a few classes, like I guess lots of new teachers do over the summer. He didn't have an official teaching degree when he graduated, but when you're an ex-pro basketball player, exceptions are made. He might drive over to Thousand Oaks to Cal Lutheran. You said you wanted to finish your degree there, so that might work out well. Sally doesn't really have a job title. She's kind of like the troubleshooter for the health clinic. Her degree isn't in nursing, but she volunteered in Boulder at the clinic, and she's worked that into helping young mothers. Sort of like a counselor. Volunteers at her church too."

"Do they smoke dope?"

"None of us did much, Mose a little more, but we've talked and they're happy to not do it anymore. Mose may drive out to the beach and toke occasionally, he said, but mostly he was kidding. Your biggest adjustment might be listening to them when they have sex. Sally can be pretty loud." Paul turned his head and chuckled.

"They can't be any louder than some of the women in prison." They both laughed. "Someday, I'll tell you prison stories, the funny ones." Abby grinned. "God! Prison. What was I thinking? Really made a difference for 'The Cause,' didn't I?" After finishing her air quotes, she reached up to her forehead and rubbed it with her palms. "I would've had a greater impact working in inner-city schools. Less screaming, more hands-on stuff." She closed her eyes and shook her head. "Could we stop somewhere before we get to the house, so I can buy some underwear. There are limits to this freedom thing, you know. Do you remember my nickname at CU?" Paul shook his head. "Bags, and it didn't usually refer to my marijuana stash."

At Point Magu, as the Coast Highway veers away from the ocean to pierce Oxnard, Paul steered into a shopping center where they found a department store. Abby selected four plain bras and panties, a pair of jeans and three tops from a sale rack. After paying for them, she asked the clerk for permission to use the dressing room to wear one pair of underwear out. Back in the truck, Abby shook her torso and smiled to Paul. "Aww, much better. I'm ready to meet my new roomies now."

If Abby had any serious trepidations about this next step, she concealed them from Paul. Nervousness, of course, anxiety that seemed more like butterflies than angst, but his antenna detected no fear. This fit his perception of her from college a half-dozen years ago when she lashed out at anyone and everyone who challenged her, but the letters they exchanged after he returned from captivity in Vietnam revealed a softer, more vulnerable Abby, someone who was in thoughtful transition. Vietnam had beaten up America and its belief in itself; it was no wonder the war still impacted individuals who had held strong opinions. Paul had taken gut punches, both physical and emotional, had left three teeth and a good deal of the feeling in one foot in that Southeast Asian nation, had returned to cold sweats at night in his childhood bedroom, so he recognized Abby's journey from Frontera to Oxnard was more than just miles to get somewhere. He wondered what physical and emotional injuries were inflicted on Abby over the previous six years.

She had made no demands of Paul on this day. Yesterday, she hoped he would pick her up and drive her to Oxnard as quickly as possible, provide the getaway car, but as he pulled into the driveway, she smiled at their day. Ten hours of, in a sense, repose. Paul had hugged her, fed her, listened to her. Obviously, he carefully planned this day for her, and his instincts were spot on. Her CU boyfriend, Jonas Cullen—the one the government wanted to get after she returned to Boulder following the bank robbery and who was arrested with her in his apartment, the one who knew nothing about her misadventure until he was arrested, the one who became the teacher she had planned to be, that Jonas—told her once that nobody nurtured friends like Paul did. Angry Abby at first resisted her parents' suggestion to have her serve her parole in California, but she acquiesced to the promise she had made to herself. Stop being so damn stubborn! Still, she stewed for months, an emotion that stayed with her until she stepped out of the prison and received Paul's hug. Instead of abetting a breakout, an escape, Paul opened a pathway.

Another hour of sunlight remained when Paul honked his horn in the Robinsons' driveway. "I'll get your things," said Paul as he climbed out. Mose was taller than Abby remembered and powerfully built with big shoulders. Sally spread her arms and hugged Abby.

"Long time. How was your drive?" asked Sally.

"Good. Thank you for this."

Mose stepped over and hugged both women together. "Welcome.

Come on in."

Inside, Sally led Abby to her room. Paul followed with her bag, laid it on the bed and left. Sally pointed to the two framed photographs of Abby's family on the dresser, sent by Mrs. Archer who also bought new sheets, which Sally thought unnecessary, but that Mrs. Archer wanted her to have. There was also an envelope from her parents on the small desk. While the two women talked about accommodations, Paul and Mose opened beers.

"How was it?" asked Mose.

"Good. Don't know what she's thinking, but I guess we'll find out. Edgy a few times; seems like that famous anger lies just below the surface."

"That's to be expected. She'll be better in your room. A little more private. Her parents have been generous in setting her up."

"So have you and Sal."

∾

After dinner on the patio at sunset, the four discussed the arrangements Abby would need to know for her meeting with her parole officer in the morning. Paul and Sally had talked to their employers about their openness to hiring a convicted felon and received positive feedback. Abby's parents were sending money, hence the envelope in her room for early expenses. Mose assured Abby that he and Sally did not need rent, but both Abby and her parents insisted she pay for that and her board. Tomorrow, Mose would drive Abby to Ventura to meet her parole agent and would wait for her. Between her gate pay and the money from her parents, she would be fine; she would not need to borrow from Paul or the Robinsons.

"I had a parole plan for Chicago, but it all revolved around my parents. Live with them, they would find me a job, and I would do tons of volunteer work to keep me busy and build my good parolee resume, safe and tight. I forgot that I had basically run away from home when I went to college. Still, I had this vision that I had grown up in prison, would be more mature, more tolerant. But I'm not sure that's true. My positions about Vietnam, especially about the people there, haven't seemed to have changed. I do know prison taught me to hold my tongue, because you stand in lines and wait for everything in prison. Hopefully, it taught me to be less obnoxious." Mose, Sally, and Paul stayed quiet and listened. Abby kept her eyes down, but the others at the table sensed she was fighting back tears—or anger. None of them ever remembered the Boulder Abby crying, or even gentle for that matter. She sniffled, and they could see her stretch out her jaw occasionally as if yawning. "Maybe I also learned to behave in prison, that the world didn't revolve around me. Let's hope anyway." She gently stirred the melted ice cream in the bowl below her face. She breathed in heavily and blew it out onto the dessert, then lifted her head. "I haven't eaten fresh fish in so long, I'd forgotten how good it tastes." Abby let go of her spoon and looked at Paul. "How did you persuade my parents?"

Sally made a sound like a grunt and simultaneously shook her head. She reached over to take Abby's ice cream bowl and stacked it with the others. She said, "The same way he convinces everyone about anything. He smiles that goofy, crooked smile and acts like he's simply working things out in his own mind, and the next thing you know, you're doing what he wanted to do all along. Do you know what his apartment was called back at CU? The Annex. The White House address is 1600 Pennsylvania Avenue. His apartment was 1602 Pennsylvania in Boulder, so it became The Annex. The list of people who met with him during the late-Sixties included Mario Savio, Jerry Rubin, Black Panthers, even Hubert Humphrey and Joan Baez. Several others. He told everyone that he was just the guy who picked these people up at Denver's airport to drive them to their appointments in Boulder, but the word got out that if you were in Boulder, you had to go to The Annex."

"What could they get at Paul's apartment?" asked Abby.

"Boulder's pulse. Paul would bring in a few local radicals, a few professors, Boulder people, you know, and just sit around in a relaxed atmosphere and discuss politics, especially civil rights and Vietnam. Somehow, the newspapers and media never learned about these meetings, so the private scuttlebutt between these, I don't know, celebrities grew. Mose and I got to sit in on some amazing conversations."

Mose nodded. "Paul participated in these discussions. Very few people knew as much about current events as he did. Does. Yeah, they were intense, but fun."

∾

Around midnight, Paul, in his new bedroom, the smallest of the three, was awakened by a gentle knock on his door. It was Abby who cracked his door. "Paul..."

"Yeah. Are you okay?" answered Paul with concern.

"Yes. Would it be alright if I left your door open a little bit?"

"Yeah, no problem."

"Thank you. Goodnight, Paul,"

Already sitting up, Paul stepped onto the floor and walked to his door. He looked to Abby's door and saw that she had left it half-open too.

 **2**  

Wally Constantine looked like a former cop, which he was, Los Angeles PD for 25 years. Now in his fifth year as a parole officer serving Ventura County, he had grown a belly, a mustache, and lost some hair. Still a strong man, tall at around 6'4", he would obviously be able to take care of himself. Abby's appointment was scheduled for 10:30, but she didn't get in to see Constantine until 11:15. Mose had driven her over from Oxnard and sat with her in the hall outside the probation office, telling Abby funny stories about Paul and Sally in college.

Abby knew nothing about her parole supervisor going in, but he knew plenty about her. Her file was just one of dozens strewn about Constantine's office. He shook her hand, offered her a seat, opened her file, and began. "My first responsibility is to the community, its safety. My job is to ensure that you comply with the terms and conditions that we establish this morning. You don't have any rights, so to speak. In a sense, you're still in jail, just a more expansive one. I'm not one of those agents who's looking to bust your chops over any little thing, but I won't have any patience for repeated minor violations either. A major violation and you're back in Frontera." Constantine paused, his eyes getting confirmation from Abby before he moved on. "I'm not your friend; I'm your supervisor and an officer of the court. If you have a problem, call me. Don't allow it to fester. I'll stop in every other week at the beginning just to check on you, often unannounced. I have the authority to search you, your vehicle, and your residence without a warrant. Any questions so far?"

"No, sir." Abby's response was offered quietly but with conviction, her eyes focused.

Constantine glanced at Abby's folder again, flipped the page, and continued. "Armed robbery, but it says you weren't in possession of one of the weapons. Still, legally, that doesn't matter. No priors. Good prison behavior the last four years. That could reduce your time if you don't screw up on parole." He smiled. "Uncooperative the first year. Complete silence. Never heard of that one before." He turned the page. "No drugs while you're on parole. None! It's the one thing that causes this office to file reports and gets parolees sent back to prison. Do any of your roommates smoke a little weed?"

"No. Beer drinkers. Some wine with dinner sometimes."

"For you, I'll allow alcohol in the evenings when you're at home. If you're stopped on the road and test positive for alcohol, that's trouble. Even at home, limit yourself to two drinks. Don't allow this to go overboard. Don't drink alone. Have a talk with your friends, especially the three people you live with. By the way, that's a pretty famous guy sitting in the lobby. Is the other guy in the house your boyfriend?"

"No. I met these people in college and then lost touch until about two years ago when Paul and I started writing to each other. He picked me up from Frontera yesterday. I suppose you have a report on that correspondence, on its content. You're aware that he was a prisoner-of-war for over a year. We were both prisoners, under very different circumstances for sure, but we wrote about our experiences and tried to help each other get through it. It helped me; you'd have to talk to him to see if it helped him."

"You have a living environment few other parolees get. The Robinsons are solid citizens, well-respected in Oxnard. Mr. Garrity's a vet who's now working for the Catholic church. Your father is a minister who has written in support of this living arrangement. I hope you understand how fortunate you are. Don't screw it up." Again, Constantine looked for Abby's acknowledgement. "I'll contact the sheriff's office, but I want you to go in and register yourself this week. Again, Sheriff Towne and his deputies aren't your friends, but recognizing your face and that you're trying to go straight can help in minor situations." Constantine handed a paper across the desk and pointed to the lines where Abby needed to sign. "Follow every one of these rules. Post them on your refrigerator and maybe another on your bathroom mirror. Make sure your friends understand them; friends won't go back to jail for breaking them and just want to make you feel good sometimes. Friends are too often willing enablers to misconduct. I'm too busy to go looking for problems, but I keep my feelers up. Follow the rules. Don't let your guard down. Keep your appointments and don't be late. Today, you had to sit for nearly an hour waiting for me. Doesn't matter. You always have to be the one who waits, not me. I'm not here to please you, you're here to please me."

As they stood to leave, Constantine asked Abby if she would introduce him to Mose, saying that he had been a little bit of a basketball player too growing up and in college. When he shook hands with Mose, Abby noticed that her parole officer was only a couple of inches shorter, two tall men who seemed comfortable with each other.

After Mose and Sally had left the house the next morning, Abby sat with Paul in the kitchen. "Tell me about The Annex. You never mentioned it in your letters. I sort of have a vague memory of being there with Jonas."

"I think I told you that I managed the rooming house where I lived. I have some skills in repairing houses, sort of self-taught. Emergency repairs. Mose and Sally and I lived on the second floor, and several students lived in the four other rooms at various times. On the main floor, there was a TV room where we had discussions about the war during my last two years. Students who didn't live in The Annex started showing up on a regular basis to argue a couple of nights a week. Sometime in '68, one of those students said he was going to avoid the draft and needed a place to hide out, so I put him in a room in the attic. Turns out he wasn't a student at CU but from Wisconsin and was a member of the Students for a Democratic Society, SDS. He had contacts. When he left after a couple of months, members of the movement who came to Boulder stayed at The Annex, not to hide out but just to stay while they met with other activists at CU. The Annex was right in the middle of every march or protest."

"Who was your most famous guest?'

"Depends on how you define famous. Israel's Yitzhak Rabin dropped in one afternoon. That was in '69; he was their ambassador to the U.S. and was speaking at the World Affairs Conference. To answer your question, Sarah had heard he was coming to Boulder and somehow sent him a message to see me. He stayed for about an hour. Amazing, humble man."

"Sarah, your old girlfriend who left you to go to Israel?"

Paul nodded. "How do you know about her?"

"I don't know. Jonas must have said something about her in one of his letters."

Wally Constantine's first home visit came on Thursday morning, a scheduled visit where he could meet Abby's friends. Paul and Sally delayed going to work so that the parole supervisor could meet them and explain their responsibilities and what they might expect housing a person on parole. Constantine walked through the house, omitting Mose's and Sally's bedroom and Paul's room, and searching Abby's room only briefly. Constantine asked if Abby was paying rent, whether there were guns or drugs in the home, if they could confirm she was actively searching for a job, and if they understood that their home could be searched without a warrant, at least the parts Abby inhabited. When he was satisfied, he thanked Paul and the Robinsons, handed them his professional card, and then took Abby outside for a few last words.

"He was satisfied," said Abby after her parole officer had driven away. "I'm not a risk to the community and have no special conditions added to my contract." She paused and turned slightly aside. "I'm sorry for this." She paused again, her jaw clenched, but Sally thought in self-directed anger. "He has the right to do this to me, but I don't think it's right that he can intrude on your privacy, into your home. I'm sorry," she repeated. "If you want me to leave . . ."

Mose spoke first. "Hey, no big deal. After a few visits, he'll see how boring we are and stop coming around. He'll see that his time will be better spent chasing down drug pushers and gang members."

Sally hugged Abby but said nothing.

"The guy's cool," said Mose. "He's got his job to do, and we'll make it easy for him. Sally and I knew what this was all about. When

Paul asked if we'd do it, we did a little research, so we knew what our requirements would be. Hell, we put up with Paul."

"Yeah," said Abby, "but you guys knew what to expect. You've been best friends forever. You don't know about me."

Sally squeezed Abby's shoulders. "Guess we'll find out then, huh." Sally turned to Paul. "I've got to go to work. Abby has a job interview in an hour." She took her husband's hand and walked out to her car leaving Abby with Paul.

Paul smiled. "See what I told you. Good people. Go get what you need for your interview, and I'll drive you. Maybe we'll find an empty parking lot afterwards at one of my churches so you can practice driving again while I work."

❧

Mose enrolled in education classes at the local community college, so Abby was on her own three times a week to get over to Thousand Oaks to restart her college education. After one week of riding the bus, Paul offered her his truck. "It's reliable and would save you tons of time. I can use the station wagon around town." Abby hesitated but agreed to try it when Paul assured her that he really didn't need his truck much during the day.

Returning on the 101 that first afternoon and just a few minutes before turning off the freeway into Oxnard, Abby pulled Paul's pickup to a stop on the shoulder. The highway patrol, with flashing lights blazing, pulled in behind her.

❧

Paul returned from one of Oxnard's Catholic churches at 6:00. "Where's Abby?" he asked Sally.

"I just got back a few minutes ago. I thought she might be with you. Wasn't she supposed to be home about 4:00?" Sally wiped her hands on the kitchen dish towel and read Mose's note on the refrigerator. "Mose is working out at the gym. Says he'll be back around 6:30."

Paul squinched his brow and walked to the window that looked out over the driveway. Abby had told the gang how excited she was about a conference with her adviser scheduled for this afternoon. Maybe the meeting had gone longer than she expected, or her professor was late, or she stopped for a coffee. She's a responsible adult, he thought, but . . . she's on parole. Little things become big things. He wondered if he should call her parole officer but decided against that. He walked back into the kitchen. "Probably nothing," he said.

Sally nodded, "Yep. Fix a salad while I get these potatoes ready. She and Mose will show up soon."

Fifteen minutes later, Mose returned. He kissed Sally and rubbed his sweaty forehead against her neck. "Did you hear anything from Abby?" asked Sally.

"No, why?" Mose took a carrot from the cutting board and looked at Paul. "Something wrong?"

"Abby's late. Probably nothing, but her parole makes me jumpy."

Just then, Abby drove Paul's truck onto the driveway. The gang waited. Entering the house, she found three pairs of eyes on her.

She smiled coyly at their expressions. "I stopped to help a stranded motorist on the side of the freeway. An older lady."

"They have people whose job that is who know the dangers of cars pulling off on the shoulder to lend assistance," said Paul.

"No one else was helping. The cop told me the same thing but then wrote me a note, sort of a "Get out of jail free" card." She smiled. There was more.

Sally drew the line. "No dinner until we get the whole story."

Abby moved her jaw sideways, took a glass from the cupboard, and poured herself two inches of wine from an open bottle on the counter. Her nod indicated she liked the taste. "Nothing like a good Pinot from the county." She set her glass down and pulled three more from the cupboard, then poured wine into each, hesitating over the third glass and looked at Mose. He nodded and she poured his. Raising her glass, she teased with her toast. "To empathetic cops."

The gang went along with its newest member, raised their glasses, and sipped.

"Any time a citizen is confronted by the police, he will ask for iden-tification. Fortunately, this citizen—me—had it. Then, the cop called Constantine, who vouched for me. The other patrolman tended to the lady whose car had broken down." She paused, smiled, and took another sip of wine. "It's all good."

Paul nodded. "That's not what we were concerned about. We want to know how your conference with your professor went. Will you get into your desired major?"

❧

Abby settled into a routine, but each day before she left for Thousand Oaks, she asked permission from Paul to borrow his truck, and the gas gauge never registered less than half-full. Abby hired on as an evening stocker for Vons Grocery, working part-time, but with an option for more hours as her schedule would allow. A month into her parole, she began cleaning two houses in the neighborhood, two houses owned by elderly women from the church where Sally worked. By the end of the summer, she added three more houses and a twice-a-week cleaning gig at the church. "A prison skill," she would joke. "I'm good at cleaning toilets and kitchens." She paid her rent on time and kept the second bathroom immaculate.

❧

A year earlier, in 1974 Sally had been stopped by the highway patrol in Isla Vista, just west of Santa Barbara at a blockade where they searched her car for Patty Hearst. The search wasn't specific to Sally; the officers had received a tip that "Tania" was in the area. Now, in late September 1975, looking like nothing she was raised to become, Hearst was captured in San Francisco. At dinner, listening to the soft jazz of Miles Davis, Abby mused to her roommates about the heiress's situation. Even though Hearst was wealthy, to Abby she seemed no less vulnerable to exotic adult ideas than the poor girls who populated much of the California Women's Prison. So naïve and in need of excitement. Abby's audience knew who she was really talking about.

Abby drank only at the house in the evening when she wasn't going out later, and even then, only a single bottle of beer or one glass of wine. Holding up her glass on this night, she turned it, looking through it to the far wall. Her thoughts went far beyond Hearst. Twenty thousand Vietnamese refugees living in tents at Camp Pendleton near San Diego, who had arrived from Guam earlier in the summer, were on the move again, this time to Orange County, San Jose, or Houston. Photos in the *Los Angeles Times* revealed the fears and insecurities of these people whom Abby, Paul, and so many others of their generation had sought to help, mostly unsuccessfully.

"What was it like?" she asked the table. "What were those last days like in Saigon? I didn't get to watch it much in the prison."

Abby and Mose deferred to Paul, who had spent his college days immersed in current events. He narrowed his eyes, tapped his fork on the table next to his plate to collect his thoughts, and cleared his throat. Mose sat back in his chair, folding his arms across his chest. "America didn't make plans for the evacuation of those people who supported us there, and when it all came crashing down, it seemed like every citizen in Saigon along with their families stormed the gates at our embassy believing we could get them on a helicopter and take them to safety. The same scene played out at the docks and the airports. Those last few days, though, the scenes that were brought into our living rooms were terrible. The rumors of an impending bloodbath terrified these people who had in any way supported America." Paul lowered his head. "We couldn't get them out, and at some point, they realized it and panicked. There were a few courageous Americans who put their own lives in danger to rescue some of our supporters, but the country failed." He stopped talking and looked up, not to Abby, but to Mose, as if to apologize.

Sally grabbed one of Mose's hands and one of Paul's. "The people who got out will be mostly fine. They brought nothing with them, but they'll be safe. It's the hundreds of thousands who didn't who will suffer or die. We failed them, and they'll pay the price of our misadventure." She looked at Abby, who had anger in her eyes. "From what Paul has told me and from what I have observed in you for the past three months, from what I knew of you back in Boulder, all of this coming apart must be torturing you too."

Abby nodded slowly, and her jaw quivered. "We lost that war long before this. The fucking Cold War. Those . . ." She stopped herself from labeling them with another curse word, "amoral people in Washington killed them for over a decade and now want nothing to do with them, with that part of the world. A country full of refugees, people with nothing and little hope. We're still responsible for them." She captured Sally's eyes. "We're still responsible for them."

Mose leaned into the table and with his free hand took Abby's. "We knew about your actions at CU; you were kind of a legend. Jonas would just shake his head, but he had this great admiration of you. We all did, sort of. Paul did what he could, but you, you fought back. You have nothing to be ashamed of."

Paul pushed his free hand over to Abby's, linking the table, waiting for Abby to respond.

"Mostly pointless. I spoiled any good things I did, but I'm not done yet. I'm not sure what stupid thing I'm going to do next, but it doesn't end in that prison for me." Abby's eyes eased. "Still have some windmills to slay."

Paul understood. "Except they aren't imaginary evils, are they?"

Mose squeezed her hand and asked, "What were you planning to do with the money you stole from that bank? Do you have a hidden stash somewhere?" It was his attempt to ease her feelings with a little humor.

Abby smiled and let go of both Mose's and Paul's hands. She wiped her face with her napkin and breathed heavily, recovering as best she could. "That's part of the stupid. We didn't know. Somehow, if you rob these corporate banks, it will help the anti-war effort. Donate it to some worthwhile organization." She laughed at herself. "God!"

"I'm getting more wine." Sally stood. "You guys want another beer?"

Four people in their late twenties with real life experiences on a Friday night talking in anger, in sorrow, in defiance. In friendship. Each one shared something, not always following upon a previous revelation. From the Vietnamese refugees, they moved to the assassination attempt on President Ford's life, to the Thrilla in Manilla, to Mose's students, to Jonas's students in Denver, to the strawberry fields of Oxnard, to basketball games both real and imagined, to Sally's patients. They even talked about jail and prison and families of the future.

Nursing a second drink, Abby said, "I'm so tired from working and school. I hate housecleaning, but I'm good at it. It's what prison taught me to do, but I absolutely hate it. In two years, I'll never do it again. You guys must think I don't like your company, since I spend so much time in my room." Mose said that the thought had crossed his mind in a way that made Abby smile. "I just don't want to be a burden or not pay my fair share or take up your space, so I try to be invisible." She paused. "And I want to be so busy I don't have time for trouble."

Sally topped off her wine and said, "You've earned the right to be tired. None of us could keep up with your schedule, stocking shelves after a full day of classes, cleaning four to five houses and my church twice a week." She smiled at her new friend. "Maybe you could pull a shift over at the docks on Sundays."

"Allow me to let you in on the family secret here, Abby," said Mose. "This house you're living in is paid off. Free and clear. We don't need your money. We take your rent only because we're afraid of you and your parents." He smiled. "After we got married, and that's a whole nother story, we moved in with my mom who was dying of cancer. While I traveled around the country getting paid a ridiculous amount of money for playing basketball, Sally lived here and took care of my mom."

Sally shook her head at her husband. "Abby, dear, he's leaving out a lot of the story or misremembering. After graduation, after living in the same rooming house with him and Paul for three years, I married my boyfriend, a good guy who I didn't love. Mose and I were in love, but we always pushed it aside. I think we both thought that if we became lovers, we might lose that special friendship. Anyway, my marriage lasted less than a year. My first husband and I had moved in with his parents, and he took a music job at his old high school."

Paul interrupted. "Are you noticing a pattern here, Abby?" Mose reached across the table and high-fived Paul and got slapped in the ribs by Sally.

"Quiet," ordered Sally. "During those months when I was married, I didn't work. I was bored out of my gourd and talked to Mose on the phone several nights each week. It was good that my marriage ended quickly. Did Paul ever tell you that I had a kid in high school? Gave it up for adoption. Another story for another night when we're confessing our sins." Sally shook her head from side to side very deliberately.

"I moved in with Mose and his mother before we got married. That house is just a few miles from here, but in a not-so-nice neighborhood, and, yes, I adored his mom and I miss her, but I was this obviously white girl living in a minority neighborhood with the most famous guy in Oxnard who wasn't always around. When she died, Mose sold her house, and then we got married and bought this one. Between what we made on his mother's house and what the NBA paid him, we bought this house. I don't work because I need to, I work because I want to."

"I was never a star in the NBA, but even reserves get taken care of, and it wasn't a lifestyle I particularly cared for. I'm not competitive enough and nagging injuries gave me an excuse to stop playing. Kicking Paul's ass on the driveway hoop is satisfaction enough. Paul insists on paying his fair share too, so he pays the utilities and for some of the groceries. Abby, Sally and I are getting rich off the two of you."

Abby looked at Paul. "How did you end up here? I mean you told me you were coming in one of your letters, but you didn't really explain why."

Paul straightened up and looked over his nose as if to say the answer was obvious. "And pass up an opportunity to live with these guys, to relive our college days?" Three old friends lifted their glasses in a silent toast. "Seriously? I had to get out of my funk. After being a POW and letting the Army try to heal me at the VA in Denver, I had to go. I sort of called and told them I was coming, making them live up to their pledge that if I needed anything, just call. So, I did and here I am."

"And he's a pain in our asses every day! Sally and I just tolerate him," said Mose.

More alcohol and more talk, some serious, some reflective, some joking. Abby stopped drinking and listened. As dinnertime moved closer to midnight, she realized she hadn't been around drunk people in over six years. This night was good though, very good, and she wanted to stop time and hold onto it.

"What are you smiling at?" Mose asked Abby.

Sally answered for Abby. "Probably at us three drunk asses, opening up our past like it might be of interest. Laughing at the stupid stuff we did years ago. Mostly at you two little boys."

Around 10:00 Paul had moved his chair from being between Abby and Sally to be between Abby and Mose. All of them had to work in the morning, except Abby who would drive Paul's truck over to Thousand Oaks for her two college classes, one sociology and one criminal justice. Mose handled his alcohol much better than Paul and Sally, even to the point of never being drunk, it seemed to Abby. Mose was stoic, cool, probably always had been, but funny. He and Sally were an affectionate couple, a trait she envied. After three months, this was the first time she had sat in with them late into the night. Usually, she retreated to her room to study or sleep. She wondered if Mose would have a hangover at school in the morning. A teacher with a noticeable hangover. She wondered if he and Sally would make love when they went to bed. Drunk sex. She knew what she would do when she went to bed. "Well, I need to say goodnight. I'm out of practice with this type of behavior, unlike you professionals. Thank you so much. Really."

"Wait a minute," said Sally leaning into the table as far as possible. "I have something to say." She looked at her friends with the eyes of a proud mother at her daughter's graduation, a tipsy mother, however. "You, my sweet girl, are no bother. You've been a treat to get to know better. We look forward to the two meals each week you cook, to hearing about your college courses, and to watching Paul walk around you gingerly."

Paul stood abruptly. "Yep, time for bed. Mose, take this drunken lady away. Come on, Abby. Leave the dishes, I'll do them in the morning."

∾

When Paul had arrived in Oxnard to live with his friends, Sally found him a job as the fix-it man at her Catholic church. The previous handyman, old and lazy, finally gave in to the ghost, as the priest said, and the diocese was hiring, and St. Anthony's was an easy walk from the house. Word got out about his skills, and within six months, Paul was on call at five Catholic churches in Ventura County. The standing joke at each church revolved around Paul's faith, with the punch line being that if he could fix the plumbing or the stairs or the lighting, then he was Catholic enough. Being confined in a jungle jail changed Paul in subtle ways, ways not noticeable by anyone but Mose and Sally, but he was quieter and more introspective, if that was possible, according to Sally. He had his moments, solitary days when he would simply go away, up into the mountains behind Ventura or Santa Barbara and walk. When he wasn't repairing churches, he worked for less than minimum picking strawberries with the Chicanos. "Working on my Spanish, a valuable skill in Oxnard."

On a Thursday in December, two weeks before Christmas, Abby watched Paul in the strawberry fields. He wore a green bandana, which was how she was able to spot him, and she hoped he could have lunch with her. One cleaning job was cancelled, freeing her up for the rest of the day. Paul pushed a small wagon ahead of him while he ran his hands among the plants, searching for ripe berries. He was one of about twenty workers in the field, and as far as Abby could discern, the only Anglo picker. Stoop labor, labor intensive, back-breaking work. At the edge of the field, two Chicano men in straw cowboy hats stood with a middle-aged woman. They were animated, their hands flapping and their heads bobbing. The woman shook each man's hand and walked into the field where she began talking with other workers. It appeared to Abby that the woman held a boss's authority, but somehow, she didn't seem to be employed by the company. Abby got out of the truck and moved to the end of the row that Paul was working. He wouldn't see her until he finished his row and stood to stretch his back. The boss-looking woman moved easily among the pickers, laughing, and sampling the strawberries as they conversed in Spanish. She strode up one row several yards to the left of Abby and walked towards her.

"Hola," she greeted Abby. "Which one are you waiting for?"

Abby pointed to Paul. "The slowest picker." Both women laughed. The lady looked familiar to Abby, but she couldn't place her. She had no reason to know a middle-aged Chicana in Southern California unless she had been a fellow prisoner at Frontera.

"He's trying, but this work is not in his blood. Why does he do it?"

Abby didn't have a ready answer, but she responded with Paul's answer when he was asked that question. "Free strawberries, I guess."

"Ah," said the middle-aged woman, "stealing from the company. Maybe I'll ask him myself." She smiled at her own joke, reached out to touch Abby's forearm, turned, and walked to Paul. He was startled and stood, seeing Abby and the lady at the same time. She asked him a few questions, but without the animated body movements she had used with the two Chicano men moments earlier. She did most of the talking, questioning, while Paul mostly nodded and smiled. The lady turned slightly, bent over to the plants, and deftly picked a dozen or so strawberries. She had done this type of work in her past. She sorted through her cache, selected two, and placed the others in Paul's wagon. She handed one to Paul and ate the other. Then, she shook his hand and walked down his row to talk with other workers. Paul indicated to Abby that he would finish the last fifteen yards of his row before he could talk.

"Who was that?" asked Abby three minutes later.

"Said her name was Dolores. Just wanted to know how I was doing and if I needed anything. Nice lady. Told me I needed to get a better paying job. I think she may be some union official, but she didn't say for sure." Paul removed his bandana and wiped his forehead.

Abby realized where she had seen the lady. "Paul, that's Dolores Huerta. She's a bigwig in the farm movement here in California; I think one of the founders of their union. I saw her back in '68. I'll never forget." Paul's face registered a concerned question. "June 5th," Abby said slowly. "She was standing on the stage with Bobby Kennedy at the Ambassador Hotel in Los Angeles when he won the California primary. The night he got shot. I was there." Abby stopped talking as her expression went back into the past.

Paul turned back to the field. Huerta was meeting with three pickers of undetermined gender, speaking Spanish. In a moment, he turned back to Abby whose face held the same expression. "What?" he asked. With both hands, he took her shoulders.

"Come on, let's have the burgers I bought, and I'll tell you."

Two burgers for Paul, one for Abby. Large fries and cokes. A pine scented cardboard tree hung from the rearview mirror in the old Ford truck, Paul's baby that now seemed to be Abby's. She had taken it in for its last oil change and was driving it to Thousand Oaks three times each week plus to her cleaning jobs in Oxnard. Bench seat.

"I was so enamored by Bobby. I campaigned for him in California, and after his victory, did a line of cocaine to celebrate. When he got shot, I called Jonas in Montana. He was back home working with his dad for the summer. Funny," Abby paused. "Jonas was a Humphrey guy because of his civil rights credentials. We used to fight about that. I fought, he parried. Anyway, I flew to Montana and lived with him and his family for a month. Sort of cleaned up for a time. Then I headed back to Illinois to live with my parents. I liked myself for a while back then, but my ugly, angry side always seemed to get the best of me."

"Especially when it came to Vietnam, I would guess."

"Yeah, I suppose, but I'm not sure I knew anyone who got so riled up over it as I did. I tried it once more with Jonas back in Boulder, but I bolted again, back out to LA. You know the rest of the story, as they say." She started to bite into her burger, pulled it back to look at it, removed a pickle slice, but set the half-eaten burger back on the wrapper. "I'm so scared of what being in prison has taken from me, of how it changed me in ways I don't understand yet. I hate being monitored! I hate giving urine samples on demand. I hate it!" She turned to look at Paul and burst into tears. She fell from the driver's side behind the steering wheel into his lap. Sobbing, shaking.

Paul had held his coke up out of the way when she fell. He dropped it out his open window onto the ground, so he could hold her as best he could in this position, his left arm around her torso, his right arm cradling her head. Abby didn't try to explain herself; she just cried until she was cried out. Five minutes, ten minutes. When her tears subsided, she continued to lay on Paul's lap sniffling. Unconsciously, he began moving his hand through her hair in the gentlest manner. Abby calmed with only an occasional sudden rise of her chest when she would sniffle. Without looking up, she spoke again, softly.

"I'd like to say that this is the first time I've cried since I got out of prison, but I think you know better. I try to do it, so you don't hear me at night, but not much gets past you. I'm so lost, Paul. Tough girl without any real plan except to finish parole and bolt again. To where, to what, to nothing. Felons don't usually get teaching jobs. I don't want to become directionless." She stopped, her eyes opened, but staring blankly. "Jonas's letters were all about his students, little etudes from his day. I sort of got to know his favorite kids, you know, like Mose speaks so tenderly about his students. Jonas even sent a few pictures of his students. When he wrote telling me that you were alive, that your name was on the list of POWs who would be coming home, I just wanted to talk with you. I knew Jonas was doing me and my parents a favor; I could tell that he was a friend who had made some kind of promise about not giving up on me or something. But any lover feelings that he once had for me were gone, probably had ended even before I robbed the bank, and he frequently mentioned in his stories this other teacher, so I suspected."

"My first year was lost too," said Paul. "Not quite a year, but too long. It takes time. I don't think I've ever thought of myself as a tough guy, but I always did think I could solve whatever I came up against. Found out differently." Paul stopped. He looked up from Abby's face out onto the strawberry field, and he shook his head. "Your letters helped me so much. I had lunch with Jonas after you and I started corresponding, and he told me he wasn't writing to you any longer, that you had told him to stop, that you were just writing to me about prison. You showed such tenderness, something, to be honest, I hadn't seen in you in Boulder. That's when my feelings started to change."

"I don't want to go backward, Paul. I don't want Jonas, don't miss him at all. He moved on, as he should have, but even if he was single, I wouldn't want him. I don't want Chicago or Boulder, and certainly not Los Angeles, but . . . I miss Vietnam. That sounds so stupid. I was never there like you were, but those people . . . I feel like I'm responsible somehow."

"It's not stupid, Abby." He measured his words. "Back in April, before you were released, I volunteered to help the Vietnamese who were coming in that second wave. I heard on the radio that Camp Pendleton needed help in setting up a tent city for them, so I drove down to see. Spent three days erecting tents and cleaning out old quonset huts along with about, I don't know, 800 Marines and some Navy sailors. A few of the Marines had served in Nam, and I could tell they felt good about helping, that it was something positive, something to help temper their remorse. That's how I felt. Something positive.

Anyway, in those few days, we put up a thousand tents, those Army brown ones, dug latrines, and re-wired the compound. I didn't stay to see the Vietnamese refugees arrive; I think I was scared, in a sense, but I watched them on TV. They seemed genuinely grateful. Very humble and respectful. These were people without a country any longer, so I know they were apprehensive." Paul paused. "Yeah, Vietnam courses in our blood."

Abby smiled. "Do you think you and I will ever let it go?"

"I imagine, but I know World War II was always on my dad's mind, his action in the Pacific, and he won. One thing more. On that last evening at Camp Pendleton, when I left the base, I sat in my truck and looked over what had been constructed; it was eerie. All those tents. There's a sign in the area for San Clemente, an exit, where Nixon lives. I tried to imagine what he would think. He should have been down there helping with the tents. I'm not sure I'll ever let go of my anger for him, for the lying that caused so many deaths."

"LBJ, too." Abby kept her head on Paul's lap, but she knew he was looking down at her. She liked the feeling. "Tell me about your CU girlfriend. Seems like I remember the guys kidding you about her. I flinched when you mentioned her before."

"Sarah Phillips. Sophomore year. She had a purpose and followed it to Israel. Runs a school for Jewish preschoolers in Tel Aviv last I heard. We stayed connected as best we could for a couple of years. Letters and monthly phone calls. Yeah, I loved her, but destiny kept getting in the way. After Boulder, when I was drafted, we never corresponded. I doubt she knows about my stint in Vietnam. That's in the past."

Abby's left hand was on the outside of Paul's right thigh. She tapped his thigh lightly. "Are you sure?"

Paul looked out the windshield. "Yeah. Very sure."

Still in his lap, Abby talked. "You're a gentleman, Paul Garrity. At pre-release I was warned about men and being vulnerable. I thank my lucky stars for the three of you. Constantine says I'm his easiest case, that he'd sign off on me if he could, and that he likes visiting with me, because it's so different than his other cases. I'm his reward, he says. Says I could work as a counselor to other parolees when my term is over. I've thought about that." Paul waited, listened to her breaths.

"At Frontera, I was several girls' big sister. I think that's why I was left alone by the guards and some of the other prisoners; I made their jobs easier. It was like so many of the younger girls grew up in a war zone and this is what they got; it's the expected outcome, and they're never going to get over it. Did you know that when I was captured, for the first month or so, all I did was yell and scream at everyone? That was in Denver where I got arrested. After I was extradited back here, I went silent for over a year."

Paul gently pushed a lock of Abby's hair out of her face to behind her ear. "What made you start talking again?"

"One of Jonas's students was killed in a car crash. He wrote me a letter about it. Evidently, she was trying to solve the entire segregation mess in inner-city Denver and was driving to the state legislature to give a speech. Hit by a drunk driver. It tore him apart, but he went on. I read that letter over and over, and then I started behaving like a model prisoner. That's what I was going to be once, a teacher in an inner city."

"I guess we can go on then, huh?" Paul smiled down on Abby who turned slightly and smiled back. She pushed herself up, scooted her butt closer to Paul's, and hugged him. "You're doing fine, you know," he said.

"I need to hear that more, from someone other than my parole supervisor. He's supposed to say it." Paul felt her smile into his ear. "Did you ever have sex in this truck?"

"I'm a virgin."

"My ass!" Abby pulled back and smiled. "Don't you have some strawberries to pick?'

∻

On an afternoon when Paul went over to watch Mose's basketball practice at the junior high, the women prepared a dinner together. Abby had some things she wanted to ask about, but Sally waited, as always allowing Abby her space. Finally, Abby opened a bottle of wine, poured two glasses, and handed one to Sally.

"You and Mose have noticed."

"Yeah. Hard not to," answered Sally as she raised her glass to Abby's.

"I'm fighting my feelings. I just don't think I'm good enough for him; not sure what he sees in me."

"It's your big boobs, Abby." They both laughed slightly.

"Seriously."

"I had those same thoughts about me with Mose once. I had baggage too, but eventually learned that it was his decision to make about me just as it was my decision to make about him."

"Yeah, but we live in such close quarters."

Sally shook her head. "I don't even know what that means. He's out in the community every day and so are you. Look, Abby, your relationship with Paul hasn't been formed exclusively over your time here. You had a bit of knowledge about each other from Boulder, but you each bared a part of your souls to each other in the dozens of letters you exchanged while you were in prison. He wrote most of his while he was living here, and I can tell you, he looked forward to receiving yours. I would like to have read the letters you wrote to each other in prison."

Abby nodded. "Everyone else did in the prison. You can if you want; I still have most of them."

"No. Paul shared a little about what you wrote, but he was careful about your privacy. In the beginning, we had no idea you would ever show up on our doorstep. That transpired late in your term. Paul asked us what we thought, and Mose and I signed on, but with conditions. We appreciate how gently you've nurtured our good friend's soul. The one thing we were concerned about was your anger. Mose and I don't fight, we don't raise our voices with each other. This house is a quiet house, a gentle house, and we intend to always keep it that way. Paul taught us that many years ago. He asked us to give you a few weeks when you arrived. It's never been an issue."

Paul and Mose burst into the front door almost like teenage brothers. Sally and Abby smiled at each other and clinked their wine glasses. "Grab your beers. Dinner's almost ready."

❧

Sally and Mose flew to Colorado for eight days over Christmas to visit Sally's mother, while Abby's parents and one brother came to California, their third trip, and stayed in a nearby motel. When they had visited in July, Reverend and Mrs. Archer found an anxious daughter, one concerned about her ability to control her temper and live up to her parole requirements. This time her mood relaxed. Her mother kidded about the benefits of a long sentence. "If we'd have known that you would stop yelling and challenging us on every issue, we would have committed you in junior high." Arriving three days before Christmas, the Archers bought and decorated a small tree, purchased several bags of groceries to donate to Oxnard's food bank, shopped in Santa Barbara, and prepared a feast on Christmas eve. Abby's mother explained to Paul that it was the Unitarians who brought the Christmas traditions of gift giving and Santa Claus back into prominence in America after those stodgy Puritans tried to prevent its celebration. "We're not much for Christmas day, but we remember the lessons of Jesus on Christmas eve."

"Paul might fit in our faith," teased Abby over the festive dinner, "except the Catholics pay his salary these days."

Paul worked overtime at his churches during this season, so Abby spent full days with her parents. Her fall semester at Cal Lutheran had ended in mid-December, but she drove them there to tour. Her parents committed to another semester of tuition since she earned an A in both courses. She introduced them to Mr. Constantine, her parole supervisor, and they took him to lunch. She received permission to drive them to the LA airport, just outside her 50-mile restriction, and they departed the day after Christmas.

Returning to Oxnard, Abby drove to four different Catholic churches before she found Paul repairing a pew at the rear of the nave. Again, she had brought burgers, fries, and cokes to get his attention. He put aside his tools, and they sat on the tile floor at the rear of the church eating fast food.

"You're good at this," she said, referring to his carpentry skills.

"I try and I enjoy it." Paul grinned and tilted his head as if to brush off the compliment. "Nice visit with your parents. Good people, Abby."

"Yeah. I hurt them pretty badly with my actions . . . with my words and behavior. I think they understood because my mom was a bit of a rebel when she was a teenager. She wasn't raised as a Unitarian. Her family came from the steel towns in Pennsylvania, tough towns. Daddy met her in Pittsburgh, and they connected somehow. They've never talked about it much, but they're committed to the service work they do in Chicago, that's for sure."

"You and your mom are close; it's cool to watch."

"It took a while. They like you a lot."

Paul smiled. "That's good because they might be seeing lots of me in the future." He took Abby's hand. "I'm not sure you're ready for a marriage proposal yet, but I'd like you to know how I feel about you. I know this puts you in a difficult position if you don't share these feelings since we live together . . ."

Abby put her index finger to Paul's lips. "Shh." She held his eyes with hers and then leaned into his lips and kissed them tenderly. "Our first kiss like this, and it's in a church." When she pulled back, she said, "I'm going back to the house now, and I'll be waiting for you in my room."

They stood together and hugged tightly, before Paul walked Abby outside to the truck, where they kissed again.

"I'll see you shortly."

∞

When Paul and Abby met Sally and Mose at the LA airport on Sunday, they returned along the same highway they had traveled in June from Santa Monica beach after her release from Frontera. The Robinsons had visited Paul's parents while they were in Colorado and brought back presents and stories to be opened or related later that night. Mose missed his seafood while in Colorado, so the four ate dinner at a waterfront restaurant in Oxnard. It was there that Sally noticed the change in Paul's and Abby's behaviors, but she said nothing. When they returned to the house, Abby had her first drink and proposed a toast.

"To the new living arrangements," she said as she lifted her wine. Sally grinned broadly and drank. Mose hesitated and looked at Paul.

Paul drank from his beer bottle and said, "Abby and I thought you guys might need the small bedroom for real guests or another family member down the road, so we moved in together." He pulled Abby into his body and kept his arm around her. Sally stepped forward and hugged them both. Mose slowly lifted his beer to complete the toast.

"We go away for a week," said Mose, "and you guys take advantage of having no chaperones. Not sure we'll be able to do that again soon." The others laughed. Mose never told jokes, but his subtle wit often skewered those in attendance, and always his principal victim was Paul. It had been that way since they were freshmen at the University of Colorado back in the fall of 1965. He turned to Abby. "I suspect you're mostly to blame for this indiscretion, since Paul's too naïve to make the first move." He paused. "But it does solve a problem we were meaning to tell you about."

Sally smiled. "I'm pregnant."

∽

Patty Hearst was convicted of bank robbery on March 20, 1976, and sentenced to 35 years in prison. The length of her sentence was not lost on either Abby or Paul. Armed robbery after being kidnapped, raped, and tortured, yet because she espoused support for the Symbionese Liberation Army and her respect for its leader, General Cinque, the prosecution went after her without mercy.

"The Government sent us a message," said Abby. "It could have been me. I've often wondered how I got parole. They threatened me with twenty years, especially those first months before my trial. It was the time; the Government hated us, the anti-war protesters. We challenged them, and as it turned out, we were right about them. Patty Hearst is just the symbol. If she serves her full sentence, she'll die in prison. She was never a rebel, just a frivolous college girl, a fabulously wealthy college girl who never marched at a rally or carried an anti-government sign, as far as I know. But because she came from privilege and then her group killed that lady . . ."

"What do you want to do?" asked Paul.

"I'm not going to do anything. I'm on parole, and it wouldn't do any good anyway. Now I realize that governments will do what governments will do. Before prison, I got caught up in the naïve belief that we protesters could actually cause the government's policy to change.

It was so wrong to invade Vietnam, to send so many Americans to die, to bomb and kill so many Vietnamese, and really what for?" Abby paused. "Well, Patty'll get a reduced sentence when they realize she was used and is no threat to anybody's safety, when someone finds a little compassion. Her family will be able to influence someone to reduce her time, and maybe a future president will commute her sentence. But not yet. She has to pay the price for the rest of us." Abby closed the newspaper and flung it to the floor. She pushed out of her chair and went out into the backyard.

Paul rose from his chair and followed her. Standing behind her, he touched her shoulders first, but then wrapped his arms around her shoulders and held her. She would do nothing while she remained on parole, but he knew her time was coming. In what form, he didn't know.

Mose sensed Sally's eyes were open even in the dark. He turned onto his side and pulled her into his body. "A lot of us had sympathy for Patty and the SLA until they shot and killed that woman in the bank. I guess we'll find out more about that, but it wasn't Abby."

Sally relaxed, her body always at home in Mose's arms. "I know, but it was clear she wondered if it could have been. I worry about her, maybe for no reason, but I wonder how she's going to channel all that anger. It separates her from us, and a little from Paul. His is guilt. Hers is guilt fueled with anger."

Mose slid his face into his wife's hair. "I don't think she'll waste her freedom when it comes, but she's hard to read because of her past."

"America's behaviors are so personal to her," Sally hesitated. After a few moments, she finished her thought. "And to Paul."

 **3** 

Wally Constantine opened his office door and called Abby in. Another parolee stood and muttered something. "She has an appointment, Ricardo. Hold on and I'll get to you as soon as I can." Abby handed the parole supervisor her obligatory monthly report and eased back into the chair while he perused it. Constantine spent a few minutes asking about her job and college courses. He laughed hard when she told him about the nineteen-year-old in one of her classes who had asked her out on a date. Abby laughed at the boy, embarrassing him unintentionally, telling him she would be happy to chaperone. The boy knew nothing about her past, only that she was smart and attractive. After a few more comments, Constantine walked her to the door.

Abby saw only a blur, but she felt his weight smash into her, driving her back into the office. She crashed into Constantine before tumbling to the floor at the front of his desk. The man continued onto the parole officer, tackling him, taking him to the floor next to Abby. She heard Constantine swear, heard him call Ricardo by his name, all the time Ricardo grunting and swearing. The parolee was wrestling, while Constantine was punching, but laying on the floor gave him no leverage, and his punches seemed to have no effect. Abby rolled away from the men and tried to stand, but her foot slipped on a pile of folders stacked on the floor. She crawled behind Constantine's desk and tried to stand using his chair as an assist. It rolled away, and she fell again. In front of the desk, Ricardo had gotten Constantine into a choke hold, and Abby could hear his labored breathing. In prison when a fight broke out, it seemed like guards sprang from the walls, but no uniforms appeared now.

She yelled something at two men standing in the doorway, but later could not recall what it was. Ricardo continued to grunt, swearing at Constantine in a rage, while Constantine seemed to be trying to say, "Get help!" At Frontera no one went for help. In fact, inmates would prevent others from going to get help, walling off the fight until the damage was done. Abby stepped around the desk, grabbed a glass ashtray, and hit Ricardo on the head. It shattered in her hand, and Ricardo kept choking Constantine, who kept punching his assailant in the side. Abby looked for another item to use as a weapon. She grabbed the closest big thing with both hands and swung it at Ricardo's head again. This time, it knocked him off Constantine, giving Constantine the opportunity to effectively fight back. He recovered to his knees and punched Ricardo twice in the face, spewing blood over both of them. The parole officer yelled a name, not Ricardo, but another name. Ricardo tried one more time to grab hold of Constantine, but Constantine hit him in the stomach and in the jaw. At the same time, two uniformed policemen barged past the two men at the door. They rolled Ricardo onto his back and handcuffed him.

From the amount of blood in the office, mostly from Ricardo's nose and head, the emergency technicians suspected greater injuries, but there were no broken bones. For the next few weeks Constantine would sport a bruised neck, and his voice would be raspy. Ricardo was immediately taken to the county jail, and three days later transported to Tehachapi, returned to prison. Abby had several small cuts on her right hand, but none required stitches. She too had been splattered with blood when the typewriter split open Ricardo's head.

"Is this Paul or Mose?' asked Constantine in a gravelly voice, holding the phone with his less bloody hand.

"Mose. Who's this?"

"Wally Constantine. Sorry about my voice. Hey, we had a little incident down here at my office, and I'm going to need you or Paul or Sally to come down here and help Abby get home. She's mostly okay."

∾

Paul, Sally, and Mose found Abby sitting in Constantine's office, her clothes very bloody and one hand heavily bandaged. She still had blood in her hair. Constantine was leaning against his desk, having changed his shirt for another white one, and a woman was on her knees scrubbing the floor. When Abby's three roommates entered, the parole agent held up his hands defensively as a joke. "It wasn't me," he said.

Paul allowed Sally to touch Abby first. He still didn't know the proper protocol for the relationship between a male friend and a female felon on parole in the office of her supervisor.

Abby was shaken. "I'm okay." She smiled. "When I process what happened, I'll tell you about it. I just want to go home now."

Constantine promised to stop by tomorrow, told Abby thanks, and pulled Paul aside. "She's a trooper, but she got slammed pretty hard. Call me later when she falls asleep."

∾

She wasn't okay. Bruised ribs, a sprained wrist, multiple cuts, and a possible concussion compounded by no insurance. Constantine assured her his department would pay for a doctor visit the next day, but Abby blamed herself for being a felon and putting herself in the position to get hurt in this way. Paul sat in their room while she slept, thinking about the day, worried more about her unseen injuries. Constantine was glad it was Abby who had been in the office when the assault took place, but Paul was not. Abby Archer had reacted with fury, as Constantine told the story, and saved him from a hopped-up druggie, but Paul worried about her legal recovery and her emotional state, especially that emotional progress. Before she fell asleep, Abby had apologized to Paul and berated herself for her stupidity. Certain forms of guilt are difficult to overcome, to heal.

∾

Stitches, slight concussion, a cracked rib, and a very sore wrist, all of which caused her to miss a week of work. She did not miss classes at Cal Lutheran, however, and when asked by both her professors and the boss at the grocery store, she told them it happened when she fell off a ladder. She healed quickly and went back to stocking groceries, the only concession being that her boss gave her light duty. "No glass. Stay in the cereal aisle." Abby's parents never were told.

During the first few months of Abby's parole in the summer of 1975, Sally assumed the role of big sister, not quite to the extent Abby had been to the young women in prison, as a counselor, but as a guide to staying busy. Without asking, Sally assigned Abby household tasks, knowing idle time would prey upon Abby's moods. Sally did not allow Abby to sleep late on any morning, which simply followed her prison routine. When Abby began her college classes again in the fall, Sally relented just a bit, but only because Paul sat with Abby late into the night and read while she studied, keeping each other company. Sally was the only avid television watcher in The House. Mose listened to jazz while he graded worksheets and made lesson plans, sitting at the kitchen table drinking strong coffee, which didn't seem to hurt his sleep. Paul had been a radio guy since college, and Abby liked study-ing to rock music. Evenings at the Robinsons' home were quiet and purposeful, and Abby's goal of graduating before her parole ended was realistic.

Growing up in Oxnard, Mose loved the beach, but never tried surf-ing, hung out with friends while cruising Saviers Road, and listened to music unique to the Chicanos of Oxnard. He paid little attention to the maritime trade there. Port Hueneme was the only deep-water harbor between Los Angeles and San Francisco, a natural location for international trade and a naval base. Many of his friends worked part-time jobs on the docks, but Mose spent his summers employed by the city recreation department working with his high school basketball coach running camps for kids whose parents worked in the fields or on those docks. Oxnard was a tough town and by 1976 was begin-ning to see rising crime rates as gangs from Los Angeles were making inroads. The neighborhood known as La Colonia where Mose had grown up, the poorest of Oxnard's neighborhoods, was particularly susceptible, but he was welcomed back because of his NBA past. A recreation department boxing coach, a hard-ass taskmaster whom Mose respected, and two local businessmen began a boxing club to provide an alternative to gangs for the new generation of teenagers growing up in a harder environment. They enlisted Mose to help, not for any fighting skills, but as a face to attract the young toughs. What surprised Mose was that he enjoyed the physical nature of the club.

Sally walked. Fast. Abby tried that first summer but could never keep up. "Big boobs slow me down." Still, the two women found time to talk in the mornings while the men did their thing. It was during these moments that Abby learned about the great friendship between Mose and Paul.

"Mose wanted to drop out of school twice. College was hard for him," said Sally. "Life was easy for him here. Between his mom and the basketball coach, he was pampered. That's my role now." She laughed. "Paul wouldn't let him quit. Then, Mose wanted to give up basketball. He's so athletic, so gifted, but he's not the most competitive person, at least in the usual ways. He's determined rather than competitive. Paul convinced him to stick with it. Lots of that stuff went on between them while we were all living together in Boulder, but it was between them. I was still an outsider, especially my first semester."

"Like I am here," said Abby.

"Yeah, I suppose. Mose loves teaching, but he didn't graduate with an education degree. We kidded him that his degree was in basketball and smiling to get his way. He was still in the NBA when Paul came home from the war, but he retired to take care of Paul. He'll tell you that he wasn't suited for it or that injuries just caught up with him, but that's not true. He had another year on his contract. We flew to San Francisco to be there when Paul returned; his parents were there too, but it was Mose who held him up. We stayed with him for a week while he was undergoing medical exams and stuff. He looked terrible, and it really bothered us, but we visited and never let on. Mose decided right then to give up basketball after the current season. He began making plans then to bring Paul to Oxnard for his recovery. Somehow Mose knew."

∾

The Robinson baby was due in early July around the time of America's Bicentennial celebration. Sally and Abby redecorated the small room where Paul had stayed before moving in with Abby. The baby would sleep in his parents' bedroom for the first year on the opposite side of the house, so as not to disturb Aunt Abby and Uncle Paul. Sally continued to work, albeit from a desk at the health clinic rather than in the homes around Oxnard. Her plan was to take a six-month leave of absence and return to work full-time at the start of '77.

As Sally's belly grew, Abby assumed more of the cooking and cleaning chores, tasks she enthusiastically embraced. Paul understood that over time Abby felt guilty less and less about receiving such kindness from the Robinsons. She shouldn't have felt that way at all but being in prison alters perceptions about sharing rooms and space. During the summer of '73 after he had returned to America from his imprisonment, Paul often found living under a roof in a comfortable house intolerable. He slept in a tent in his parents' backyard several nights a week. It was irrational, but it helped get him to the next day. Irrational guilt. Of the over 500 American POWs in Vietnam who returned in April of 1973, fewer than 100 were grunts, the infantry. Most of the prisoners were college-educated pilots shot down from the skies rather than privates and sergeants captured in the jungle or rice paddies. One of the similarities between Abby's and Paul's confinement had been the depth of guilt they carried on their shoulders—and into their souls.

In June of '76, The House wanted to celebrate Abby's one-year anniversary with Sally cooking a special meal, but Abby asked them not to, that it only reminded her that she still had more time on the front end than on the back end, that counting days of successful parole forced her to look backward rather than forward. She still had much to recover, but the one thing she could never reclaim was that lost time. They would celebrate on December 11, 1977. Abby circled that date in her mind. So did Paul. She would be off parole, would not have to receive anyone's permission to do anything, would no longer have to look over her shoulder for "The Man," whoever that was. Paul looked to that day as the date when she would be able to give all her emotions to their relationship, to each other, to start a family if they wished, to work where they wanted rather than where they must, to remove the conditions from their lives.

Mose hugged Abby around her shoulders, a six-foot-seven-inch giant accepting her request and then altering the moment. "Did Sal say party? She meant gang initiation. We eat the meal and then you do the dishes—tonight and for the next week." He squeezed her body and then teased, "Now, go set the table."

∾

While Sally and Mose had made it abundantly clear Abby was a member of the family and not an intruder, while her parole supervisor often remarked on the stability of her home environment, and even though the room she shared with Paul was comfortable, Abby imagined a place of her own, where she and Paul could be "untethered." She itched for another step toward freedom. Often, after her college classes, she would drive the streets in Thousand Oaks looking at houses on the market. In the evenings she would describe them to Paul, who quickly realized that the outstanding feature of each house she described was its exclusivity, that it would be theirs alone, a place with a yard where he could pitch his tent. It was unrealistic; they would leave the area when her parole ended. Home ownership was for another place, another time. For now, just the tent in the trees seemed a more realistic scenario.

Mose continued to push Paul toward teaching and said he could get him a job in the Oxnard district. Tempting, but Paul had an itch like Abby's. Now, nearly 30-years old, it was time. His twenties were what they were, as he told Mose on the driveway during one of his one-on-one beatdowns, but he needed to go and wasn't accepting Mose's offer. Teaching, maybe, but not in California.

During Abby's most recent parole visit with Constantine, he urged her to petition for an early discharge, or as he had called it, "early termination." The parole board would probably refuse, these were rare, but he would strongly support her request. Her last four years in prison and her time on parole had been exemplary. And there had been the fight. Give it a shot, he suggested, it may only reduce the sentence a month or two, but it was something. She agreed to file if there were no conditions, no detainers, attached to her Discharge Certificate.

∾

Baby Robinson arrived on July 9, 1976. Mose had picked out several names—Count, Dizzy, or Duke—but Sally was not wild about any of them. Fortunately, Baby Robinson was a girl. Ella Pauline Robinson.

∾

On July 15, the Democrats nominated Jimmy Carter, a Southerner, an outsider to run against the Establishment. A month later, Gerald Ford's supporters held off the serious challenge from the more conservative Republican wing, those who wanted former California governor and movie star, Ronald Reagan. While Abby and Paul weren't wild about Carter, they couldn't forgive Ford for pardoning Richard Nixon for his Watergate crimes and his prolonging of the Vietnam War.

Mose's junior high school was looking for volunteers to help in the fall with a new silent reading program, and he asked Abby if she was interested. She was but couldn't as it would violate the terms of her parole, a felon working in schools. Mose wanted to talk with her supervisor, but she told him no. She wanted no special favors; she would live under the original contract. She did, however, give up half of her house-cleaning jobs and began volunteering at one of Paul's Catholic churches serving food to the poor. She also worked to collect food for the charity, driving Paul's truck to various grocery stores and the docks to pick up old or damaged vegetables and fruits. The church didn't care that she was on parole for bank robbery, only that she showed up regularly and worked hard. In prison Abby kept her hair short, maybe four inches long, but since her release, she had not cut it and it reached to the middle of her back. *Oh, gimme a head with hair.* It was a subtle expression of freedom, but more importantly, Paul liked it.

On Saturday, September 11, Abby treated her friends to dinner. Despite her earlier protestations about counting days, she wanted them to know that she was half-way plus one day through her parole, and she was succeeding because of them. Ella, Sally, and Mose returned home after the meal, and Abby and Paul drove out to a beach "to park"

46

in private. Paul produced a small diamond ring and proposed.

Abby stared at the ring for a minute without saying anything, then she took it with both hands to inspect it, but not in a critical way. Without looking up, "I'm kind of damaged, you know." She slid the ring onto her finger, turning her hand as she did. "It fits."

After a long hug, they talked. She had one condition, that they wait until her parole was over before the wedding. She was beginning to formulate a plan for that next life.

∾

Late in September, a new judge reduced Patty Hearst's sentence to seven years.

∾

Abby received permission from her parole supervisor to travel out of state to visit her parents in Chicago in October. When she flew out of Los Angeles, it marked the first day since her release from prison sixteen months earlier that she would not be saying good night to at least one of her new gang members in person. Anxious to see her family and her old neighborhood, she wondered about their routines and health. Now in their 60s, Reverend and Mrs. Archer continued to run a soup kitchen on Chicago's Lower West Side, assistance they had been providing since Abby was a child. Originally set up nearer The Loop, they had moved the charity farther south, into Pilsen, after the city cleared out the area for the building of the University of Illinois Chicago, uprooting thousands of poor Latinos. Poverty was the main characteristic of the neighborhood, with hopelessness a close second. First and second-generation Hispanics, the largest portion being Mexican but with sizeable numbers from the Caribbean, pushed the Eastern Europeans out in the Sixties. Abby's father started the soup kitchen in 1951, taking over a dilapidated restaurant north of Hull House on Halsted. With the creation of UIC, he moved it in the mid-Sixties to Pilsen where it remained. Abby grew up serving meals at least once each weekend to men mostly "down on their luck" and needing a "hand up." It was where Abby as a pre-teen began to observe the systems of social injustice.

O'Hare International Airport sat only a few miles from the Archer home in Des Plaines where Abby had grown up, her only home until she left for college in the mid-Sixties to Colorado. The house was seventeen miles from the soup kitchen, but it was a world away from the poverty of Pilsen. She hadn't been back in Des Plaines since the summer of 1970, six years earlier, two chapters of her life ago. The first evening back was like reunions most middle-class families would recognize: dinner, laughter, photographs, time spent mostly around the dining room table. However, the main topic of discussion was Abby's ring, her engagement to Paul. Her parents were happy, with the one caveat, Paul's Catholicism. When the laughter subsided, Abby explained that it was a joke in Oxnard too. She would be in Illinois only five days before returning to California on Sunday.

On Wednesday morning, Abby helped load the family station wagon with groceries for the trip to Pilsen. The routine. They made a half-dozen stops along the way to collect free food. At the kitchen, five volunteers waited, one man and four ladies. Abby met them all and had to tell them about "back when." And then the work began, the food preparation. More food was delivered to the alley entrance, sometimes by individuals who felt generous or by boys who were truant from school but working to make a few extra dollars for their families. Abby thought the level of poverty was greater than she remembered. The front door swung open precisely at noon, the line already sixteen deep. Meals were served until 2:30. Clean-up lasted until almost 4:00, with Abby washing more dishes than she ever had. Still, it was a wonderful day full of smiles and pats on strangers' shoulders, laughter with the volunteers, hugs from mom and dad, and a general feeling of worth.

At home, after dinner, Abby called Paul from the kitchen phone after her parents had gone to bed. "I'm exhausted. I don't know how my parents do it."

"Yeah, I miss you too."

Abby smiled on her end. "I love you, Paul. I wish you could have shared this day with me; it was so different from any day I've had in so long. I can't even remember. Every day in California, I feel like I'm under a microscope, but today I wasn't. What my parents do is valuable work. They make a difference. Maybe not in the grand scheme of things, but for their little part of the universe, they do."

Abby's enthusiasm passed through the phone lines in more ways than her words, and Paul listened with curiosity to the side of Abby that she kept mostly hidden, that she revealed cautiously. Confinement knocks enthusiasm out of a prisoner, and it takes time to replenish it, if ever, as he well knew. Paul observed signs in his fiancée at the Oxnard food drives, but it was measured. At this moment, her sentences were choppy, full of exuberance. Sally walked past him, lifting the phone cord in the kitchen, and silently mouthed "Abby?" He nodded. "Mose is at practice," she mouthed again.

"Oh, Paul, you can never underestimate the value of a hot meal. I grew up hearing that message, but I didn't understand. Back then, this place was mostly a chore for me. Today, it was something else." Abby spoke about specific individuals, their mannerisms, their accents, their kindness, and their appreciation for the meal. Most of the recipients were regulars who depended upon Abby's parents' service to survive, but many came in to get warm and eat a healthy meal. "I'm going back tomorrow if I can convince my muscles not to spasm all night. Did I tell you how tired I am?"

Abby ended the conversation to shower and fall into bed. Paul understood that kind of tired; he remembered from his first weeks of picking strawberries for twelve hours, but he had not received the rewards Abby was feeling tonight. Picking was penance, in a way. He sat with Sally and told her of Abby's day, then opened a book when Sally put Ella to bed. The words didn't register, however, and he closed the cover. Abby's recovery was brewing. He wondered about his own.

Three quick pops, like firecrackers to Abby, and then a delayed fourth shattered the front window spraying glass over the front tables. Diners dived onto the floor, locals who knew the sound well, yelling, "Get down! Get down!" Several men who were standing out front of the soup kitchen ran inside for protection, getting away from the front door as rapidly as possible. One of them, an older man, grabbed Abby and took her to the floor, shielding her body with his. Abby listened to both men and women lamenting, "Oh, God! Oh, God!" Within minutes, the street was wailing with police cars, all with their lights ablaze, and it reminded her of an episode in her life when those sounds and lights were behind her as she ran out of an apartment just ahead of the police. The older man raised up and helped her to her feet. "It's done now." He looked her over, and when he was satisfied that she hadn't been injured, he said, "When you hear shots, kiss the floor or the pavement. One shot usually leads to more." Abby turned suddenly to find her parents. They were already checking on the conditions of their guests, helping them to their feet or sitting them at tables to reassure them.

Following the lead of her parents and the volunteers, Abby began straightening the tables and chairs, returning order to the room. The only injuries were small hand cuts on a few of the guests who had been sitting near the front, the result of diving onto a floor covered with glass shards. Three volunteers pushed brooms across the floor collecting the debris. Two police officers entered the soup kitchen to ask if anyone had seen anything. Two men had been shot and were laying on the sidewalk with ambulance EMTs kneeling over them. It became clear that the shots were not intentionally aimed at the soup kitchen; it had merely been the backdrop for a drive-by shooting. "Gang warfare," said the police. "Probably La Raza, Ambrose, or the Kings. Mexican gangs, as far as we can tell."

Within fifteen minutes of the shooting, hot meals were again being placed in front of the guests while volunteers boarded up the shattered windows. Life went on in Pilsen.

∾

"My mom calls them guests, while my dad usually says visitors. Regardless, they're mostly homeless," said Abby on the ride back from Los Angeles with Paul on Sunday afternoon. "One of them is always at the kitchen unless it's Sunday, then they're both working with the congregation near the house. My dad has other duties, an occasional wedding or funeral, but I think his heart is with the kitchen. I know my mom's is." She paused. "She works there more now than when I was home, probably too much."

"So, those guests are mostly homeless too? Certain parts of the year in Chicago must be really cold!" said Paul.

"They don't operate a shelter, but there are nights when we open up for precisely that reason. This past week was chillier than normal for this time of the year, but not like it will be in January. Lake Michigan's wind just blasts through all your clothing," said Abby.

"Sounds like they provide much more than just a meal."

"They do. I always remembered that part, what my mom referred to as hospitality. She wanted them to be treated as guests with dignity. They don't have much of that in their lives. To eat as equals, which is why it's important to my parents that the volunteers often eat with the homeless. Our volunteers are from the area and know homelessness themselves. There are always more men in the lines than women, but over the past few years, my parents have commented on the number of children who are showing up, often unattended. The economy hits the poor first and hardest and lasts the longest."

Paul had chosen to return to Oxnard via the 101 instead of the more congested 1 this Sunday. Abby wanted to know about Ella, while Paul questioned her about her time with the family. She sat next to him on the bench seat and kept her hand on his thigh.

"It's odd," said Abby, "I was only going to help at the kitchen for a day or two, but I enjoyed it so much that I spent every day there. I'm looking forward to getting back to the church to help. Maybe I'll sign up for extra days."

"The shooting sure scared me. I imagine you too. When you called, I wondered if you were hiding some details from me, protecting me from worrying. I was glad to see you with no bandages at the airport. Make me a promise; no more gunfire in your life."

Abby put her arm around his shoulders and laid her head against him. "I would have told you. I probably would have had to call my parole officer too, but we were all okay. A couple of the guests have minor cuts and scrapes, but nothing serious. Neither of the boys who were shot died, but one was pretty serious. Chicago's gangs are much more violent than Oxnard's, but I did think about Mose and his boxing club." She kissed Paul's cheek. "But thank you for worrying."

❧

That evening, Abby and Paul babysat Ella so the Robinsons could have a date. Mostly, Abby held Ella while Paul read *Roots*, by Alex Haley.

"Where did you pick that up?" asked Abby softly.

"Mose was reading it; said I'd like it. Follows a slave from Africa to America and then his family up to about now. Supposedly, it's the author's family."

"Hence the title, huh?" Abby kissed Ella's sleeping head. "She's ready for bed."

"You're good with her," said Paul. "Will she let go of your finger when you set her down.?"

"I hope not. Keep reading, I'm going to sit in the rocker and sing her a lullaby, practice for the day when I have one of my own." She stood and kissed Paul. "When we have one of our own."

Abby returned a half-hour later and sat on the carpet between Paul's legs, forcing him to put down his book. She indicated she wanted a shoulder rub. "So, the book..."

"It talks about a person's ties to his land, to his home, that the attachment never dies. Kunte Kinte is forcibly taken from Africa, but he will always remain an African . . . in some way."

Abby stayed quiet as Paul massaged her scalp, neck, and shoulders and told her more about the book. She loved when he talked books, because he absorbed meanings and could project the ideas into his own life, his own times. The massage ended abruptly when Mose and Sally returned.

"How was Ella?" asked Mose as Sally went to check on her daughter.

"Perfect, as always," answered Abby. "You could have stayed out longer."

"You used to wear those huge hoop earrings, if I remember," said Paul. "Why not now?" His face only a few inches from Abby's, he traced his fingers over her face. Minutes earlier, she had done the same, spending time on the wrinkles above his eyebrows, asking him if he really was just 30-years old. Mose and Sally had taken Ella to the hills north of Ventura and would be gone all afternoon, so Paul and Abby went to bed to make Sunday afternoon love.

"I wore them to stand out, along with heavy eyeshadow, sort of my personality in Boulder. I try to be as inconspicuous as possible these days. You're the only one I want to notice me." She smiled, moved into his face, and keeping her eyes open, kissed him. "I came out of the prison door, and the look you gave me told me I was still pretty. I had no makeup on, but your eyes said I was pretty . . . and in more than just a physical sense, like you recognized me. That meant so much to me."

Paul rolled onto his back and pulled Abby on top of him. "You know what I miss? I miss our letters. Nothing helped my early recovery like your words. Then, when I came out here, they stopped being therapy in the sense of curing my war wounds and began, I don't know, giving me my spirit back. I'm still not where I'm supposed to be, I still have my moments, but I think the old Paul Garrity is at least recognizable too."

"It's difficult to concentrate on your words just now with you getting a hard-on again." Abby's body moved against his, and she bent her head into his neck, sucking slightly. "Want a hickey?" she teased. She rose up onto her knees and took him inside her again.

❧

On November 2, Jimmy Carter narrowly defeated Gerald Ford in the presidential race Carter had once led by 25 percentage points. Ford's pardon of Nixon, a staggering economy, and the shadow of Vietnam almost guaranteed that he would lose. Almost. An "un-Christian-like" *Playboy* interview where Carter revealed he lusted about women in his heart, although not in deed, collapsed his Christian evangelical support. He managed to hold the South and carry the Northeast, but the election's outcome wasn't decided until after midnight. The three votes from the Robinson house could not push California into the Democratic column, and Abby was prohibited from voting. She hadn't been eligible to vote in the '72 election either. Carter became the first Southern president since before the Civil War, a born-again Christian in an era of cynicism and deep division in America. Mose stayed up with Paul and Abby to get the result, Sally retiring with Ella around 10:00. Carter was proclaimed the winner just before 1:00 a.m., and Mose turned in, but the two current events geeks stayed up to listen to the president-elect's speech.

Listening to Carter speak, Paul waited for him to say something about a specific campaign promise, but he never did. "I like Walter Cronkite," said Paul.

"You probably liked him a lot more when he came out against the war," said Abby.

"I remember that night. He had gone to Vietnam to see for himself. I thought it might mean something toward ending the war sooner, but it didn't help."

Abby shook her head slightly, stood up and turned off the TV, and then climbed into Paul's lap. "For you or for me." They held each other for several minutes before going to bed.

❧

On his second day in office, January 21, 1977, President Carter pardoned all Vietnam draft evaders through executive order, fulfilling the campaign promise Paul had hoped for.

❧

Paul made dinner on Friday night. What else but spaghetti, but he took his time using fresh ingredients from the open-air market instead of canned sauces. Sally would note that he had grown as an adult. The wine was from one of the California vineyards up near San Francisco, and because Mose would be late due to a game, Paul fixed a plate of hams, cheeses, and olives for the women.

"So, what did we do to deserve such a feast?" asked Sally when everyone sat down to eat around 9:00. As Paul lit a single candle for faux ambiance, Sally turned to Abby. "Back in the old days, when spaghetti was served with meatballs or sausage, it signified that Paul had a major announcement. It's a tradition worth preserving." Her husband nodded in agreement.

Paul sat. "Fill your plates first." When they all had a full plate and a refill of wine, Paul congratulated Mose on another victory, his eleventh straight since an opening defeat. His freshmen squad, the D team, was dominating its opposition.

"Coaches are usually about as good as their talent, and I've got some talent, that's for sure," said Mose, deflecting the compliment.

"Well?" asked Sally staring at Paul.

Paul raised his goblet. "To James Earl Carter. He freed me today. Had I run off to Canada after college to avoid being drafted, I could come home now." He tried to say this with a little humor, but his eyes welled up and he swallowed hard. He set his wine down on the table but left his hand on the stem. His friends and lover waited. In a few moments he said, "Sorry." Abby reached over and took his free hand. "I've always wondered what if. In many ways, it would have been easier, but . . ." He took another deep breath and bit the inside of his lower lip and looked at Abby. "Mose and Sally know how much I thought about it, about heading north, but I had this stupid idea that if I didn't go into the Army, I would miss the great event of our generation, and that, somehow, I owed it to those men who couldn't get multiple deferments like we had. . . and to my dad who served in World War II. It would have been six-and-a-half years, but a safe six-and-a-half years, albeit locked away from everyone I love. As it turned out, I spent a little over three years in the Army, two in Vietnam. Shorter prison term physically, but . . ." He leaned over and kissed Abby on her cheek. "I think you know the difference between two years and six years." He bit his lower lip again, but this time smiled gently and apologized a second time. "Food's getting cold. Dig in."

"I wondered if you'd noticed," said Mose.

The remainder of the evening was festive rather than somber, four people who loved one another sharing a meal, good wine, and memories after carrying a terrible burden for too long.

∾

Naked in bed, holding each other close, Abby and Paul talked. They had shared similar thoughts in letters while Abby spent her years in prison, but that time of affinity had altered their perspective in important ways.

"Do you wish you would have gone to Canada?" asked Abby.

"No," he answered with a whisper. "Not that I have a soft spot for the alternative. You once said you wished I had."

"You could have died in Nam, in that jungle. You almost did. Many soldiers did."

"I had to survive to come here to you."

"You know what Mose would say about that, don't you? You're full of bullshit sometimes."

"If anyone would know, it would be him," said Paul.

"He's a good friend. So's Sally. I've been so lucky to have this, but mostly to have you." Abby loved his eyes, eyes she once said saw nothing but what was directly in front of them. She moved up and softly kissed both of his eyes. "What color will our children's eyes be?"

"I won't care about our boys, but I want all of our girls to have your brown eyes."

Abby smiled. "How many kids are you planning for?"

"It was a frivolous response. I've never given serious thoughts to having children."

"I have. Lots. I want ours." She kissed him again. "I want to make our own, bear them, birth them, raise them. I hold Ella and feel the future. I watch Mose and Sally hold Ella together and feel the love they share as a family. I want that for you, a different dimension for our love." She hugged him for a long moment. "You'll be a wonderful father, you know."

Paul moved his forehead to Abby's very gently. He studied her eyes and she waited, knowing he was exploring another part of her. They went quiet for a few minutes, just holding each other.

Abby agreed silently. "Sally asked me a few days ago where I thought we might end up. I told her about wanting to run away from California on the day my parole is over, but I'm not sure about that anymore. Oxnard has been so good for me. I know it's not Oxnard but what you guys have provided, but it's the setting, so I associate this place with all the rest. Father Serna wants me to work for the church when I graduate. A paying position maybe. Both of us."

"We don't have to decide yet. We have time."

"I know, but I'm planning. I don't want to drift." Abby finally pulled back slightly and looked up at Paul. "Sally has made it clear that she wants us to stay here with them, but I also know she wants another kid someday. It's their house, and at some point, we need to leave. It's not large enough for two families."

Paul laughed softly. "You mean actually pay rent? On our wages? In this economy? We'd be like those homeless people in La Colonia. Or we could work with your parents in their soup kitchen."

"I spoke with Constantine about moving, and he told me I would be crazy to go. He understands my desire for a place of my own, for privacy." She paused there and kissed Paul. "He knows we're a thing, but he advised me to stay and finish my parole in a stable environment. He talks with Mose a lot and has assured me that they don't want us to move out."

"I guess Constantine is pretty involved in community affairs, at least that's what Mose told me. The old cop in him. Anyway, they talk at the boxing gym."

Abby kissed his lips and moaned softly. She pulled back, looking intently at Paul. "I love our gentle talk, these moments in our life now." She kissed him tenderly again. "Where do you go when you go off alone?"

"I don't do that to get away from you guys," he said. Abby tilted her head slightly and waited. "I could ask you the same thing."

She nipped his nose. "You're avoiding my question. I don't mean going silent, going off in your own skin. I mean when you drive off alone."

"I know what you mean," said Paul. He slid his hands from her butt to the small of her back. "I'm a Colorado guy. What that means is that I find, I don't know, solace, I guess, in the mountains. When I arrived here to live with Mose and Sally, I was still suffering from my captivity. That captivity was in a mountain valley. I still had my mountains. I firmly believe those mountains in Vietnam, in a sense, wrapped their arms around me and helped me survive. Does that sound crazy?"

"No, I think you find solace when you're nestled in my mountains too."

"In my Vietnam prison, I mostly focused on daily survival, but so did the old people who were my guards. They were protective of the grandchildren, hiding them from their own soldiers, almost like they were afraid they could be taken from them, which of course they could once the children became teenagers." Paul paused as if looking over his shoulder to check for traffic as he turned a corner. "My brother and I aged my parents. They lost us both, my brother permanently due to drugs, and I think they were good parents."

Abby put two fingers on Paul's lips. "Don't go there. That's guilt that was laid on you by others or circumstances beyond your control. There are many reasons not to have children of our own, maybe adopt, but I won't allow those to stop us. I want your children and someday I want a family like what we see here."

Paul blinked. "You're not pregnant now, are you?"

Abby smiled coyly. "And if I was?"

∾

On the other side of the house, Mose rocked Ella while Sally slept, another casualty of too much wine. This was the best part of his day. His daughter hadn't learned to sleep through the night yet, or maybe had learned that her papa would cradle her if she made that subtle cry to wake him. For the first time since the late-Sixties with The War hanging over their heads, Mose stopped worrying about Paul. He was still recovering and would be for a while longer, but it seemed as though President Carter's blanket pardon had closed a door behind Paul, that he had breathed tonight. Mose gently touched Ella's nose,

"Uncle Paul taught me that we are complete in what we do for others rather than what others do to us. I want you to remember that my little angel."

∾

Abby revealed her anger through her eyes; they narrowed and focused on what was behind them rather than what was in front of them. Paul's anger registered in his jaw; visible to an alert observer, which Abby was. Tonight, he was stewing, moving towards boiling over. Before dinner, while she was studying her sociology, he went for a run to settle down, but it hadn't worked. Over dinner, he told her and Sally and Mose about the renewed fighting along the Vietnamese-Cambodian border, another of the sporadic clashes between these two Southeast Asian nations. The never-ending war in that region. "If you wouldn't read the newspaper," advised Mose. But Paul devoured the LA Times daily. Sally had reminded him that dinner was a no-politics zone when Ella was at the table. Paul smiled, and the conversation shifted to the NBA playoffs, which meant that Abby wasn't interested. She finished her meal, excused herself to study, and immersed herself in social stratification, the last course in her major. She had first enrolled in college to become a teacher, but her felony conviction nixed that. She continued with her sociology major while dropping all her education classes. On a whim, she chose criminal justice for her new minor, finding that it was a fascinating area, and she had some real-life experiences there.

Paul joined her in the bedroom around 7:00. He set his beer down on the end table next to his well-worn, green chair, a chair Mose had carried around since their college days and which had finally ended up in this house. Paul stood behind Abby and rubbed her shoulders. She leaned her head back into his chest, enjoying his touch.

"I'm proud of you, you know," he said.

"Mmm-um." She waited.

"The never-ending war. The Chinese, the French, the Japanese, America. I think war gets into your system and never lets go. An evil force that takes on a life of its own. Vietnam finally gets its independence, reunifies, and should be happy, but it can't move on." He was interrupted by a soft rap on the jamb.

Mose and Sally came in with beers. "Do you want us to take him off your hands, so you can study, Abby?" asked Sally. "We can take him into the living room to rant, so you'll have some quiet."

Abby took hold of Paul's hands and shook her head. "I'm mostly done for tonight, so let's all go. I think I'll have hot tea though."

When they were all settled, Mose said, "Well, get it out."

Paul tapped his beer on his thigh and began. "It's hard to find the good guys over there, but the Khmer Rouge are maybe the worst. Pol Pot." Paul paused there. "That murderer is completely financed by us, by the good old USA, just because he calls his government a democracy and opposes our old enemy, but he's killing his own people by the thousands." Paul halted again. "Cambodia!"

"Kampuchea," corrected Sally.

Paul shook his head slowly. "No, not to me. Always and forever Cambodia. It's where I was captured." He had never shared this information with anyone. The Army knew, but Paul had never told anyone. "For the record, it was the Viet Minh operating with a Khmer Rouge unit who got me there and hauled my ass back across the border. I'll spare you the details, but the soldiers who controlled me were kids, didn't seem more than fifteen or sixteen. Child soldiers. Not nice. Savages." Paul went back in time for a moment. Then, "Anyway, what set me off this afternoon was the reports that Pol Pot and the Khmer Rouge were doing our work for us, finishing our war against the Viet Minh. Whoever wrote the story obviously didn't do his homework or is from another planet. There's nothing good or democratic going on in Cambodia. Hundreds of thousands of Cambodians have been relocated out of the cities. Forced labor. Stalinism. Pol Pot won't last forever, but the people of his country will be destroyed all over again. This one isn't directly our fault, but we have our part. A major part." It wasn't the word Paul was looking for.

"Our lingering shadow," said Abby gently.

"Seems like nations can be prisoners of war too," said Mose.

"God," grunted Sally. "If there was one thing I could change about you, Paul Garrity, it's your damned attitude that you're personally responsible for America's war in Vietnam. Get over it! The war began before you started school as a little boy. You know the history." Mose touched her thigh. He wanted her to stop, but she had one more thing to add. "You too, Abby. LBJ and Nixon didn't call you for your advice. Both of you tried harder to stop that war than anyone else I ever knew. You did what you could."

The room went quiet. Paul and Abby were touching, Mose and Sally too. Finally, Mose spoke. "I think I understand you both, and I have enormous respect for you. That war tore us all a new one. We just hate to see what it continues to do to the two of you. You hate someone, but it's a faceless someone, so you don't know how to fight him. The bad guy, the antagonist in all of this, is the soulless entity that makes war, the one who kills innocent people or at least forces them into exile. I think you both need to quit battling windmills, get off those imaginary horses you ride, and get your hands dirty doing things like your parents do." He spoke directly to Abby. "You came back so happy after Christmas, so relaxed and yet so energized."

When he paused, Sally apologized. "I'm sorry. I just see you both making such great strides, and then something sets one of you off, and you take steps back into yesterday. I can't imagine what either of you went through, but you're both tough people. Quit allowing that fucking war to hold you back. Abby, you don't think we notice your anger, but we do. Less and less, but we see. Your time on parole is coming to an end. You're almost there. Do more of what you're doing at the church. It's special and it makes a difference."

Abby sniffled. "I don't know how. Vietnam has been the driving force in my adult life. I continue to see the people who fought with purpose and are now left, I don't know, left to suffer."

"I think," said Mose, "in a strange way, Vietnam might have helped get you through prison by giving you a rationale for your . . . actions . . . for the robbery. You went in when we were at war; you came out and it was gone, and you hadn't done anything to end it." He turned to Paul. "Remember when we talked about that? You said you felt guilty being a POW, that you didn't do anything to change the war one way or the other. Hell, when you sleep in a four-by-four bamboo hut at night and are tethered to a rope during the day for over a year, it's not your job to fix the war. It was your job to survive, and you did."

Abby turned to Paul with a shocked look on her face. "You were tethered? Oh, God!"

"It's okay," said Paul in a whisper. He took both of Abby's hands, squeezed, and turned to the Robinsons. "When I call your husband dumbass, it's a term of endearment." He smiled at Sally. "Maybe I need to call you dumbass also, so you'll remember how much I love you too. At the VA, they told me that this would happen, that I was suffering from combat stress, and that it might show up unexpectedly for years to come. I told them I saw very little combat, that mostly I was a desk clerk in Saigon. One doctor said it wasn't combat stress, that my fatigue came from being a POW. They wanted to medicate me. I said no to their drugs, that I could recover on my own. Not the first time in my life I've been wrong, not about the drugs but about doing it alone." His eyes went back to Abby. "I think that might apply to you, too." He lifted both of Abby's hands a short distance and shook them gently. "We're quite a pair, you know."

Abby smiled. "You're stuck with me though."

Paul turned back to Mose and Sally. "We're trying, and I appreciate your advice. Gotta stop looking back and start looking for a job that has more value than fixing broken pews or packaging strawberries."

In bed, in each other's arms, Abby spoke softly. "No secrets. Let's get our prisoner stories out."

"You know the basics from my letters. I told you there were three of us captured that night. The two others were chubby draftees, both twenty. Kids. No college. The NVA marched us for two days and then they separated us. I never saw them again, but they weren't on the POW list, so I can only assume they died, since no one ever escaped. The reason my foot hurts occasionally is from the metal collar they fastened around my ankle. They put that on after a week or so when they started letting me out of the hut, my jail, to work in the fields. That's how I was tethered. They would tie a rope to the collar which gave me some room to roam, twenty feet or so at a time. The thing about working was I began exercising and ate better. Not good, but better. I was malnourished but not starving. I think I lost about 40 pounds." He paused.

"If you were in such a small hut at night, you couldn't even straighten out to sleep."

Paul smiled. "Pythagorean theorem. I slept diagonally. Propped my head up usually. That way I could stretch my legs and feet. Really, that part wasn't so bad. What was bad was not knowing what was going on anywhere else. I began watching the moods of the family who held me, especially the grandma. When news was bad, she was angry and took it out on me with a long pole. Stinging blows. Never broke anything. The only time she did any lasting damage was when I flinched, and she missed my shoulder and hit me on the jaw. Lost a couple of teeth. The VA gave me new ones." Again, Paul smiled. "While I was a prisoner, I never again heard any fighting. What I did hear were the jets flying back and forth on bombing runs, but my farm never got bombed. The other worst thing was wondering if I would ever get home and how my mom was doing. Funny. I didn't worry about my dad. Somehow, I knew he could be proud of me for serving and not running away; that he could rationalize the whole prisoner thing. But not my mom. I knew this would be killing her. When I returned, she had aged so much."

"Did you ever talk to anyone while you were a captive?"

"Not really. They gave me commands in Vietnamese. I got so I understood what I was supposed to do and stuff, but we never conversed. By they, I mean the old man, grandma, and his daughter who operated the farm. The little kids. All the young men were off fighting. I was held by a family, probably the only POW who was. Nobody has ever figured out why, or if they did, never told me. I got the feeling that the old man had been important once, and they gave me to him to help with his farm during the war. But I'll never know. I was relocated near Hanoi those last few weeks."

"Do you ever think about why you survived?"

"When I was there, it wasn't why, it was how to survive. But, yeah, when I got home, even now sometimes, I wonder. Logically, some of it has to do with the fact that I was in really good shape when I was captured. I think that may have had something to do with why I was dropped off at the farm, to help. But that's just speculation. I was also older and educated. I kept processing the discussions that I had had in Boulder with Mose and people like you. I created a friend and talked out loud, sort of using a different voice for him. Kept me company."

"Did he have a name?"

"Mario."

"Don't tell me it was after Mario Savio."

"The one and only. Who better to resist with? He needed to experience Vietnam in some way. Anyway, we had some wonderful discussions, and he was angry all the time, so I didn't have to be. That sounds funny, but it's true. I worked, I slept, and I hung out with Mario."

"Why not Abbie Hoffman?"

"I never met him. I had a brief conversation with Savio in Boulder once. Fascinating guy."

"What are you leaving out?" asked Abby.

"Nothing intentionally. If you think of questions, ask. No more concealing hard things from you. Promise." They both went silent for a moment, and then Paul asked, "What about you? What hurt you the most?"

Abby averted her eyes to contemplate. Paul heard her roll saliva in her mouth and swallow. He waited, understanding that, like for him, to name just one thing was impossible, for it changed almost daily.

She brought her eyes back to him. "Not being touched in . . . a loving way. Not sex exactly. No hugs, no kisses, no handholding, no one that I truly trusted just to sit with. I never knew how addicted I was to physical contact. Early on, I refused to play anyone's game, and it just became me. I had almost no visitors in my time at Frontera. My parents came out once a year, but my brothers and sisters never visited. That hurt, but I understand. They're not rich." She paused. "And I never turned." Paul's eyes said that he didn't understand the term. "Became homosexual. There's pressure to do that, you know. I had advances made that were more seductive than threatening, but I decided I wasn't going to do that. And I didn't. My advantage was that I didn't need any of the items that were traded for certain behavior. Cigarettes, drugs, candy. Later, after I settled down and settled in, a blockmate told me the talk that went on among the lesbians was intense over who would get me. To be blunt, because I was attractive and built, I would be a catch. Never happened though. Those girls who had been on the street dived headfirst into that culture, the inmate code. I understood. Understand." Abby kissed Paul tenderly. "That six years without sex, I'm trying to catch all of it up with you."

"We've got a good start."

She kissed him again, pulled back, and smiled deviously. "Did you have sex in Vietnam?" When Paul delayed his answer, she said, "No secrets, remember."

"Okay. Once with a prostitute. A couple of times with a nurse from Ohio. Once with the sister of a buddy in Hawaii when I went on leave." He paused. "Satisfied?"

"Yeah. Any feelings attached to these encounters?"

"No. Pure sex."

"Do you want to know how I survived?" asked Abby.

"I thought you said you abstained."

"I sinned. Masturbation." She giggled in a junior-high way.

∾

Sally apologized to her husband. "A little blunt, huh?"

Mose nodded. "You and me and Paul have been together long enough that we can say anything, but maybe a bit too much with Abby. I think she'll be okay though." He held the covers up for Sally while she climbed into bed. He pulled her into his body, a body 60 pounds more muscular than when she first met him in the fall of '66 at the University of Colorado.

"I forget that she can't just break away and do what she wants, what she needs. In a way, she's tethered like Paul was, at least for the rest of the year."

"They're a good match, Sal. They really look out for each other." Mose kissed Sally on her forehead. "Like you and me."

"Abby would like to get her own place, and I know she thinks she's an imposition to our privacy. I told her once that when Paul moved in, you and I stopped running around naked, so her presence didn't change anything. I was jokingly serious, but she accepted that," said Sally. "She'll be here until she's free."

Mose hugged his wife. "Prison knocked the shit out of her just like it did to Paul, but they're both regaining their old spirit. It's hard to be as sure with Abby since we didn't know her as well. I was thinking about what they could do permanently, and I talked to Paul again about teaching with me or at the high school. The district would hire him. His military experience would go a long way in getting him the job. He told me he wasn't going to stay here to teach, but we'll see."

"Did you talk to Dr. Romero about him?" asked Sally. "He'd be such a good teacher!"

Mose nodded. "And I think Abby could find work in the county doing charity stuff with a paycheck. Kind of seems like the type of career she's been working toward." Mose could feel his wife smiling. "What?"

"You accuse me of scheming." Sally bumped her head into Mose's shoulder. "Have you picked out a house for them to buy too?" She giggled. "They're sort of like our kids, you know."

On Monday, February 14, Valentine's Day, Abby didn't return from Thousand Oaks until late in the afternoon. Sally worried. "Where have you been? I always worry about you in that traffic."

"I spent some extra time with my advisor and then the registrar." She hugged Sally. "I'm going to graduate this spring! I'll need to finish my senior essay before April, but I can do that. I have enough credits with these two classes that I have now to graduate."

 **5** 

A Bachelor of Arts from California Lutheran University awarded to Abigail Anne Archer, to be issued on Saturday, May 21, 1977, twelve years after starting college in Colorado. Mose and Sally informed Abby that her next gang responsibility was a graduation party. No discussion as to whether, but only who would attend, who to invite.

St. Anthony's by itself needed enough maintenance to keep Paul busy throughout the week, but he also worked four other Catholic churches in Ventura County. He had gone over to Sacred Heart before breakfast to unclog the plumbing and now was back at St. Anthony's painting the walls in the narthex. Father Thomas came in with an armload of paraphernalia to collect money for another project.

"What charity today, Father?" asked Paul.

"Not a charity this time. Two new churches. A few dollars from each diocese goes a long way."

"Well, Father, since every town in America has a Catholic church, I'd say you'll fund that church completely by the end of the month. Will they be needing my services too, Father? Where are these new churches going to be located?"

"Indonesia and Mexico. When will you and Abby be converting? You've both done so much for us, I think it only fair that we do something for you. Save your soul maybe?" He laughed at his little joke. "You could join and then give your friend Moses a nudge. Such a biblical name." Father Thomas placed a slotted metal box on top of the wooden stand with an explanation of where the new churches would be constructed.

"At least Mose allowed Ella to be baptized here at St. Anthony's. Keep working on him, and I'll put in a good word for you." Paul laid his brush on top of the paint can and picked up a roll of masking tape. "Abby's sure enjoying her time here. She's going to be graduating from Cal Lutheran next month, and we're throwing a little party that afternoon. Saturday the 21st, I think. She'd like it if you were there. No gifts."

Father Thomas said he would try to make it. He jokingly warned Paul not to knock over the new collection box but to feel free to donate. Hours later when Paul finished and was cleaning up, he slid the collection box back next to the door into the nave. The informational sheet asked that funds be provided for a small church on the tiny island of Galang where already several thousand Vietnamese refugees were being housed.

❧

The conversation began when, unexpectedly, Abby said, "Oxnard grows on you." They were all in the living room doing what they did: Mose grading math papers, Paul reading, Sally sitting on the floor with Ella while trying to finish reports on unwed mothers, and Abby studying. Mose gave a flippant response, "And that's why I shower daily." He stood, stretched, asked if anyone else wanted a beer. Only Paul said yes. Mose returned from the kitchen, handed Paul his beer, and stood over Abby waiting.

"It's a beautiful place," said Abby with a coy smile, as if the conversation was over. Mose didn't move. "Something's always growing. Lima beans, strawberries, flowers for greenhouses. The smell of the ocean is everywhere. Look north and it's mountains. Go sit down, you big giant." Sally patted the couch behind her and Ella.

"It's a boxer's town," said Paul. "Your buddy Tiny is really a good guy and funny as hell." Paul turned slightly to Abby. "Don't know if you've ever met him, but he's the guy who convinced Mose to work out at the boxing gym. It's Tiny's gym, and he runs it like boot camp."

"You would know boot camp, wouldn't you," said Sally.

"Bad metaphor. The Colonia is much, much tougher than basic training ever was. When I go over to lift with Mose, I'm the only white face there. Tiny doesn't care, but some of his homies do, I think. Intruding maybe, but it's all good since I'm seldom there. Mexicans, and proud of it. No gangs in the gym though. Tiny's Oxnard."

Mose leaned over and picked up his daughter. "Tiny likes you. Respects you. He's a veteran too. Tells me you're a survivor, and once a survivor, always a survivor."

"Shit! If I ever got in the ring with one of the boxers he's trained, I'd get killed. No survivor here."

Mose lifted Ella above his head and made faces at her. "Boxing's the sport of heroes. Win in the ring, especially here in Oxnard, and you don't pay for many street tacos. I grew up here, obviously, and was the best basketball player they ever had, but I was no big deal compared to those guys who were boxing champs." He looked at Abby. "I still don't know why you seem so enamored with Oxnard tonight."

Abby smiled inwardly and fiddled with her engagement ring. "When I'm at school in Thousand Oaks or even just in Ventura, do you know what I see? Shoppers. The few times we've gone to Santa Barbara, do you know what we see? Tourists. What do I see in Oxnard?" She allowed her question to hang in the air. "Workers." She let her answer hover for a moment too. "Mostly brown, tight, short men and women in the fields, but in town too. Your description of Oxnard as a boxing town, I like it. Tough. Tenacious. Hard workers doing hard work. The unwed girls I try to help are mostly white girls. Unwed Chicano girls rely on their families. Maybe that's not always positive, but it's also part of that toughness. And family. Family matters here."

Sally took a drink from Mose's beer. "So, you and Paul will be buying a house here after your parole ends then?" Abby's smile did not reveal her plans. There was a minute of reflection in the Robinson living room before Abby spoke again.

"Paul and I will always have Oxnard, our Paris." She kissed Paul on his cheek. "That's a *Casablanca* reference, my love."

∾

Wally Constantine constantly found news coming from the judicial side of his job something to swear about. Daily. Ricardo Gomez had been released from Tehachapi again. Gomez was once a cop, one who took bribes, a bad cop. Bleeding heart judges! At least they didn't reassign him to me, thought Constantine, but Los Angeles is no place for an angry, violent man with no ties other than the street. Prison overcrowding, my ass! He opened his desk drawer and removed his service revolver, loaded it, and placed it in his briefcase.

∞

"Who's the graduation speaker?" asked Sally.

"Some Presbyterian minister. They tried to get Kurt Vonnegut, but he declined. What's for dinner?" asked Abby.

"More ham. Still working on our Easter leftovers. Paul called and said he might be a little late, something to do with meeting a buddy in Ventura. He didn't give me a name. Hey, I'm putting together the guest list for your graduation party. Write down anyone you would want to attend that we wouldn't think of."

Abby shook her head slightly. A part of her wanted her graduation to be low-key so she could thank those closest to her who had made it possible. Paul, Mose, Sally, and her parents. Maybe take them to dinner. But there were others who deserved her thanks too, especially Wally Constantine. From their first meeting when he seemed so impersonal, so unconcerned about her rehabilitation and reentrance into society, until yesterday's monthly meeting when he took her to lunch. He hadn't heard back from the Department of Corrections, but neither he nor Abby had expected any reduction in her sentence. Still, he commended her on her commitment to right a wrong. She would never call him a teddy bear, but she realized his no tolerance policy had set a tone that worked perfectly for her. Nearly two years in with eight months left. Then there were the women at Cal Lutheran, Dr. Scudder and Dr. Clark, her adviser and favorite professor, who had taken similar approaches as Constantine. Prove to them she was serious. After that first semester of earning two As, they sat her down and made out a schedule allowing her to graduate next month, one semester early. Scudder even talked about graduate school. Maybe journalism. Yeah, these people should be my guests too.

～

"People see me as a coward." He kept his head down. "And a liar. That hurts. I just told them how I felt about the war, but I didn't reveal any sensitive information. Hell, I didn't have any to give them, but I still went over when I was drafted and killed VC. I never thought anyone would have to worry about me killing myself. I never suffered from depression, but since I've been home, I can't get going."

"It's an unforgiving world, isn't it?" It was a rhetorical question, a comment of support, an "I understand" response. "Are you still going to counseling?" he asked.

"Nah. None of those other guys were POWs; they don't get it."

～

"Need a junker. Cheap one." The parolee slid a fifty across the seat of the Olds. "In a couple of weeks. I'll be around."

～

Paul missed dinner, but he reheated the remains of the ham and potatoes when he returned around 8:00. The big news from Mose was that he had secured three concert tickets to hear Jackson Browne in Los Angeles for early May, a first Mother's Day present from Ella for her mama to see her favorite rocker. Mose would stay home with Ella. Had Paul and Abby not been around to go with Sally, Mose would have escorted her, but it would have been two hours of musical torture for him. Abby spoke with her parole supervisor and received permission to attend, but with the admonition to be careful about the drug use. Paul stood at the counter while he ate, and Abby stood with him.

"So, tell me about your day," she said.

"Around noon, I got a call from a VA doctor who I didn't know, wanting to know if I had any time today to talk to a patient of his who had attempted suicide. I thought he meant on the phone, but he wanted me to come by the clinic in Ventura and visit with the guy. Turns out he was a prisoner-of-war too. That's why he wanted me to talk with him. Messed up." Paul stopped for a moment to finish off his meal and rinse his plate before putting it in the dishwasher. He stepped into Abby and enveloped her in a bearhug, holding it for several seconds. He relaxed his hold only slightly when he spoke again. "He evidently put a pistol in his mouth but backed off before pulling the trigger. That was two days ago." Abby tensed. "He was a Marine sergeant, captured near the DMZ and imprisoned for four years. When he got home, his wife only stayed for a couple of months before leaving him and taking the kids." Paul stopped again but continued to hold Abby. "I think the whole ordeal was almost as hard on the families as on us."

They held each other before Paul continued.

"It's been four years since we came home, but sometimes, it seems like only yesterday, and I think I'm one of the lucky ones. A day hasn't gone by without me knowing that someone cares. My parents, Mose and Sally, and you." He turned his head into her hair and kissed it. "But our country hasn't been supportive, so I can understand this guy's despair, especially without his wife and family. I don't know."

Sally came into the kitchen with Ella on her hip. "Don't mind me, I'll only be a sec."

Paul tousled Ella's dark hair. "Not a problem. We're just keeping each other warm."

Abby broke off from Paul's arms and hugged Sally. "Oh, one of those moments, huh?" said Sally. With her free arm, she hugged Abby back. "You're welcome, for whatever I did." She kissed Abby's cheek and then rejoined Mose in the living room.

Abby returned to Paul's hug. "She told me a while back that a child never understands a parent's love until that child has a child of her own."

"All the time I was talking to this guy today, I was thinking about you and Mose and Sally. My family. It's hard for me to see myself as that guy, but he's lots of the men who came back. He's evidently an alcoholic now, at least that's what the doctor said. I guess the clinic got my name from a VA list that tracks us all, or at least some of us. The guy wanted to know how I did it. I told him about you, but that it hadn't been easy during that first year when I was living with my parents."

"Did you tell him how lucky you got?"

Paul pulled back. "I think so." He kissed Abby on the lips, and they rubbed noses. "I am, you know."

"Yeah, I know. Still can't believe I'm sleeping with such an ugly man."

❧

Jackson Browne more than lived up to Sally's expectations, and she rewarded Mose for his thoughtful gift when she joined him in bed that night. Neither Paul nor Abby had attended a large venue concert before, but they had seen several prominent performers and groups in Boulder in bars and concert halls. As much as they enjoyed Browne, they were blown away by the warm-up singer, a red-haired guitarist named Bonnie Raitt who performed a mixture of blues and country rock. "Mose might even have liked her."

❧

On the same night as the concert, in another neighborhood of Los Angeles, a faceless man rolled down the window of his Oldsmobile and unwrapped a rag revealing a .38 special, a snubbie, and motioned to the man on the curb to take the weapon. "I don't want to know why you want it." The standing man jammed the gun into his coat pocket, tapped the car door, and walked away.

❧

Constantine called Abby on Tuesday to reschedule her monthly parole meeting, wanting to know if she could come in on Wednesday instead of Thursday because he needed to be in Los Angeles for a court hearing. Abby agreed, reminding him that her college classes had ended, so she would not be in Thousand Oaks on Wednesday. She asked him if he was going to be able to attend her graduation party on Saturday afternoon.

Abby left the church office at 10:30 for her 11:30 meeting at the Ventura County Courthouse. She brought with her a graduation announcement to give to Constantine, a reminder of the time. As always, when she arrived outside his office, she had to wait in the hallway with two or three other parolees, all of whom she recognized and exchanged greetings with. She wondered what parole would have been like under the supervision of another agent, but Constantine took no credit for her rehabilitation. He always remarked that Abby was a model client. Client. This morning, she brought with her a pocket notebook. Her only paying job now was stocking at the grocery store. She would be taking on more hours beginning in June, a mindless job that she could probably do in her sleep, but it had been constant, reliable, and acceptable to her parole conditions. Maybe she should invite a few of her co-workers to her party. Abby wrote down two names in her notebook. Life was less scheduled without her college classes, the biggest reason she carried a notebook now. Too much free time. Free time in Boulder meant marijuana time. She had no desire for it any longer; she lived in a drug-free house with friends who watched out for her best interests. Two years earlier, it would have been called babysitting, but that was no longer the case. She was rehabilitated.

Abby once asked Jonas Cullen to help her cut down on her drug usage, but try as he did, it didn't help. At certain moments, she would do what she wanted. That applied to most everything growing up, probably the main reason she and her mother butted heads so violently growing up. Stubborn, intransigent, willful, disrespectful. Abby made another entry into her notebook. "Apologize sincerely to mom." It wasn't in the plan, but Abby would like her mother to observe her daughter now, how disciplined she had become, how appreciative she was of those whom she worked with or around, at Cal Lutheran, at Vons, at St. Anthony's, here at the courthouse.

Constantine walked into the hall with Curtiss and sent him on his way. He told Marvin to go in and have a seat, that he'd be right with him, and then he sat down on the bench next to Abby. "I'm going to miss our little meetings," he said. There was something in his words, and Abby tilted her head. "The parole board approved your petition. Just got the word this week. July 14. Hang tight, and we'll sign the papers when I finish with Marvin. Shouldn't take too long." Constantine nodded and gave Abby a long stare before standing.

She sat alone in the hall now, no other scheduled parolee meetings over the lunch hour. She held her notebook with both hands in her lap and stared at the painting of a sunrise or sunset on the opposite wall. It was a copy of an Impressionist work, probably by Monet, but she wasn't sure. Abby had seen this painting every time she was here over the past two years, the lonely man standing in the boat with the orange sun in the background. Were there two people in the boat, one standing and another sitting? It wasn't a painting she would have in her home, too blue, and she had always been drawn to yellow in her art choices. She stood and stepped to the painting, reached up and touched the boat. Yes, two people in the boat.

∽

Abby found Paul at Mary Star of the Sea at 2:15 after driving to three other churches first. He was standing on a short ladder trying to muscle off a wooden window frame and didn't see her walk up. She watched him for a moment before speaking. "Need any help?"

Paul turned with a start. "Hey, I didn't hear you. How long have you been standing there?" His smile always showed how happy he was to see her.

"Not long. Get down and give me a hug."

Paul did as ordered, a hug that Abby held onto far longer than a usual afternoon hello. When she relaxed her hold, she pulled back only far enough to look into his face. She slid her arms from around his shoulders and placed her hands on his upper chest. "Can you get away right now?"

Paul nodded. "Why? Do you want to go have sex?"

"As a matter of fact, . . ."

∽

The graduation speaker for California Lutheran University in the spring of 1977 was Fred Rogers, Mr. Rogers of children's television. He gave a gentle speech without a challenge to save the world, but instead "to give the gift of an honest self," to look to be of service in one's own neighborhood, one's tiny piece of that world. Six guests sat as close to the stage as possible to see and be seen by Abby in her gold gown with purple tassel. The guests had ridden over in Sally's new station wagon, except for Paul who had driven Abby to Thousand Oaks earlier and then staked out the good seats. Abby's father wore a tie, but Paul and Mose were in their best Southern California casual attire. Two women from St. Anthony's were already at the Robinson house preparing food and drinks for the afternoon party, a gathering that might number up to twenty people. Abby's request for no gifts would be ignored by several of the guests.

When the graduation ceremony ended and the photographs of Abby with every person in California had been taken, all with her diploma prominently displayed, the group returned to Oxnard, to a neighborhood crowded with cars. Respecting Abby's parole conditions, the church guests, and Abby's parents, alcoholic drinks were kept to a minimum. It seemed at all times that Abby was hugging either Paul or her mother. Wally Constantine sat with Mose for much of the time and talked basketball. He was a huge Laker fan, a team that Mose had never played on. Abby's two professors from Cal Lutheran showed up for an hour as did three workers from Von's grocery store. Two priests and three congregants also attended. As the festivities wound down, Abby walked each guest to his or her car and thanked them profusely. Around 4:00, she and Paul and Mose walked Constantine to his car.

"Thank you so much for coming by. This means a lot to me," said Abby. She touched his arm as she spoke.

"Wouldn't have missed it. By the way, I have something for you." He bent over to retrieve his briefcase from the back seat of his car. As he did, across the street a man opened a car door and ran directly at the group. About twenty feet away, he fired his first shot. Another step closer, he pulled the trigger again. Mose tackled Abby, shoving her to the grass behind Constantine's car. Constantine rose quickly with his weapon but hesitated when his target was blocked out. Paul had reacted to the shooter, drawing his focus from the others. The shooter squeezed off one more shot before Paul tackled him.

Gunshots in Oxnard were not rare, but in this neighborhood in the afternoon, they were. Squad cars and an ambulance arrived within minutes. Ricardo Gomez was unconscious, handcuffed, and lying on the pavement next to Constantine's car. Forty or 50 people from the neighborhood gathered to witness the aftermath, to speculate on what had just happened, to wonder about what was happening to the neighborhood. Reverend and Mrs. Archer wanted to take their daughter into the house, but she refused. When Mose had allowed Abby to rise from the grass, she ran to where Paul lay on the street. As she rolled him over, he said, "He missed me. I'm good." She was furious that Gomez had disrupted such an important event in her life, threatening her guests. Somehow, no one had been hit by the three bullets fired from the .38 Special. Except for the blow Constantine inflicted on Gomez's head with his pistol, Paul sustained the worst injuries, two scraped forearms when he tackled Gomez to the street.

∾

Constantine returned to the Robinsons' house on Sunday afternoon to check on everyone.

"Parolees with spotless records aren't supposed to be this much fun," he said when Abby let him in. "You're more paperwork than my derelicts." He inspected Paul's arms and gave an update on Ricardo Gomez. "Fortunately, a snub-nose isn't the most accurate weapon." Mostly, it seemed to the group, Constantine wanted to reassure himself about everyone's state of mind.

"We're all okay," said Abby. They sat and drank beers and laughed nervously. Abby's parents were taking them all to dinner at 5:00, but they had some time.

"How are your parents handing all this?" asked Constantine.

Abby told him of her drive-by shooting adventure in Chicago the previous year. "They were a bit shaken. Thank God they were in the house with Ella when all the action occurred."

They talked for a few minutes and then Constantine pulled a badge from his pocket. "I was going to give you this yesterday, sort of a token of saving my life the first time. Maybe I need to get a couple more." It was an LAPD badge. "I don't have kids and I'm divorced. I have a couple of these, and I want you to have one. It's the real thing."

Paul knew Moses Robinson almost as well as he knew himself, maybe since his captivity, better. He was, at base level, a quiet, introspective man who liked himself. Mose's four-year stint in the NBA provided a nest-egg to buy a home and begin a family without a looming debt, but it had never been Mose's goal nor passion. His life had a far different purpose. Taking Paul in first and then Abby had not been an imposition; it was sheltering his best friend and then providing refuge for another needy soul. Moses Robinson had discarded his cool back in Boulder and learned to filter out life's noises. In the summer of 1977, when the Oxnard school district offered Mose a position at the high school and the assistant head coaching job, Mose declined. Being a junior high math teacher and coach was important, and he believed he was suited for it. Moreover, it allowed him to be Sally's husband and Ella's papa full-time.

What Paul believed was that Mose's philosophy on life was the result of growing up in a tough neighborhood as a working woman's only child. What Sally knew after being a roommate of Mose and Paul for three years in college and then Mose's girlfriend/wife for another six was that her husband's philosophy on life was never static. He was a keen observer of those around him and selected information and experiences from them that pertained to his future. From that first year in the rooming house on Boulder's Hill, Sally watched Mose grapple with ideas and issues. While Sally worried about Paul's and Abby's future, Moses Robinson studied. He had had a plan since Paul drove up in his old pickup in 1974.

∾

"I got a raise," said Abby as she slid into the front seat of Paul's truck. They leaned into each other and kissed. "I didn't even ask for it. Juan just told me I'd see a bigger paycheck at the end of the week. I thought he meant because I was working 40-hours a week now, but he just gave me a raise. I think he wants me to stay forever."

"He'd better be careful. You'll have his job at the end of the year if you stay." Paul parked in front of the post office. "Be right back." He returned with two packets and handed them to Abby. "Paperwork for passports. We'll submit after you get freed. We have some traveling to catch up on. Besides, a honeymoon should involve some exotic place farther than 50 miles away."

"I was thinking a camping trip to Yosemite or the Grand Canyon, something we can afford." Abby perused the packet and chuckled. "I'm not delaying our wedding, so you'll need to be content with a honeymoon night in a motel in Cambria."

"Remember when you told me you'd bolt out of California on the day your parole ended? What happened to that plan?"

"I was young and impetuous when I said it. Can't you see how I've matured?" Abby put the packets on the dashboard. "I think I said I'd leave on December 11, so I'm pretty sure we'll be gone by then." Abby turned the rearview mirror, so she could see herself. She made a face and replaced the mirror.

Returning home, they found Mose feeding Ella in her highchair. "What did you find out?" he asked Paul as they entered the kitchen.

"Father Thomas said no, but he'd bless us in his own way. He said just get some minister to do it, so I was thinking maybe we'd look in the yellow pages for a not-so-devout guy to marry us. Seems like Catholics take the ceremony pretty seriously." Paul sat next to Ella and began making faces, much to her delight. Abby pulled cheese and lunch meat out of the refrigerator for sandwiches.

"That's what Sally and I did. Or you could have the justice of the peace do it at the courthouse," said Mose.

"No!" said Abby with conviction. "Too much of my life has been directed in courthouses. Our marriage won't be tainted." She made sandwiches on two plates, then put them on the table, one in front of Paul. "We'll find a church that will take two damaged people. You and

Sally can stand with us while we say our vows. Ella can be the flower girl."

"She's not so steady on her feet yet," laughed Mose.

"Honorary flower girl."

"Playing the devil's advocate here," continued Mose, "aren't you worried Gomez might show up again?"

"I might invite him. He's the reason I'm getting a five-month early release."

They all knew that wasn't true, but it made for a good story. This time, he wouldn't be getting out of jail for any reason. It's one thing to tackle one's parole officer because you're frustrated and on drugs, quite another when you shoot at him at a party. Premeditated assault.

Mose put a spoonful of peas in Ella's mouth, used the spoon to catch a dribble, and then wiped her chin. "Have you guys set a date yet?"

Abby answered. "We're thinking a week after Freedom Day. If they're any glitches on the 14th, we'll have a little wiggle room."

Mose laughed aloud, something he seldom did. "What could possibly go wrong in either one of your guys's lives?"

"What are you thinking?" asked Abby. They were alone in their room, watching TV. She slid off his lap on the green chair, reached over, and shut off the tube. She slid back onto his lap and shook her body. "So, what's going on inside that head?" She tapped his temple with her finger.

"Well, thinking about what's next. You and I . . . need purpose. Survival, I guess, is sort of purpose, but not what I set out to do a decade ago." Paul huhed and shook his head slowly. "A decade plus a little more. I had a professor at CU . . ." Paul stopped and went inside himself for a moment. Abby waited but tightened her hug slightly. "He told me I was something special." Paul's eyes welled up, and he curled his lips inward.

Abby asked so gently, "What was his name?"

"Dr. Orr. Seems like I had him for every class my sophomore year, the year I changed my major to history, but it was only two classes each semester. He moved on to Yale after that year. He almost never answered any of my questions, just kept asking me new ones when I thought I had answers."

With the same tone of voice, Abby asked, "What would he ask you now?"

Paul breathed in deeply. "He'd ask me what I'm going to do with my life now, now that I've survived Vietnam, now that I survived being a prisoner-of-war, now that I've found my life partner." Paul kissed Abby.

"Would he congratulate you now?"

Paul nodded as he answered. "Yeah, I think he'd understand. I think he'd like you . . . a lot. I know he would. He always respected curiosity and courage."

Abby smiled, maybe more inwardly than outwardly. "How about stupidity?"

"I think he'd see you for how you recovered from that mistake and took hold of your life. Maybe when we're passing through New Haven next, we'll stop in, so I can introduce you to him."

"You'd still have to answer his question. What are you going to do with your life now?"

∾

July 14, 1977, was not Freedom Day. A prison sentence ends at midnight on the scheduled day, so the 14th was the final day of her term. Constantine told Abby to come in at 10:00 on July 15, Friday. The process of discharge can take many forms, he said, but because she had been a model prisoner, he would have her certificate at his office. All the paperwork, the notification to the county clerk, the sentencing court, the local law enforcement, all of it, he would take care of.

Abby and Paul arrived at her parole officer's office and found it crowded as always. The Impressionist art copy seemed comforting, indeed, a sunrise. None of the other parolees knew this was her release day. They had their own concerns. At 9:57, Constantine's door opened. He ushered out a young man, telling him to have a seat, that he'd have him come right back in, but he had to deal with the lady right now. It would only take a moment.

And it did. There was no ceremony. Wally Constantine handed Abby her Certificate of Discharge and card for her wallet or purse, as the case might be. He shook Paul's hand first and then turned to Abby. He took her hand and held it. "If I ever see you in here again or find out you've messed up somewhere else, I'll see to it you never get parole."

Abby nodded, let go of his hand, and hugged him. She left with no detainers, no conditions, and only a full life ahead.

∾

It was Sally who decided the wedding would be in their backyard. Mose stood with Paul, Sally with Abby. Ella was the flower girl of record but held by Abby's mom. Paul's parents attended. The small, but meaningful ceremony was officiated by Abby's father. Over dinner on Freedom Day nearly a week earlier, Abby had told Mose and Sally about the conversation she and Paul had had about their future. What to do now? Mose and Sally laughed about Paul's sophomore year, laughing especially about the night his peace booth was blown up, about the inordinate amount of homework Dr. Orr assigned him, about the night Paul's father had exploded over his son's political beliefs. The journey to here had been painful, no doubt, but it was filled with wonderful memories too. In bed that night, Mose and Sally made another decision. The other guest at the wedding of Abigail Archer and Paul Garrity was Dr. Orr, and he liked Abby a lot. And he did ask, "What now?" He suggested graduate school at Yale. "We once talked about you being a college professor."

The Garritys left on their honeymoon to Cambria the next afternoon, after both sets of parents and Dr. Orr were driven to Los Angeles by Sally. Before Paul and Abby departed, Mose handed each one an envelope.

"A little wedding gift from Sal and me," said Mose. "We've never needed your rent money, so we set up bank accounts. Figured it might cover all those missed rent payments you covered for us back in Boulder. Don't even think about giving it back." He smiled like a father might on the day he was sending his children off into the world.

SEGMENT II
REDRESS
1979-1980

In the late spring of 1979, over 430 miles from Ho Chi Minh City south-southwest across the South China Sea, 23 days at the mercy of the currents, now just twenty yards off the steep, rocky coastline of Bidong Island, Malaysia, so close to safety, a trawler heaved sideways, pounded by the surf, and began taking on water. In a vessel designed for three dozen, 80 Vietnamese refugees, weakened by hunger, thirst, and violence, clung to the boat's small cabin and siderails. On the rocks, scores of half-naked men stood poised to help. Some held grappling hooks, others innertubes. One refugee worker standing alone on a rock shivered slightly. The next wave spilled several people into the water and further flooded the boat. Two dozen men leaped into the water to pull children, too small to conquer the tide on their own, to safety. Relief workers ignored instructions to stay out of the water and dived into the sea to help the refugees get to the rocks. Suitcases bobbed in the water, deciding on their own whether to join their owners on the shore or whether to return to the sea. The trawler sank within minutes, becoming another submerged monument to the courage of families trying to escape to freedom despite overwhelming obstacles. A drenched woman crouched on the rocks and wailed inconsolably, her two children lost, dragged under by the tide, and carried out to sea with the suitcases.

Above the rocks, anxiously monitoring the rescue/tragedy unfolding below, and unlike the rest of the world which didn't want to see, dozens of earlier refugees and relief workers watched, waiting to assist the survivors when they ascended the steep path to the camp. Abby Garrity held her arms around her chest. It wasn't until she saw her husband finally climb out of the turbulent sea that she realized she had been holding her breath. At last, knowing her husband was safe, Abby moved to help the Boat People who braved the crossing despite the dangers and uncertainty. An unwanted band in search of refuge.

❧

"Why does God direct some boats to the sandy beach and others to the crags?" asked Abby almost as an accusation. "And you shouldn't go in the water. You're not a good swimmer. You're not a lifeguard." Paul kept his head in her lap, enjoying her touch.

Paul reached up to brush a lock of hair from Abby's eyes. "And you're not supposed to be watching me."

"I don't go there to, but you stand out. You're six inches taller than every Vietnamese person here." She breathed out heavily as if changing the subject. "I can't get them to give me a Polaroid camera; they say the film's too expensive."

"I heard you and Norm got into it again."

Abby tugged Paul's hair slightly and shook it. "He's so damned focused on budget, but he needs to see the bigger picture. The sooner I can post photos of the children on the wall, the more likely it is that someone will recognize them and tell their family. Norm continues to call them orphans, but they're not, most of them anyway. They're unaccompanied minors, displaced persons. They have family here or down at Galang. Every one of the children must be tagged and registered!"

"Yelling at him probably won't soften his stance."

"No, probably not, but it makes me feel better."

"Do you want me to talk to him?" asked Paul.

"No. I'll fight my own battles, besides you have enough on your plate. Are you still going to Kuala Lumpur tomorrow?"

"I am, but I thought you were going with me and then on to Galang." Paul looked at her with concern.

Abby sighed. "Oh, Paul, it's such a mess, and if I leave, those girls just get abused. The volunteers work so hard, but they can't do this." She swatted hard at a fly, missed, but followed it with her eyes. "They're last in line for everything; I think even for getting on the boats back in Nam. That's why there're fewer of them than males. I need to be their guardian." She returned her eyes to Paul. "This last boat was boarded by Thai pirates twice. Several of the women were raped, and three were taken . . . along with most of their possessions. So tragic."

"Their guardian angel, huh?"

"No one has ever called me an angel before." She smiled and nodded.

His eyes registered agreement. "I got the new census for Bidong today, if that's what you want to call it. Almost 20,000. When they set it up last summer, it was designed for a tenth of that. We can't build shelters fast enough, so they construct their own out of old boat wood and tarps. One of the American news stations is coming to do an expose next week, to enlighten the people back home about the conditions here. Just what America doesn't want to be reminded of . . . another aspect of our failure in Vietnam." He reached up and touched her cheek. "You're beautiful, you know."

Abby kissed her index finger and placed it on Paul's lips. She smiled warmly. "Good thing the Vietnamese have us or they'd have no one." She allowed her sarcasm to rest for a moment and then sighed. "I'll stay here for a couple of days before going back to Galang. You'll be flying to Saigon day after tomorrow, so I'd be alone anyway, and I'd be angry at myself if I left. I was able to talk most of our volunteers out of their film. I'll take as many pictures as I can of the children and then take the film back to Galang to see how fast I can get it developed and then bring it back for the photo wall. I also have a meeting with the security forces to see if they can provide more protection for my girls." She scratched his beard. "We can meet up when you get back." She paused again, this time to alter her position on the bamboo mat/couch. "You're excited about going back, aren't you?"

"To be honest, I'm apprehensive. My emotions are all over the place. Saigon will trigger some memories, I'm sure, but I won't get near my special place." Paul raised his eyebrows when he said that. "Still . . ." He allowed that thought to hang silently.

"Did you ever think how many doors would open just because you were a POW?" She laughed coyly. "Hey," she announced in an elevated tone to the empty room, "we're forming a committee to go to Vietnam to see if we can slow down the mass exodus of refugees that are overwhelming the other nations of Southeast Asia. Any former

POWs around who want to go? We're pretty sure the communists will listen to you in particular."

Paul smiled. "Somehow, I missed the real conference in Geneva where they stayed in luxurious hotels. Let's see, we arrived last winter in Galang as simple volunteers working for our local Catholic church, and now we're employees of the United Nations High Commissioner for Refugees doing jobs we've never been trained for with minimal language skills. On the job training. Weren't we just going to stay for a few months to assuage our guilt? Father Thomas would be proud of us. I guess I'm supposed to talk with some minor Vietnamese officials about who they're willing to part with and who's acceptable to America. I can see that going well."

"Just use your charm, dear. Tell them that you're a construction engineer at Bidong and Galang and that your wife is a grief counselor and community sociologist specializing in reuniting families. And your Spanish is pretty good." She shifted her position. "My turn," she said, indicating he was to massage her scalp.

"Better?" he asked when she stretched out. They went quiet while Paul massaged Abby's face tenderly. "Our stint in Mexico was a picnic compared to this, wasn't it. Knowing the language helped us navigate their culture far easier. Without the interpreters here, we'd be lost." Paul paused again. "We could have stayed home and bought a house, started a family," he finally said. That had been their plan, but they didn't know where to settle after Oxnard or what career paths to pursue, so one night they decided to take Father Thomas up on his offer to work at a church in Mexico for ten months. When that time ended, he asked them to go halfway around the world to continue working with the Catholic Church, only this time with refugees whose lives were in danger. They agreed.

Without opening her eyes, she answered. "What fun would that have been, I mean having our own bathroom or a bedroom to make love? Besides, how would Vietnam progress now without our help?"

Paul tapped her nose. "Yeah, pretty boring, I suppose. Maybe a few years down the road then?" He often wondered about this choice of theirs. Just two years ago, she had graduated from college and completed her parole, finished her prison term. Then, nearly a year in Mexico as volunteers with Catholic Relief Services. Now, they were half a world away from California living in aid workers' quarters that were only slightly better than the tenements that he had helped construct on Galang, Indonesia. Tonight, they were sleeping in a simple room on Bidong Island, off the east coast of Malaysia, with 20,000 Vietnamese refugees, all of them crammed into a one square kilometer camp.

Abby sensed he had gone inside himself. She opened her eyes and studied his face from below. Shoulder length hair parted in the middle of his forehead that he frequently shoved back with both hands, a full beard with flecks of gray at his cheeks. He was aging faster than she was but carrying this new physical maturity well. She knew that being older than most of their fellow aid workers and with less idealism now, but with a true understanding of the mission, gave them an air of distinction and authority and had pushed them into leadership positions rapidly. They came under the auspices of Catholic Relief Services in December 1978 as volunteers but had recently taken paid positions with the United Nations High Commissioner for Refugees. This would be a short stint here in Malaysia and Indonesia. Already they had been asked to head north to Thailand to do similar work along the Cambodian border where reports of a Khmer Rouge genocide had occurred. Because of the reports of violence, the thought of relocating there concerned them both, but they had accepted with the condition that Abby be allowed to complete the framework of her program, of setting up the structure and of training two other aid workers to reunite Vietnamese children with family members. "You have to promise me something tonight," she said bringing Paul's eyes back to hers.

"Anything for you, you know."

"You won't let anything happen to you while you're in Vietnam."

∽

Abby respected the Malaysian government's position on the Vietnamese refugees. It didn't want them, to be sure, but it also didn't want to tow the boats back out into the South China Sea where the passengers would most assuredly die. Malaysia did not believe the

Vietnamese were culturally compatible with them, either politically or religiously. The years between 1976 and 1979 had been tense, but by agreeing to be the place of "first asylum" for the Boat People, Malaysia afforded tens of thousands of Vietnamese refugees a chance. Receiving guarantees from the United States, Australia, Canada, and a half-dozen other countries that refugees would not stay permanently in Malaysia or Indonesia or Hong Kong, it set aside Bidong Island for a refugee camp. When Abby and Paul signed on with the UNHCR, they became part of an international group of aid workers committed to turning an uninhabited island with no infrastructure into livable camps. Volunteers with little or no understanding of the refugees' culture, but a desire to learn, understand, and help. Indonesia had agreed to the same contract as Malaysia, establishing refugee camps on Galang Island south of Singapore. The similarities ended there, however. Abby referred to Bidong as the hell hole, as it was flooded with refugees. Shelters were primitive: boat parts and blue tarps in the early months with no plumbing or running water, which had to be transported daily from the mainland. Galang's camps had wells and barracks early on. Families could remain together in two-story barracks, hundreds of them stretching across the gentle slopes. Neither camp looked like the camps California had constructed at Camp Pendleton in the months after Saigon fell in April of 1975, but at least Galang provided a sense of security.

Two days after Paul left Bidong for Vietnam as part of a delegation to set up the processing of refugees, Abby boarded a fishing boat for the often-terrifying two-hour ride on choppy seas to Malaysia's mainland. From the coast, it was an all-day trip in a smelly, rented van to Singapore. The last leg was several hours by ferry to Galang, Indonesia. Abby hated this day. She could neither work nor sleep on the journey, and few of the other passengers spoke English. She missed Paul terribly when they were on separate islands or even at separate camps on Galang, but she felt strongly about her role in the refugee crisis. Today, she outlined new procedures in her mind for protecting the young women and small children housed on Bidong. She had spoken with the Malaysian security chief on the island and been given assurances, but he didn't carry the same conviction for justice as she did. "Many of these girls were raped on the boats," she said with a raised voice, "and some have been raped here in the camp! The girls who are here without their families are especially at risk." Abby reminded the security chief that more young men made the journey from Vietnam to the camps, and these boys posed a serious threat to the unattached girls. They had to be protected. The chief responded that these pork-eating, half-Chinese would need to monitor themselves better. Abby tried to conceal her disgust and felt her resolve to protect the girls strengthen.

She arrived at Galang after the sun had set, but she checked in with her supervisor, a Canadian in his forties with a decade of experience. He was more concerned about reuniting families than protecting lone females. "When the new processing begins," he said, "our first priority will be keeping families together."

The way he said this hit a nerve in Abby. "No shit! That's been my priority since day one, and now Canada and America are finally on board," she said in anger.

"This takes time, Abby. Have a seat."

"No, I'm not staying! You need to get your ass up to Bidong to see firsthand. Your fellow countrymen are doing the best they can. They're busting their asses to make this work, but they need your help. Screw the bureaucracy in Ottawa and turn your people loose to process these refugees. Give Margaret and her people the authority to move them all. Get them off the island and on planes in Kuala Lumpur. Let the suits back home deal with them when they arrive. Fill up the damn airplanes." Abby didn't wait for a response. She pivoted and went to her apartment to miss Paul even more. She couldn't sleep, so she wrote to Sally.

These Vietnamese are people without a country, praying for some country to claim them. Most were farmers or fishermen, but now they have no work, especially on Bidong. For Paul and me, this has been a crash course in cultural awareness. There are barriers to understanding that didn't exist in Mexico, but we are learning rapidly. So many of the aid workers are young and determined; I'm so proud of them, so fortunate to work with them. (As far as I can tell, none of them spent time in prison for bank robbery.) My world here is the children who have been separated from their families, and I spend my days devising ways to reunite them. The obstacles that exist with adults are minimized compared to infants and small children. Most of them understand kindness and touch, which transcend boundaries. Their young lives have been lived in chaos which can't be good for their overall development. They are all undernourished, and I have been able to find a bit of success here in Galang, but my efforts on Bidong have been less successful. Still, the new agreements between the U.S. and a few other Have Nations with the countries where the Vietnamese have escaped to are encouraging. Paul is in Saigon as I write this, setting up processing procedures to get more Vietnamese out. I've had a long day, so I'll close. Our plans remain the same, to return to California around Christmas and look for gainful employment and start a family. My love to you and Mose. Hug Ella for me.

∾

Several statements made at the initial meeting in Saigon left Paul confused. Part of it was the translations, but not all of it. Paul always did his homework. The lists provided by the Communists seemed incomplete, because those people seeking asylum were mostly from Saigon. That was to be expected, but not one family on the roster listed Bien Hoa as its residence. The second meeting was to be held the next morning.

"Tell Brown I'll be back before dark," Paul said to the young man who acted as the aide to Edmund Brown, the head of the U.S. delegation. Paul had a knapsack strung over his shoulder and was wearing a baseball cap. He asked one of the interpreters, a man named Tran, to accompany him, and outside, he hailed a cab, which was no more than a two-seat bench on wheels pulled by a motor scooter.

"Bien Hoa," instructed Tran. Bien Hoa was seventeen miles east from central Saigon on Highway 1, the crowded artery of the nation. The driver asked again as if he had misunderstood the interpreter. Paul repeated the directions and motioned with his right arm to head out.

Weaving in and out of traffic, the cabbie hunched forward. As the ride unfolded, so did the onion that Paul called Saigon. Four years and several months after the U.S. defeat and the fall of Saigon to the NVA, all the city was in a state of disrepair, but as the modified rickshaw took the two men farther from the city center, conditions grew worse. Paul expected that. He knew that beginning in 1954 Bien Hoa had been resettled by Vietnamese from the north, across the Seventeenth Parallel, who opposed the communists led by Ho Chi Minh. Most who put down new roots in Bien Hoa were Roman Catholics. These people had been some of America's strongest, most loyal supporters during the war and now found themselves without sponsors. The U.S. established its primary air base there, and many of Bien Hoa's residents worked for the U.S. military. Only a couple hundred of these people were evacuated in 1975 when Saigon fell to the communists, and they escaped only because of the daring and courageous efforts of two State Department officials acting outside their orders.

Entering Bien Hoa just after three in the afternoon, the driver asked for specific directions, translated to Paul by Tran. Paul waved his hand to continue driving.

"I've never been here, so I'm not sure what I'm looking for," said Paul.

They drove on through the crowded streets, markets really, the buzz of scooters steady in their ears. Paul saw the faces of desperate Vietnamese, faces he had seen in Bidong and Galang, and wondered how desperate a person needs to be to give up citizenship and ancestry. How desperate did a parent need to be to risk the life of his children on the journey? As many were dying in the South China Sea as were making it to the refugee camps. Paul looked at soldiers, mostly young, all of whom had pledged allegiance to the Hanoi regime. True believers. A sudden stop by the driver jerked Paul back to the present. Three of those young soldiers stuck weapons in the faces of Paul, Tran, and the driver and yelled commands Paul could not understand, but obviously demanding they exit the rickshaw.

"What the hell was Garrity thinking?" thundered Edmund Brown when he was told that Paul and his translator had not returned. "Do we have any leads on where he could have gone?"

"Not exactly, but one of the other taxi drivers thinks they may have gone to Bien Hoa."

"In a rickshaw?" Brown spoke his thoughts aloud. "That's nuts! There's nothing to be gained by one aide worker getting lost in Bien Hoa."

"The other rickshaw drivers are sure their friend wouldn't get lost. He has family there and knows the streets well. They think the army may have them."

Brown narrowed his eyes and looked at his assistant. "Son of a bitch! First, don't tell anyone about this, especially not anyone outside our delegation. Then, get me an appointment with Colonel Do; I may have a favor to ask." Brown paused. "Nobody goes to bed tonight until we get them back."

∾

The soldiers had taken Paul's watch, but he sensed it was nearing midnight. The room was more spacious than the bamboo cell he had lived in for over a year up north. He had tried to communicate with his translator but had been told, in commands he understood from years earlier, to shut up. An armed soldier stood by the open doors of both Paul and Tran. Paul wondered where the taxi driver had been taken. During the morning meeting, both sides tried to spin optimism about the refugee removal, but Paul sensed the paranoia emanating from the Vietnamese. Years of war, a terrible, destructive, senseless conflict. He got angry with himself about his reckless action, about what Abby would feel when she found out he was again a prisoner of the Vietnamese, or worse. He thought this confinement wouldn't last long for himself, but he worried about what might happen to Tran and the taxi driver. They were Vietnamese and vulnerable. He had put their lives at risk.

Paul crouched at the back of the cell, his eyes locked on the space just outside the door, trying to discern light. Subconsciously, he rubbed his ankle and foot. He listened to the muted conversation between the guards; he understood some of their words but not their meaning. He tried to imagine Abby in her prison cell, staring through the bars at "lights out," criticizing herself for an act of stupidity, blaming herself for hurting others. Light from a flashlight bounced on the hallway wall, and Paul saw Abby's face. She had a slight smile and was tenderly shaking her head at him. He held onto that light.

∾

"Colonel, this mission is too important to allow the spontaneous action of one of my assistants to sidetrack it. Your soldiers' response is understandable, an American with no reason to be in Bien Hoa. Of course, they would respond as they did." Brown stood as he spoke on the phone, playing on his own weakness and the Colonel's obvious ignorance of the incident. Brown was sure Colonel Do had not ordered the taking of Garrity and Tran and pretty sure the Vietnamese officer did not want an international incident either. Brown wished he could see into the eyes of the colonel. "I apologize for my associate and assure you he will be punished for any embarrassment he might have caused you and your government. If you could help me here, I would remember your generosity in the future."

∾

Shouting and overhead lights suddenly broke the darkness. Almost immediately, Paul's young guard began yelling for Paul to stand and exit his small room. When Paul did, he was pushed toward the end of a short hallway where another soldier stood, a soldier older and with rank. Paul stood before the man, and both men inspected each other.

The soldier's question surprised Paul. "Why Bien Hoa?" he asked in English.

"I needed to see for myself," answered Paul. The soldier stood rigid, almost, Paul thought, angrily.

"This is not your country any longer. You don't get to decide."

Paul blinked but otherwise stood still. A moment of uneasy silence passed between them. Finally, Paul answered. "It never was."

"You acted like it was."

"I was mistaken. We were mistaken." Paul thought he saw an easing of the soldier's shoulders.

"Were you a soldier?"

"Yes." Paul paused. "No longer."

"Did you kill any of my comrades?"

94

Paul answered truthfully. "I fired my weapon. I don't know if any of my rounds hit your soldiers. I wasn't a very good shot at night."

A moment passed. "And you are back," said the soldier. "Did you see anything here that helps you understand?"

"No. Your soldiers took me before I learned. You have trained them well."

The soldier hmphed at Paul's answer. "They are too young to be trained well. They should be in school." He turned to one of the boy soldiers and said something. The boy left quickly and returned with Paul's pack. He handed it to the soldier who then handed it to Paul. "The roll of film has been taken. My soldiers will take you back to your hotel in Saigon. Ho Chi Minh City." He kept his eyes on Paul, indicating that he had more to say. In a moment, he asked, "Will you come back again, Paul Garrity?"

"Only if I'm invited."

The soldier hmphed again. "That may be a long time, maybe never. We have deep wounds. We have much healing to do."

Paul nodded ever so slightly, but the soldier noticed. "Has the healing begun?" asked Paul.

"Only recently. Time has frozen since you left as if it were imprisoned. Your country had a civil war once, so you might understand." The soldier seemed to Paul like a teacher at that moment.

"May I ask a favor?" asked Paul. The soldier listened, giving permission with his eyes. "Will you allow the translator to leave too?"

The soldier glanced at the translator's door. "He's Vietnamese."

"Yes."

The soldier thought about Paul's request. Finally, he turned to his soldiers and motioned for them to bring the translator. Tran was brought out and stood next to Paul. The soldier spoke to Tran in French. "My men do not understand this conversation. I expect that you will not translate any of it to anyone else, as if you were not present, maybe in another room. When you are an old man and our country has healed, then you can tell your grandchildren about this night." The soldier looked to the interpreter for confirmation. When he got it, he turned to Paul. "Do you have family?"

"A wife. No children."

"No children? You must not be optimistic about the future." The soldier nodded, took one step to the side indicating to his men to take Paul and the translator away. He was no longer a teacher but a soldier again.

Paul and the translator returned to his hotel in Saigon in the back of a half-ton truck. Children, thought Paul, a decision that he and Abby had delayed. They had never thought about it in the way the Vietnamese officer had responded.

∾

It was dawn in Vietnam when Paul met with Edmund Brown. After a severe reprimand, Brown settled down. "You're not a young man, Garrity, and this was pretty irrational. What were you thinking?"

"I apologize. It was stupid and put our mission in jeopardy."

"That's not what I asked," said Brown.

Paul swallowed. "At yesterday morning's meeting, one of their representatives said we would never understand. I wanted to prove him wrong."

∾

In the middle of August 1979, on the islands of Bidong and Galang, with both the temperature and humidity hovering in the low-80s, Paul, Abby, and dozens of aid workers, working in close conjunction with translators, began processing Vietnamese refugees by the thousands. Five to ten minutes per interview with interpreters, a thousand each day. Immigration laws in Australia, Canada, and the U.S. prohibited criminals, drug dealers, and those with communicable diseases, but everyone else was eligible for relocation. Paul and Abby worked at Bidong, so tired at night that they ate their meager dinners on the picnic tables under the tarps where they had interviewed refugees, and then slept on those very tables before beginning again eight hours later. The Orderly Departure Program had begun.

∾

Sitting opposite Abby on the floor in their quarters in the glow of a single candle, Paul chuckled. "I need a shower." Tired after a week of

96

interviews, on an evening when they finally found a few hours alone, they touched gently and talked softly.

"No, because if you take one, then you'll be able to smell me." She raised her arm and smelled herself for effect, an underarm she hadn't shaved in months. "My pit-hair is longer than your beard. Pretty sexy, huh."

He smiled and then slid his body closer to hers so that her legs crossed over his. He kissed her tenderly, pulled back slightly, and said, "Yes, you are. Always."

Abby moved her hands from his thighs and wrapped her arms around his neck, pulling his lips back into hers. Deftly, she removed her clothes, blew out the candle, and in the one-room island amid a sea of Vietnamese refugees, they made love.

Two months later, the UNHCR transferred Paul and Abby Garrity to Thailand to work with the refugee crisis along the Cambodian border. They spent one weekend in Bangkok, a vacation of sorts before heading to the border. Abby wrote to Sally that she doubted if she would ever do anything again that made her so proud, that was so fulfilling, as their time in Galang and Bidong had been. The Garritys had been bitten.

"The hand of the United States is everywhere," bragged the American mercenary who stood with the three Khmer Rouge soldiers. Abby set her jaw but remained silent. He seemed comfortable with his remark. "People back home never understood the scope of our war. It wasn't just Vietnam; it was all Southeast Asia." Abby evaluated the mercenary. Maybe 35 to 40 years-old, a handful of years older than her and Paul, probably a veteran of the Vietnam War, short and lean much like a feral African cat. Wild. He had a cigarette tucked behind his ear. She wondered if he had a woman back in the States who loved him, who waited for him. She doubted it. The mercenary stepped forward one pace, extended his hand to Paul, and said, "Call me Bear. Make sure you stay on this side of the border; things are pretty hairy over there," he said referring to Cambodia. "The Cambodian army is disbanding, but we'll just reform as a guerrilla force and take it back. No more rules." He grinned and rolled his chin into his mouth, rubbed his right eyebrow with the palm of his right hand, slung his M-16 over his shoulder, and walked away with the three KR soldiers.

"My God," said Abby.

"Yeah," said Paul. "Those are the good guys. Foster wanted us to meet them. Now, I think I know why." He paused and watched the four men walk up the trail that led back into the forest. "Full day. Let's go get something to eat."

"That bastard never acknowledged my presence," said Abby.

Back in the refugee dining hall, they were joined by Carl Foster, an Englishman assigned by the International Red Cross to manage the string of refugee camps along the Thai-Cambodian border to help the desperate Cambodians fleeing the four-year genocide in their country.

He sat down wearily next to Paul, across from Abby, and spoke. "I had one of the volunteers take your bags back to Aranyaprathet. None of the aid workers stay here overnight. The bus'll take you there when we finish here. This past week has been something; I'm glad you're here. I hope I didn't wear you out." Foster paused. "By the way, what day is it?"

"Thursday, October 18th," said Abby.

"Still 1979?" joked Foster. "These people you see here and in the two other camps that I had you tour today have been holding up on the other side of the border, just trying to stay alive. Over there, there's maybe 300,000 Cambodians living under the rule of warlords. Most won't be able to cross the border. The KR put land mines around everything, the biggest mine field in the world. A week ago, the Thai government finally allowed some of them to cross the border at Poipet. These small camps can't hold them, so we'll need to build a bigger one. That's what you're here for, Paul, to help with the construction of a new camp. They told me you could build anything and keep it functioning." Foster raised his eyebrows to get Paul's confirmation.

Paul smirked. "I helped build the one-room church on Bidong and some of the barracks there and on Galang. So yeah, I guess so."

Foster turned to Abby. "You're going to take over coordinating the children's relief center here at Kamput. It's daunting. The two men who I had put in charge left. Overwhelmed. I've been warned that you tend to yell at your supervisors when you don't get your way." He smiled. "You'll start tomorrow. I'll make up some official title for you and give you our best interpreter. A truck and driver will be at your disposal in the afternoon, so you can visit a few of the other camps, see what they're doing there." Foster turned his attention away from Abby without getting her consent. "Paul, we're going to drive to Sa Kaeo to map out the new camp there. I think the Thai government will give us the go-ahead to build a big camp there. Questions?"

"Hundreds, but I'll wait," said Abby.

"Food distribution is going okay; not great, but okay. Medical treatment is slapdash, but I think you'll see that our doctors and nurses are unbelievable. We're seeing people this week who are starving and missing limbs. It's terrible. What I want you to do is somehow coordinate the movement of the refugees, so they feel safe. I can't tell you how. Don't allow our staff and volunteers to stake out their own fiefdoms. Get families under tents together. You'll have my full backing. Give orders and directions and move on. We don't have time to soothe feelings right now; we have lives to save immediately." Foster's eyes bore in on Abby. "And it's only going to get worse in the days ahead." He allowed that to sink in, and then took a piece of roti bread from a metal plate on the table. "The buses back to Aran leave at 5:00. Thai soldiers guard the camps at night."

Paul guessed Foster's meaning. "Not so safe then for the refugees, huh?"

∾

Forty aid workers from various international agencies speaking a dozen languages departed on the bus. At Aranyaprathet a slender woman from Australia greeted Paul and Abby with plastic containers of water, made small talk, and led them to their room in the staff apartments. Stark. There were two chairs, a small table, and two single cots.

"I'm exhausted," said Paul.

"Poor baby." She kissed him and then hugged him with her head against his shoulder. "This is my life, hon, our lives. We're here and we'll do what we can, but when we solve this crisis, I want to start a family."

Paul squeezed his wife, and they remained quiet for a moment. Finally, he spoke. "This afternoon at one of the camps we toured, I can't remember the name, I spoke with an old man. At least, I think he was an old man, but he told me about his land. He pointed over a hill and said it was just over there, but he could never go back. He said the whole area was filled with land mines. He said his son lost both legs and then finally died last week at the camp. He wanted to bury his son on his land but couldn't. He wondered what would happen to his son's soul." Paul paused. "Abby, don't go over there under any circumstances. That's no-man's land. These camps are the last chance for those people, but it's not the land of their ancestors."

∾

They traveled in a white van with UN painted on the side. Foster found that Paul knew much of the history of Cambodia, both recent and past, and was curious to learn more. While much was known about the genocide occurring in Cambodia, much more was coming out as the refugees told their horrifying stories of killing fields near every city and village.

"Everyone has a story. This tragedy has touched everyone. They're numb. These people just wanted to farm and live their lives as their families had done for centuries, but the war put them in harm's way. When the Vietnam War spread into eastern Cambodia, the bombs fell on Cambodians who had no part in the conflict." said Foster.

"My country bombed the hell out of them, I know." Paul knew all too well. He had been there. "The bombing forced the citizens off their ancestral lands, and they began congregating in Phnom Penh. The Khmer Rouge took over those areas. A hundred-thousand civilians were killed, and the survivors hated the U.S."

"More like 300,000 according to new estimates. Your government backed the loser in Cambodia just as it did in Vietnam. Lon Nol." Foster paused. "You were a POW about then, huh?"

Paul nodded. "'72 mostly."

Foster knew. He had been briefed. "Both Saigon and Phnom Penh fell in April of '75, but conditions in Cambodia fell completely apart. The Khmer Rouge set out to destroy the old culture and began killing anyone and everyone who they even suspected of not supporting them completely. Muslims, teachers, religious leaders, soldiers, anyone who had traveled out of the country. And their families. Once it started, it was like a wildfire that couldn't be contained. Pol Pot and the KR emptied the cities to create their agrarian utopia. These people you see in these camps are the survivors of a man-made famine designed to exterminate them."

The van pulled to a stop at a Thai checkpoint at the edge of the jungle. Foster spoke with the soldiers briefly before the van was allowed to proceed. "They're cautious, rightfully so. Thailand is about to be invaded by a half-million desperate Cambodians. I don't think they really understand how many."

"The Vietnam invasion last year . . ." Paul didn't know how to end his sentence. "No good guys anywhere. Looks like the KR is finished, but then what? You would have thought Vietnam would want a little peace after so many years of war."

"You'd think, but I don't believe for a moment that the KR will give up the fight. Your government is still supporting them, despite the slaughter." Foster paused. "My government too. The fighting could go on for another decade."

"The damn Cold War created strange alliances, that's for sure," said Paul.

Foster pointed to the handful of buildings on the side of the road, and the van stopped. To Paul, it looked like rice fields. Foster lit a cigarette. "If the Thai government gives us permission, this is where we'll build."

"When do you think they'll decide?" asked Paul.

"Within the next few days, maybe a week."

"How many refugees will it support?"

"I'd say we'll receive 8,000 the first day. We hope to lend support to almost 90,000."

"God! How long will we have to set up the camp?"

"Two or three days." Foster let out a loud laugh.

Returning to Kamput, Foster and Paul met with a handful of other international aid agencies to see what they could provide. The Catholic Relief Services and the Christian and Missionary Alliance promised more building materials than Foster thought possible, and he was encouraged. He told them to collect the materials immediately. From this meeting, Foster met with Thai officials in nearby villages to get workers. "What else will you need, Garrity?" asked Foster.

"Local engineers and a bulldozer."

On October 22nd, at the request of the Royal Thai Government, construction began on the first truly organized refugee camp for Cambodians inside Thailand. Shelters made from bamboo and thatch, a medical center, mess tents, thousands of individual shelters made of tarps or beach umbrellas. The bulldozer carved roads and shaved hills inside the fenced area. Somewhere Foster had procured a backhoe which was used to dig latrines around the perimeter of the camp. Local Thai workers from Aranyaprathet were paid two dollars a day to help, and the NGO volunteers performed gallantly. A basic infrastructure was in place on the first day. There would be no permanent housing, just shelters. No running water. But where once there was bushland and some rice fields, a safer camp grew. On day three, 8,000 refugees arrived, many of them children with no family, all suffering from malnutrition. All were in some state of shock from the months—or years—of neglect, victims of a decade long war brought on them by their neighbors and world powers.

☙

"I don't know how they've done it for these past few years," said Paul to Abby as they lay on their cots in the dark. Paul had rebuilt them to resemble a double bed.

"Which they are you talking about?" She rolled sideways so she could see her husband.

"This they are the aid organizations. From all over the world. I can't imagine being the first refugee agencies to arrive here. I guess it was the natural place to start. They couldn't go to Vietnam or Laos, but still, establishing a foothold here for the Cambodians who look like death along a hostile border. Seems like every fourth person in the camp is carrying a rifle or some kind of weapon. I just can't wrap my head around what it must have been like a year ago."

Abby placed her left arm on Paul's chest. "There are so many languages being spoken. My limited French has helped a little. The French have been so good. Their doctors and nurses patch wounds both visible and invisible. And all the college-age kids, volunteers from New Zealand and Australia and just everywhere. Why didn't America send our kids to Vietnam as volunteers instead of soldiers with guns?"

Paul turned into Abby. "If only we would have dropped supplies instead of bombs. I know that's too simplistic and it's hindsight, but still." As always, when he spoke of these conditions, he searched Abby's eyes for understanding and forgiveness.

And she always gave it. "We can't change the past; we just move forward. You showed me that, my dear." Her eyes glistened. "Any word on the two volunteers who've gone missing?"

Paul shook his head slightly. "No. We're hoping they're at one of the smaller camps down south."

"Rumors are flying. One of those rumors is that they crossed over and were taken by KR guerrillas." She watched carefully to see if Paul's face would divulge a secret.

"That's a possibility. They all think they're invincible. If they did go into Cambodia," he paused, "I don't want them wandering the back roads or fields. They'll get blown up by a mine. But if the KR has them, we don't know how to get them back."

"The Thai army won't cross the border, that's for sure."

Paul mused, "All those land mines put out to keep their own people from leaving the country. Not to deter the Vietnamese, but, in a sense, to imprison their own people. Look around the camps; hundreds of refugees missing legs." He paused. "I guess I don't have to tell you that, do I. You see it up close and personal." A moment passed. "I admire you so much."

"What's Foster going to do if the volunteers don't turn up tomorrow?" asked Abby.

"He's already made calls to anyone who might be able to help, but no one seems to want to take responsibility. He's hoping just like everyone else. He's got every UN bigwig making calls, but it's all bluster, he thinks. If those two kids are on this side of the border, we'll get them back. If they're over there, we might not." Paul's eyes looked past his wife.

Abby spent the morning in the hospital taking pictures of wounded children, the Displaced Persons of Sa Kaeo. Two German NGOs set up a dark room to develop her photos immediately, and the "reunification board" in the mess tent attracted the largest crowds and was having some success. Around noon, Paul and Foster met with KR representatives about the missing volunteers. They were told that the two young men, both from Italy, may have been taken by a unit of the most desperate KRs near the border camp of Nong Samet, a camp of tens of thousands not too far inside Cambodia, but dangerous for those without leverage, which was most anyone entering the camp.

"The Red Cross and the UN stopped sending food there months ago. It never got to the refugees. The KR kept it for themselves or sold it on the black market. Maybe as many as 40,000 refugees are there trying to survive. It's a lawless camp under the thumbs of four or five warlords, mostly the soft caps, the KR that get supplies from China. The worst. Even if the Thais were willing, they wouldn't know who to contact."

"The Thais won't go. Who else can we turn to?"

Foster shook his head. "Maybe the International Rescue Committee, but they won't go anytime soon."

Later, Foster was informed that President Carter's wife would be coming for a tour around November 9th. Maybe she could secure the release of the volunteers. "If they live that long. That's ten days off. No, we can't wait that long."

Paul took hold of Foster's arm and ushered him out of the room. "We gotta go. Not you, but us. Me. I'll load up one of our little trucks with rice. Give me a handful of ID passes, the ones we give to our refugees, and I'll go. I'll trade food for the kids."

"No, Paul. They'll just take the food and you. Then, we'll be missing three people. I won't let you do that."

Paul stared at Foster but didn't say anything.

"Son of a bitch! You're going to go whether I give you permission or not. I ought to put you under arrest."

"We don't have a jail. Load up the truck, one that runs and is clearly labeled. No driver. Just me. Six passes. I'm going to see Abby. I'll be back in a half-hour. Don't tell her anything."

Just after 1:00, Paul found Abby at Site 2 North meeting with a small group of teenage girls. Through an interpreter, she was instructing them on how to avoid the camp soldiers, the Thai soldiers who wanted their bodies. He listened for a few minutes until she noticed him.

"Hey," she said. "Any word?"

"Maybe a lead. Across the border at one of the KR strongholds. We're going to make a trade. Rice for the kids. We'll have them back by sundown."

Abby curled her lips inward, stepped into her husband, and hugged him tightly. "I can't talk you out of this, can I?"

Paul dipped his face into her neck. "I'll be fine. Save me some dinner."

Abby squeezed him more tightly, as if she would never let him go. "I'll hold you to that."

∾

"This is the deal, Garrity. You take an interpreter, or you don't go," said Foster. He would not budge on this issue and Paul saw it in his demeanor.

"Not a young kid, though. He can't have any illusions about what we're doing."

"Trust me on this one, he's not a kid." Foster walked Paul to a Toyota pickup parked by the mess tent. Standing there leaning against the truck was a swarthy man who appeared to be in his early forties to Paul. Five-ten, short hair, a bit balding, strong, roundish face. Mediterranean maybe. As they approached, he stepped forward and extended his hand.

"Paul, this is Mario. He'll accompany you across the border."

The two men shook hands and sized each other up. "Are you sure you want to do this?" asked Mario.

Paul thought about his imaginary friend from his captivity. "Have you ever been into Cambodia?"

Mario nodded, not knowing what Paul was referring to. "Sort of grew up there." He smiled. "We'll talk about it on the way."

The pickup carried two 100-pound sacks of rice for barter, or trade as the case might demand. Foster handed Paul a manila envelope with UNHCR papers inside. "Just so you know, I'm totally against this." He handed Paul a cloth sack. "Single malt scotch. Maybe whoever is holding the two kids appreciates what I had to do to get this. If you give it to him, tell him you might be able to get another bottle in a few weeks." Mario tapped Paul on the shoulder. "If we're going to do this, we'd better get started. I'm not interested in driving after dark." He turned to Foster. "I'm driving straight into Nong Samet. No back roads."

They left the compound at Aranyaprathet and crossed into Cambodia at Poipet. There they stopped at the checkpoint, which had been advised of their travel. Thai guards looked at a set of papers and shook their heads. A foolish gamble. Mario drove Route 33 only a few miles before turning north onto a well-traveled dirt road. Along the sides camped hundreds of Cambodian families unable to cross into Thailand. Khmer Rouge soldiers walked the road, menacing with their M-16s. Oxcarts clogged the road. A hundred thousand or more Cambodians trapped between the retreating Khmer Rouge and the advancing Vietnamese army, prevented from entering Thailand by its army.

"What do you know about the aid workers we're going to pick up?" asked Paul.

"I know they're stupid as hell. Reckless." Mario was driving only fifteen miles an hour, careful of the potholes, refugees, and soldiers. "They're from my country. Italy. Do-gooders. College students. They're assigned to the Catholic Relief Services. Both of them are from the Milan area."

"Any guess what they were thinking then when they decided crossing the border was a good idea?" asked Paul. "Did you volunteer for this because they're your countrymen?"

"Their friends at camp said they wanted to go to Angkor Wat to see the temples. They must not have gotten the message that the Khmer Rouge were killing people there." Mario's low-key assessment masked his anger. "Yes, I'm responsible for them."

"If they're still alive, then they've used up all their good luck," said Paul. "You said back at Aran that you grew up in Cambodia. Was your father a diplomat or something?"

"I was making light of myself. I came to Cambodia in '67 when I was 27. I was probably as naïve as the volunteers we're going for. I'd heard so much about the peacefulness of Cambodia, and I was drifting in life. Phnom Penh and this country exceeded my expectations.

A perfect country untouched by the wars in Vietnam and Laos."

Paul started to speak but was jerked forward when Mario slammed on the brakes. Seven KR soldiers stepped quickly from the side of the road into the path of the Toyota. They were teenagers, the soldiers least predictable, least disciplined, most angry. Mario yelled and waived his hand as if he was driving in rush-hour traffic in Rome. The soldiers stood firm and moved to surround the truck. Mario kept talking, partly to the soldiers and partly to Paul.

"Remember, Paul, we're supposed to be here. We have papers to prove it. Take one of the sheets out of your folder and flash it at them. Be authoritative and show contempt. Say anything, and I'll interpret based on my understanding. They won't understand English."

The false bravado kept the child soldiers at bay for the moment. Paul yelled loudly about nonsense unrelated to the situation. Mario translated quickly and waved his arms. Quickly, Mario and Paul ascertained which soldier was in charge. All of them were barefoot and wearing the black pajamas of the KR, but one boy stepped slightly forward and held out his hand for the paper Paul was waiving.

Mario spoke to Paul. "He can't read it. He's posturing, but we'll play along." Mario turned back to the soldier and began speaking in a calmer voice. Speaking Cambodian Khmer, he informed the boy that they were on their way to Nong Samet to see the warlord in charge, and that the warlord would be very angry with the soldiers if they delayed the visit. At the rear of the truck, a soldier stabbed a knife into a sack of rice, spilling some of the rice.

Paul turned and yelled at the soldier who seemed to defy him. Mario cautioned the boy leader about the consequences. The leader stepped to the soldier with the knife and cuffed him on the head knocking a cigarette from his mouth and staggering him. The soldier with the knife handed it to the boy leader.

Mario spoke again to the leader. "Have each of your soldiers take two cups of rice from the open sack. I will speak to the warlord and tell him of your assistance in directing us to him."

The leader responded, telling Mario the name of the warlord he was looking for. "Sek."

The soldiers took their rice and Mario drove off. Fifty yards down the road, he took a huge breath. "That was hairy to the max," said Mario. "Not sure what I would have done had I seen the one soldier pull out his knife."

"Thank God their hunger outstrips their savagery. They live on the brink of evil without a clue as to what they exist for, what they're fighting for. Whatever will happen to them if this war ever ends?" Paul reached over and squeezed Mario's shoulder. "Should be a piece of cake from here on in." The two men laughed.

They continued to pass KR soldiers along the road and scraggly-looking men, women, and children just off the road as they neared Nong Samet. They had been briefed that the once small, peaceful hamlet had swollen in size, but they were stunned by its size and filth when they arrived. Paul estimated around 25,000, but Mario thought even more. Their speed dropped to a crawl, and they wondered if they would make it into the village center at all. They knew they were being watched.

A couple of blocks into Nong Samet, they were again stopped by KR soldiers; this time though, the men were older and more disciplined. Mario exchanged words with one, and Paul understood that the soldier was directing them to Sek.

"Maybe it would be safer if we had him climb in the back and escort us," said Paul.

Mario interpreted Paul's words to the soldier. The man shook his head no, but then ordered two of his men to jump in the back. Then he waved the Toyota on.

"This Sek must be the real deal. He'll either have the kids or know where they are," said Paul.

"By the way," cautioned Mario, "do not speak any French. The KR hate the French influence in their country. Anything remotely French is associated with Phnom Penh, which was sacked back in '75." Mario looked over at Paul. "Do you speak any French?"

"Just a few phrases. I agree it would be prudent if we only spoke English. The KR hate everyone and everything, but I'm going to bluff my way by reminding them that the US of A pays their salaries."

"In a manner of speaking," said Mario.

Within minutes the two KR soldiers jumped off the bed of the truck and motioned for Mario to stop. One soldier held his rifle in a ready position just next to Mario's head, while the other went inside the house, an old structure damaged by war. Mario and Paul waited. Cautiously, Paul reached under the seat for the bottle of scotch, then shuffled through his folder in the manner of a confident diplomat.

"Are you a betting man?" asked Mario.

"Not so much. Why?"

"I'll give you two-to-one odds that this truck won't be here when we come back out."

"Three-to-one and you're on," said Paul as he watched the soldier reappear. "Showtime."

Paul and Mario were escorted inside to a room with a ceiling fan. As they waited, Paul handled Mario the bottle to hold. Minutes later, three soldiers entered the room: the one in the middle, obviously the warlord Sek.

"Good afternoon, gentlemen," said Sek in French. "What is it you are risking your lives for?"

Mario held up his hand with his thumb and forefinger a half-inch apart. "Very little, I am the interpreter," he said in Khmer. "This is Mr. Garrity from the American embassy."

Paul nodded to Sek and spoke. As he did, Mario interpreted. "Two of our volunteers . . . two stupid volunteers . . . from Aranyaprathet crossed the border two days ago without permission. I have come asking that I take them off your hands, so they can be sent home. I'm also here to apologize for their behavior. As you are aware, two bags of rice are in the back of the truck."

Sek stared at Paul but remained unmoved. Paul remembered a North Vietnamese soldier from nearly a decade earlier who stood before him with the same air of authority. That soldier then struck Paul in the face, knocking him to the ground. When other soldiers picked him up, the soldier struck him again. Sek finally asked, and Mario translated, "Your two volunteers are arrogant. Are they American also?"

Paul wanted to say yes, to keep the discussion simple, but he thought Sek might already know. "No, they are Italian. Two of dozens of students who have come to help the refugees. They are old enough to know better."

Sek maintained his stare. "Obviously not. What makes you think I know where they are and have the authority to give them to you?"

Paul considered the bluff. "I didn't know anything for sure when I left Aran. The young soldiers who stopped us on the road and opened one of the bags of rice directed us to you." Paul paused. "What is happening here in Cambodia is complicated, but if you and your men are to continue with any chance of success, you will need the support of my government. It is a tired government, and many in my country want to end any involvement with your war. Don't give them any more reasons to walk away from that commitment."

"Commitment." Sek said this word with disdain. "Like you gave to South Vietnam?"

"My country gave Saigon fourteen years." Paul allowed that statement to settle in. "In the end it wasn't enough. We made many mistakes, too many to chronicle right now, but I'm not here to either apologize or beg. I'm here to exchange rice for the two volunteers. I'm authorized to tell you that if you release them to me today, another load of rice will be given to you at Poipet tomorrow. If I return empty-handed, there will be no more rice. Stupid as the actions of these boys were, they meant no harm to you. They are in Thailand to help the Cambodians who have been hurt by the Vietnamese invasion."

Sek continued to stare into Paul's eyes. "And if these boys are already dead?"

"Then I will take them back anyway, but there will be no more rice."

Sek nodded and his eyes shifted to the paper bag Mario held. Sek reached over and tapped the sack. "Bourbon whiskey, I hope."

Paul shook his head. "My apologies. Single-malt scotch." Mario handed the sack to Sek. "I can arrange for bourbon to be delivered with the rice in the morning."

"Your volunteers are waiting in the back of your truck. They are a little worse than when they arrived, but their bones are intact. Two of my men will ride with you back to Poipet. You had better go now before the sun sets."

Back at the truck, Mario spoke with the volunteers who looked as if they had lost a bar fight, but Sek was correct that there were no permanent injuries. The bags of rice had been removed, and two KR soldiers sat on the wheel wells with their M-16s. One of them ordered Mario and Paul into the truck with instructions to drive.

As Mario started back to the border, he warned Paul not to say anything. "One of the soldiers understands English." They rode in silence until they reached the checkpoint on the western edge of Poipet where the two KR soldiers jumped out. Shortly thereafter, Mario pulled the Toyota up to the hospital in Aranyaprathet.

∽

Foster set aside dinner for Paul and Mario. Abby had waited for Paul at the hospital and hadn't let go of his arm or hand in the hour that it took to debrief Foster and then clean up. Now, the three of them sat at the table in the mess hall of the aid workers' quarters.

"No secrets now, remember," said Abby.

"Once we made contact with the warlord, I felt better. It was the kiddie-corps that scared the shit out of us." Paul hesitated but remembered. "About three or four miles out of Nong Samet, we were stopped by a squad of KRs, really young kids. A couple of them couldn't have been more than twelve. Their rifles were bigger than they were. I started yelling at them in English and Mario in Italian."

Mario made eye contact with Abby. "It was a combination of Italian and Khmer. I think it may have confused the boys." He smiled. "Has your husband always thought of himself as invincible?"

"He doesn't think about himself." Abby smiled back and laid her head on Paul's shoulder. "Pretty much he is."

"Paul said the two of you came over with the Catholic Relief Services. Are you both Catholic?"

Abby laughed. "Neither one of us is. Hell, neither one of us has religion much."

Mario hmphed and took another bite of rice. "So, you're both carrying around guilt from America's failed adventure in Vietnam?" Paul nodded as if the answer was obvious.

"Why are you here?" asked Abby.

"I already explained that to your husband; he can fill you in on the details. The bigger question is why I'm still here. This work gets in your blood. These people, at least the ones who have been beaten by the war, need help. They didn't ask to be bombed and starved or have their children's futures taken away. None of these poor Cambodians ever sat around after twelve hours in their fields and discussed Marx. And the people I work with," Mario paused, "you will never find the likes of them anywhere else. They will drive you crazy at times, but they will show up and do what they can."

"The Khmer Rouge being the exception," said Paul.

"The Khmer Rouge." Mario let their name hang over the table. "In all of Southeast Asia, these people are the most vile, terrifying, evil creatures. How a gentle culture like Cambodia can give birth to such demons, I'll never understand. When this savagery ends, I don't know how Cambodia will resurrect itself."

"They come straggling into camp," said Abby, "looking for food, looking like they'd like to tear your heart out. Jumpy, sullen. They stick together all the time. Sleep together, their weapons never far away. Like wounded, beaten dogs. They scare me."

"All those land mines out there," said Mario, "were put there by the KR . . . to keep their fellow countrymen in the country, to prevent them from escaping the terror. The mines are directed inward. Nobody in, nobody out. America didn't create the KR; you just gave them justification by bombing the eastern regions of Cambodia, created the incubator for their growth."

Paul stirred the last grains of rice on his metal plate and started to say something but stopped. He laid his fork in his plate and breathed out heavily. Abby's look asked him to say what he started. "Refugees are nothing new, people fleeing war who had absolutely nothing to do with its creation. All those decisions were made at the heart of government. We took in what, 130,000 Vietnamese and thought we were done with the problem, but our war destroyed the way of life of millions more in Cambodia and Laos, and we aren't going to bring them to America. So, yeah, I have an enormous amount of guilt about this. I know my country isn't entirely to blame, but it has some responsibility. I have some responsibility."

∾

The monsoon struck with a ferociousness reserved for people who are already desperate, turning Sa Kaeo into a muddy bog. Cambodians weak from hunger and disease died on the paths of red dirt only bull-dozed into streets two weeks earlier. When the camp had been opened, Abby estimated nearly 100 refugees died each day, and these were the people who actually made it across the border into the Thai camps. Weaker refugees, especially children and the elderly, were left in the weeds on the other side. *"On the other side,"* Abby would say almost with contempt. Experienced aid workers like Foster were critical of the unpreparedness of agencies like UNHCR and the Red Cross in not having predicted and arranged for the flood of refugees now streaming into Sa Kaeo. *"Bureaucracy!"* Western journalists and politicians came to Thailand to witness the refugee crisis firsthand, and Foster's time was constantly being taken to show them around. Today, however, the rains kept most of these people holed up in Bangkok hotels or Aranyaprathet bars.

Abby and Paul hitched a ride to Sa Kaeo in a pickup truck because the road from Aranyaprathet was impassable for the buses. Abby went to the Children's Center, while Paul donned a raincoat and rubber boots to troubleshoot. The winds blew the rain into the shelters that were really just tarps hung over bamboo stakes. Compared to the situation two weeks earlier, conditions had improved a hundred-fold, but today, it seemed negligible. Paul picked up and carried a body from the side of one lane to the morgue. The cause of death could have been one of a dozen diseases; it could have been starvation; it even could have been drowning, but it didn't matter. Another Cambodian dead hundreds of miles from her farm.

Being 40 miles west of Aranyaprathet and the border, Sa Kaeo provided security not found in the border camps, but as Paul slogged through the red dirt streets, he concluded that the lack of proper drain-age would always prevent the camp from providing the sanitation and cleanliness necessary for housing the thousands of refugees it was set up to shelter. Sa Kaeo was an emergency camp, and it was better than the border camps, but it wasn't the final answer. Khmer Rouge soldiers still intimidated large numbers of refugees, as they would in any new camp, but because of the physical limitations, the living conditions were overwhelming the relief efforts of the UNHCR and the Catholic Relief Agency. And always, there was the murderous Khmer Rouge.

Paul worked his way over to the Processing Center looking for a small group referred to as The Posse, a handful of officials with the reputation for ignoring protocol to get things done, individuals not on the payroll of worldwide relief agencies. Despite the rain and wind, a few journalists had made it to Sa Kaeo and were looking for the story of the day. Paul knew they were essential in reporting the ongoing tragedy, but at times they missed the forest for the trees. Many Western journalists, especially from America and France, tended to be pro-KR, because of those nations' anti-Vietnam bias. These journalists purposely overlooked the KR atrocities.

In one corner three men and a woman, the very people Paul was searching for, stood smoking with their heads together. Paul had learned during his short time in Southeast Asia that many of the most determined and dependable individuals were those who had a stake in the region: former Green Beret soldiers, State Department employees, and long-time residents of Cambodia, those like Mario, people who hadn't turned tail and run when America left in 1973 or 1975, people who bucked the bureaucracy and side-stepped the aid agencies to help individuals, especially those brave people who had helped the United States during the war like the Montagnards, the people of the Central Highlands. The Posse cared about their fellow allies and were fiercely loyal to them.

Paul walked to The Posse, keeping his back to the journalists. "Excuse me. My name is Paul Garrity, and I wonder if I could have a minute?"

"Garrity." A bear of a man with thick hair and a big face rotated to see Paul better. "Are you the guy who drove over to Nong Samet the other day to retrieve those kids?"

"Yeah," answered Paul, "I'm that fool."

The woman, who appeared to be slightly older than the men and had a reputation for using her charm to raise money from reluctant sources, offered Paul a cigarette, which he waived away. He knew her to be a French woman who had lived in Cambodia for several years, a businesswoman of some wealth. "That stunt buys you a few minutes of our time," she said.

Paul spoke. "This camp isn't going to cut it. We need to find a location that's sustainable." He stopped to get a reaction from the group.

"Are you with the UNHCR?" asked the big-faced man almost as if the acronym was a swear word.

Paul nodded. "And I haven't been here that long, so my credentials are suspect." He held his cards for a moment.

The shortest man scratched his beard. "How did you end up in this part of the world, and how did you end up with the UN. It's not like they were hiring in the States."

"My wife and I were working for a Catholic church in California and volunteered for some home building in Mexico. The church asked if we would continue their work in Southeast Asia. Didn't have anything planned, so we took a chance. Worked at Galang and Bidong over the spring and summer, then took jobs with the UN because they paid. They sent us here last month. Ironically, neither of us is Catholic."

Big Face nodded, raised his hand, and shook his finger at Paul for a moment. As if remembering, he said to his associates, "This is the guy Foster put in charge of building this camp." He exhaled his cigarette smoke.

Paul couldn't tell whether The Posse was accepting him or ridiculing him. He waited.

The short man offered his hand. "Art. This is Camille. Will. Roy." Paul shook each person's hand while Art continued. "What's your stake in this game? All of us are a little crazy, but you don't have that look yet."

"Just one of those guilt-ridden Americans?" asked Camille.

"Leftist with a conscience?" asked Will, the big-faced member of The Posse.

"Once, maybe. Spent a few years in Nam, one and a half as a POW." Paul played his card.

Roy spoke for the first time. "Green Beret?"

"No. Draftee. Just got lost in the Highlands one day and ended up as a guest of the NVA."

Will tapped the ashes from his smoke, took a deep drag, and dropped it on the wooden floor. "When you were putting this camp together, didn't you notice that it was a former rice paddy?" He said that with a bit of humor, but it was a serious question.

"I didn't pick the site. Foster just gave me a bulldozer and a backhoe and told me to make it livable. Gotta tell ya, when it's not raining, it's like the Hilton."

"Yeah, right," said Art, "but it rains in Southeast Asia, or didn't you notice when you were marching around during the war?"

They all laughed, including Paul. Will looked over to Camille and smiled before turning back to Paul. "Do you have a site in mind?"

"No, but somewhere with a slope might be good. Thought you guys might have a lease on a plot like that," said Paul.

"How are you going to convince your employer to close this one?" asked Camille referring to the UNHCR.

"I'm not. Hoping when President Carter's wife arrives next week, it rains again."

∾

Abby guessed the boy with the amputated leg was maybe thirteen. Sullen and alone, wearing the black pajamas of a KR soldier. A boy with no name. In the three days she had watched him, his only interaction was taking the food from the volunteers and then retreating into himself, facing the wall. No words. No one touched him. Abby looked around for the right person. She decided on another child, another amputee, another child without her family, but one who spoke some English. Kim was nine and near death when she was brought to the hospital on the first day Sa Kaeo opened. She was one of the first to be operated on and had made a remarkable recovery. Another miracle performed by the doctors who worked without the benefit of modern technology in this remote corner of the world.

"Hello, Kim," said Abby standing next to the small girl's mat. "My name is Mrs. Garrity. I would like to take your picture, so it can be posted on the bulletin board to help your family find you." Abby smiled. "Would that be okay?" The young girl nodded but did not smile back. Abby helped Kim sit up and then adjusted the focus on her camera. Abby lowered the camera. "I'm going to need a smile."

Kim's dark eyes couldn't smile, hadn't smiled in years. "The soldiers got angry if we smiled."

Abby understood but still recoiled. Families throughout Cambodia taught their children to hide their feelings; emotions were not allowed by the Khmer Rouge. Open displays of affection could be punished, even with death. Keep your eyes down, don't hug your family in public, don't smile and laugh. Rules to live by—literally. Abby lowered her body toward Kim. "May I sit with you?"

Kim was hesitant to give permission, but finally nodded. She pulled back slightly as Abby settled onto the mat. They sat in silence for a moment, Abby allowing Kim to accept the fact that a stranger was in close proximity but not making any demands.

In a voice barely audible over the rain, Abby spoke. "The doctor said you might have been a tennis player once." A pattern developed, a soft statement and then quiet. "When he operated on you, he said you mumbled something about tennis. In English." Abby tilted her head to get a better angle on Kim's face. Abby set the camera down next to Kim's thigh. "When I was a young girl, my family played badminton. It's a game a little like tennis, not as difficult, but still fun." Abby paused and waited again, this time a little longer. She noticed that Kim's head had tilted toward the camera, and Abby wondered if Kim had ever seen a camera before. Then she realized that if Kim played tennis once, she certainly was in a family that took photos. Lots of photos. "Who was the picture-taker in your family?" asked Abby.

Kim rocked slightly but remained quiet. Abby waited. Without lifting her eyes, Kim answered softly. "My father." She used the French term for father. "He burned them all."

Abby understood her meaning, the intentional destruction of records. Families from the cities, especially Phnom Penh, were slaughtered, and the educated were singled out. At Galang and Bidong, Abby was optimistic about finding the relatives of displaced persons, but here along the Thai border, there was little chance that Kim's family survived. An orphan. Ever so slowly and gently, Abby slid an open palm toward Kim, not to touch her but to give Kim the opportunity. Abby remembered Paul's first hug on the day she was released from prison. This, however, was different. She waited, and the rain continued. Amid the commotion of a makeshift hospital trying to save hundreds of patients each day, a woman and a girl sat alone, each with her own thoughts.

After several minutes, the girl's head moved slightly, from the camera to the outstretched hand, as if studying it. Abby watched her own hand and waited. Kim's chest rose and fell as if it made the decision for her, as if saying, "Oh, go ahead." Kim's hand slid past the camera, touching it briefly, and then slid into Abby's. A tiny, calloused hand, not like a nine-year old's should be. Abby gently closed her fingers around Kim's hand. The rain didn't stop, but it seemed to let up slightly, along with the wind. After a few moments, Abby placed her arm around Kim's shoulder very gently.

"I see you are a brave girl," said Abby. "I would like to get to know you better."

Without looking up, Kim allowed her body to fall into Abby's lap. They continued to hold hands, and Abby left her arm on Kim's shoulders. The camp hospital had wooden planks covering a gravel base which allowed for the best drainage at Sa Kaeo, the one structure that didn't turn to mud during the heavy downpour. Abby had things to do, but none seemed more important than holding on to this Cambodian girl at this moment.

∾

Back in Aranyaprathet, Paul told Abby of his meeting with Will, Ray, Art, and Camille. Abby listened on the outside, but her mind was on a little girl in the hospital in Sa Kaeo. In time Abby stopped her husband.

"I learned something today," she said. "Across the border there are hundreds of thousands of nameless refugees. From what we're hearing, a million more have died at the hands of the KR. I tell myself this cannot be happening, but the flood continues every day." She split the word to emphasize every day. "I, we, are a part of something much larger than ourselves, something that needs to be done and can only be done by the people we work with. I've seen Camille in the hospital and at the bulletin board scanning the photos, trying to put another face with another family. She gets it. For her, it's about saving one and then two; she doesn't waste her time trying to save millions. She knows she can't. Yet, as I watch her, saving is not her only goal, I don't think. It's more." Abby paused.

Paul took his wife's hand but remained quiet. Abby's lip quivered, and tears formed in her eyes. She looked tired. Paul couldn't tell if they were tears of sadness or anger. Maybe both. Months of sixteen-hour days, with the Vietnamese families on Galang and Bidong and now in Thailand, seeing the injuries and pain up close, and yet trying bravely to carry on.

"I'm so glad we came, but what keeps coming into my mind is that I want our own family, and our time will run out soon. We're 32-years-old. I want to feel our child inside my belly, our children." Her eyes focused on Paul's. "Do you want that too?"

Paul leaned in and kissed Abby's lips tenderly. "Yes," he whispered, "yes, I do."

"Would you feel like we're running away if we left here and went home?"

"No. We only said we were coming here temporarily, never as a career. Remember?" He squeezed his lips into a single line. "I don't know where our home is though."

Abby's tears dripped down her cheeks. "This is what I've learned. Families in their own place are everything, but they must have a place." She sniffled. "I want to be closer to ours, to mine and yours. Chicago is a possibility, Oxnard too. Mose and Sally and Ella are family. I just want a safe place for our children." She squeezed Paul's hands hard, lifted them up and shook them. "But I'm so touched by these Cambodian refugees who have survived."

"What happened today that brought this out?" asked Paul.

"I sat with a bright little girl, probably an orphan, most likely from the Phnom Penh elite. Held her hand. She had one leg blown off by a land mine not two miles inside the border. Malnourished. I was looking for someone to use to make a connection to one of the child soldiers, a boy who was obviously KR but had lost his humanity. He too was an amputee and starved. In every way this boy is disgusting, except that he didn't choose this life. He was dragged into it. As I held Kim, that's the little girl, I watched the boy. Like a beaten dog. So far gone, detached from reality, from what a thirteen-year-old boy should be. I wondered if there was any way to get him back, any process, and I couldn't think of one. The boy will become the man who destroyed Cambodia, who blew off one of Kim's legs." Abby paused. She had stopped crying, and Paul sensed her legendary anger rising.

"Did you have Kim meet the boy?"

"No. That was a bad idea. She's so traumatized. To think that having her say hi to that creature would automatically save him was stupid. Hell, just a few days ago, she was fighting for her life. She's this butterfly who needs, I don't know, tenderness and love. She can't be used as my vehicle to enter into the world of a child soldier."

Paul tilted his head slightly. "Nobody has a good solution for them, neither Kim nor the boy. Foreign countries don't want damaged orphans; nobody is looking to sponsor them. Kim might find a home, but even that's iffy. The boy has no future. He most likely was forced to commit horrible acts by the KR adults to make him unacceptable in his community ever again, maybe even killing one of his own family members. He had no choice; kill or be killed. How in the hell do you patch a boy like that up or put him into society again? When I went to Nong Samet, he was the soldier I most feared. Not the adults, but these boys who've been tortured and starved themselves."

Without saying anything, Abby leaned into her husband and hugged him tightly. She held him for a minute before speaking. Finally, "I left work a little early because I was so, I don't know, distraught. I curled up in the corner and cried. In prison lots of the younger women would have these breakdowns, but I was too tough." Abby hmphed. "When the guards shut off the lights, some prisoner always started crying, holding it in until she couldn't be seen. So many nights, I sat curled up in a corner of my cell but without giving in to my tears." She hugged Paul even more tightly and kept her face buried in his chest. "Tonight, I want to make love to you, to hold you inside me and take your seed, to show you again how much I love you and want your children, to begin that family now."

Paul intensified his hug on Abby. When he was sure she was done talking, he said, "You know that there's no guarantee you'll get pregnant tonight. I think maybe we ought to have sex every night for a while."

It didn't rain on November 9th when Rosalynn Carter toured Sa Kaeo. To those who built the camp in three days or worked there for the two weeks prior to Mrs. Carter's visit, conditions were immeasurably better, but to the untrained eye, to the politicians and dignitaries who came for one day, conditions were squalid. Women, children, and old men were dying in plain sight, or to these visitors, about ready to die. Tarp shelters, mats instead of beds, no privacy, distended bellies, swollen feet, and vacant eyes. Mrs. Carter held a child in her arms who died hours later. She promised to tell her husband of the desperate conditions at the border, and within days, the United States authorized a hundred million dollars of aid for the Cambodian tragedy.

Sa Kaeo's deficiencies magnified as the population of starving refugees swelled. Even as supplies began to arrive in adequate numbers, chaos ruled. Will exploded in frustration at Red Cross and UNHCR officials over bureaucratic delays. Camille and Art dragged him from the RC office to keep him from punching one official. The various international aid agencies bickered over territory, and the miscommunication and lack of understanding of the local culture caused the operation to be less effective than it should have been. And always, there were the Khmer Rouge who came to the camps to escape the Vietnamese army, to use the border camps as a protected refuge. The fact that war raged 40 miles to the east between Vietnam and several guerrilla Khmer Rouge units could never be ignored. At times, gunfire and mortar fire crossed the border and put volunteers at risk, as well as the refugees in the border camps. Having the Vietnamese army engaged with the Khmer Rouge served everyone's purpose except the Cambodian people. Caught in the middle of a brutal war, they died by the millions. Thirty miles west of the poorly-defined border, Sa Kaeo provided a modicum of safety from the actual war.

Paul, Will, Ray, Art, and Camille got their wish. Sa Kaeo could not sustain its operation, so Thailand approved a new site, one selected with greater care by Will and the US Ambassador. The new location had access to wells on a sloping plot of land to the north and only six miles from the Cambodian border, but it was sustainable. The UNHCR, under the new direction of a British field officer named Martin Gray, regained a measure of trust from the other aid agencies, and especially from mavericks like Will and Camille, when it constructed the new camp. Khao-I-Dang took four days to build and began taking in refugees on November 21st. Paul wanted an extra day or two to make it perfect, but Gray knew that some of those "frills" could be added after the camp became operational. Paul wanted the wells to be operational at the beginning, but that had to wait; water would be trucked in early on. Paul also wanted to build permanent structures at KID, but the Thai government refused to allow it.

∽

At the KID Children's Center, Abby organized the volunteers daily to facilitate the treatment of hundreds of children coming in. Some wounds were visible, some were not, but every child suffered trauma. Information about the desperate nature of Cambodia had gotten out to the Western world, and adequate supplies were arriving. The numbers of volunteers also increased, and Abby had enough to staff the daily needs, except too many allowed their hearts to interfere with the process, and the multiplicity of languages often slowed the most basic of jobs. Many volunteers were tourists whose help could last only a day or two.

Abby directed six new volunteers at the Children's Center on December 7th, two weeks after KID opened. "Don't let any child sit without a checkup! Even if they look fine, they are not. Each one is traumatized. If you aren't sure where to send them, ask! The nurses will take those with wounds, but many of the children are just dropped off and left alone. Record each arrival and tag them."

A mortar shell exploded in the compound.

"Get down!" yelled Abby. She pushed two volunteers to the floor of the giant tent and moved quickly to grab three children nearest the door and shove them to the ground.

A second mortar round exploded, this one destroying a bamboo and thatch structure that held UN supplies. Voices outside the Center screamed for help, some from the victims and some from camp personnel.

"Stay down," warned Abby. She duckwalked to a child who seemed oblivious to the explosions outside. Abby stood only long enough to envelope the child in her arms and guide her to the floor. She remembered a large man in Chicago who forced her to the floor in her parents' food kitchen years earlier. "Kiss the floor!" the man had said. Good advice anywhere. At that moment, gunfire exploded on the periphery of the camp. Abby decided it must be a firefight occurring between two factions of KRs who couldn't figure out who the enemy was. She assumed it wasn't with the Vietnamese on this side of the border. Laying on a small child, her arm around another, Abby's anger surfaced. She wasn't scared; she was furious that these people who were receiving the benefits provided by thousands of volunteers here at KID and other border camps could not stop fighting, would not stop killing.

The tent flap opened, and a woman carried a bloody child into the Center. Abby rose immediately, took the child from the woman's arms, and ushered the woman to a volunteer, a young man who had also stood to help. He rushed to cover the woman with his body, trying to soothe her with his gentle voice. Abby did not recognize his language. Ignoring the sound of gunfire, Abby left the Center to take the child to the hospital next door. Inside, she handed the child to a doctor and returned to the Center to tend to her charges.

The firefight ended as quickly as it started, and the activity resembled an ant hill after it had been stomped on by young boys. Abby directed her volunteers to tend to each child in the Center, one volunteer to one child. If nothing else, hug the child. A Red Cross official who worked in conjunction with Abby at the Children's Center noticed the blood on Abby and wanted to take her to the hospital to be tended to. Abby thanked him but said it was the child's blood. The

Center had not been damaged in the fight. A few benches had been overturned, but within minutes, order was restored, and the processing of children continued.

Three minutes later, Abby collapsed.

∞

Gunfire could always be heard at Khao-I-Dang since it was just six miles inside the border. While tens of thousands of refugees were housed at KID, thousands more fleeing, homeless, terrified Cambodians huddled in the forests and grasslands on the Cambodian side, prevented from crossing the border by landmines, Khmer Rouge guerrillas, and Thai Rangers. The border camps in Cambodia were not recognized as official refugee camps, because the people there had not crossed a border. At KID and Sa Kaeo, refugees were cared for with food and medical treatment, plus a measure of security, despite the occasional gunfire. They were dangerous places for sure, especially for women and teenage girls. Inside Cambodia, just miles away from KID, fugitives were not eligible for asylum nor given basic rights. Prisoners in their own country. These camps were run by KR resistance groups which had organized after being routed by the Vietnamese army and were now carving out their own tiny spheres of influence. And the Cambodian people continued to die.

Paul rode in a UN truck with Camille and Art when the shooting started at KID. They were unaware that shells had exploded inside the camp, even though they heard them. "Close," said Camille.

"Maybe we ought to go back to check the damages," said Art. "I'm not real excited about driving back to Aran if those bastards are playing wargames. Our meeting with Will can wait." He laughed. "Maybe he'll fly back to Bangkok, and we'll miss the meeting completely."

Paul nodded. "He operates at a level beyond my metabolism. Amazing guy."

Art slowed the truck and made a U-turn. "Camille, you okay with this. I know you want to see him." Art knew that her reasons for going with Paul and him today extended beyond the professional level.

"Yeah. He wants me to fly with him into Laos to see about helping some Montagnards. We can't go this week anyway, so this is fine."

She bumped Paul's shoulder. "Have you ever flown in one of the small planes we use to get around in the bush?" Paul shook his head. "I'll have to take you up sometime. Exciting as hell!" She laughed, and Paul knew her definition of exciting probably wasn't his definition of the word.

"Where do you land the plane?" asked Paul.

"Any old clearing. A dirt road, a field. A few hamlets have a short strip. I'll fly, you ride," said Camille.

Art pulled the truck into KID ten minutes later. "We'll try again tomorrow if Will is still in Aran. I'll let you know before dinner." He left Paul off at the Processing Center, and he and Camille drove back to the motor pool.

When Paul stepped into the tent, Martin Gray nearly assaulted him. "Come with me, Paul." He took Paul by the arm and rushed him to the hospital. At a table near the back of the room, blood was being pumped into Abby, and a team of doctors and nurses worked to stabilize her. Gray guided Paul closer to his wife, just steps away from the table. Abby's face was pale, and she was obviously unconscious. Paul shook off Gray's hold and stepped closer to Abby, close enough where he could touch her head. One doctor looked up to Gray and nodded, indicating Paul's presence at the table was okay.

The doctor continued his procedure but spoke quietly. "When your wife was brought in, we feared it was a chest wound because of the location of the blood. Turns out it was the child's blood. Your wife had carried the child in just minutes earlier, handed her to a nurse, and went back to the Children's Center. That's where she collapsed. Volunteers carried her back. She's stabilized for the moment, and we've located the wound. I first thought it was a bullet, but I finally found where she was bleeding, and it turns out it was a wood splinter to the lower torso. I think it missed her liver and stomach, but she's suffered significant blood loss. It's serious but I think we've got it under control."

A nurse held up a four-inch dagger of wood covered with Abby's blood for Paul to see. Bamboo. Paul's fingers moved tenderly against Abby's scalp. He curled his lips inward, and his chest heaved.

The doctor lowered his head to get a better view of the wound in Abby's side. "I think we got it all. Pretty routine since it wasn't a bullet."

Paul identified the accent as German. He looked at the other medical personnel and realized the team was from several countries. One nurse appeared to be American. Much like the volunteers in Malaysia and Indonesia, the rescue of Abby was being performed by men and women from around the world, people whose main concern was saving lives, regardless of nationality.

∾

Abby stayed one day in the KID hospital and was then transferred to Aranyaprathet, a better equipped facility. The main medical concern was infection, or as Will jokingly put it, "You never know where that bamboo sliver's been." Aran was where most of the volunteers stayed. They were bused to the various camps in Thailand, not those in Cambodia, and returned to Aran before dark. Aran became a wild west Sixties town for the aid workers. Bars, brothels, casual sex, and drugs. It was the hub of the relief community where mostly unmarried volunteers found respite from their fourteen-hour days. It was a border town, just across from Poipet, Cambodia, where the black-market trade flourished. Before the war Aran was the last Thai town on the way to Angkor Wat, a stopping off spot for those who flew into Bangkok rather than Phnom Penh. Bangkok may have been sin city, but Aran was its little brother.

For three days, Paul stayed with Abby in the hospital as she recovered. He drew sketches for improvements at KID, held meetings with Camille, Art, Foster, and the indefatigable Will on infrastructure at the camp, and played the devil's advocate with Martin Gray on the topic of resettlement versus repatriation of the refugees. KID's population became the new home for the Cambodian middle class, the group of people who had been the main targets of the Khmer Rouge genocide that began in 1975 when Phnom Penh was overthrown, and Pol Pot became communist "Brother Number One." The people who had been forced to dig their own graves when they were ordered to evacuate Phnom Penh were now coming out of the forests and reclaiming their families—or what was left of them.

On the evening of December 11, 1979, Paul sat with Abby in her hospital room and held a meeting with The Posse and the head of the UNHCR, Martin Gray. The Englishman was adamant that the Cambodians needed to be repatriated into their own country even though that would be a dangerous proposition. No one in the room disagreed, but Paul argued the US position that forcing the refugees back across the border where the Khmer Rouge guerrillas fought with the Vietnamese army was tantamount to surrender.

"Why are you arguing what you don't believe?" yelled Will at Paul.

Paul smiled, which drove Will crazy. "You're arguing a position that you fully don't stand behind. You really think that if those refugees at KID are all sent back, the old Cambodia will magically reappear?"

The discussion raged over two hours with the non-patients drinking several beers. Abby said nothing, but worried about those she had tried to protect during her time in Malaysia and Thailand—the children and young girls. She reached out her hand, a signal to Paul that she wanted a taste of his beer, took a sip, and said, "No solution fits everyone's need, does it. The refugees won't be allowed to stay in Thailand or the other half-dozen Asian nations forever, but the rest of the world won't take them either. Americans are already pushing back against the numbers being let in." She winced as she took another drink. "Has Paul told you?"

"I'm taking her home," said Paul. "We've got a van set up as her personal ambulance. Leaving tomorrow for Bangkok. The doctor said she can travel."

"I'm more of a burden at this point than a help," said Abby.

Martin Gray already knew. Camille shook her head and asked, "When will you be coming back? I mean, Paul, you can stay in the States, but, Abby, we need you over here."

"I'm holding out for Martin to raise our salaries," said Paul. "New titles, bigger office than this, better truck." Everyone laughed, especially Gray. Paul took Abby's hand and spoke seriously. "We'll see. She needs to fully recover, and we're kind of a team. We're going to be staying with her parents in Chicago, but we'll play it by ear."

"Are you leaving your bulldozer?" asked Will.

"For now," answered Paul. "Martin won't let me put it on the plane.

You need to get it out and just plow a road into Nong Samet. We've done pretty well with the refugees over here, but the others who exist just over the border still need your help." Everyone nodded, and they raised their beers in a silent toast.

"Ashford's already got a plan to truck rice to Nong Chan," said Martin. "That young man is a stud."

"Listen, asshole," said Will to Paul. "You get your wife fixed up and get back here. I'm not done with you yet. Maybe I can get the State Department to pitch in a few extra dollars to entice you. I spend too much time with do-gooders and not enough time with vets, present company excepted," he said looking at Abby.

"Noted," smiled Abby. "Apology accepted."

"With you gone, Abby, I'll have to do all the yelling at these male bureaucrats," said Camille. "You'd think the State Department or the UN could find a few capable women for leadership roles. If it weren't for wives, this would be the all-boys club. Almost is now." Camille shook her head.

Art stood, a signal that the meeting/party was over. "By the way, Paul, did you hear the latest rumor?" Paul shook his head. "Rumor has it you're CIA."

The room exploded in laughter.

∽

Later that night, Will knocked at Paul's door, or what passed as a door. "Got a few minutes?"

Paul let him in and offered him a chair. "More beer?"

"Maybe just one." The two men settled in with their beers and a few minutes of silence. Finally, Will spoke. "The doctors aren't jivin' ya. Abby's going to be okay." He smiled at Paul and continued. "Tough lady. She's been a true hero these past few months." Paul raised his beer in a silent toast to his wife and waited for Will to get to his point. "You too, Garrity. I've been thinking about your captivity. Never heard anything like it, and when I was a Beret, I thought I'd seen everything." Will flexed his jaw and nodded, a sign he had asked his question.

Paul started slowly. "Yeah, unique, but mostly easy, especially when compared to the other POWs. I farmed from sunup to sundown."

He grinned. "A POW tied to the land sort of like one of them nine-teenth-century Russian serfs. Lonely, but I'm pretty comfortable being a hermit." He laughed slightly at his description. "Got whacked by a stick a few times but was never shot at or beaten. I have a good friend back in California who maintains it was penance for allowing myself to be drafted." Paul knew Will once held the opposite view.

"So," said Will, "not a true believer, huh? Never gung-ho?" He looked into his beer. "What now?"

"Mario thinks Abby and I have been infected. I don't think it's guilt any longer. These refugees need help, that's for sure."

Will nodded. "Ya got another one of these?" Paul pulled another beer from his cooler and handed it to Will. "I was in Saigon in '75 trying to get some of our friends out at the last minute. That was a real clusterfuck. This is different."

Paul agreed. "It's still a clusterfuck but with more deaths."

"Yeah, and they're going to die if we can't get our shit together. Ashford has a bold plan to get rice across that border. Hope it works." Will gulped his beer down before standing. At the door he shook Paul's hand. "Get your ass back here as soon as you can."

Wearing a Santa hat with bells, Paul worked Christmas day at the soup kitchen in Chicago's Pilsen neighborhood. Still recovering from her wound, Abby stayed at her parents' home with a brother. Despite the hardships of living in Third World environments, both missed the work along the Thai-Cambodia border, but for Paul, serving food alongside Abby's parents gave him purpose. A thousand pounds of turkey, tubs of mashed potatoes with gravy, stuffing, cranberries, and dessert. Donors from the area neighborhoods had been especially generous this year. Abby spent her time outlining procedures to reunite families in war-torn regions, using her experiences at Bidong, Sa Kaeo, and Khao-I-Dong as guides. One group of displaced persons baffled her—the child soldiers, those wild, dangerous, and unwanted outcasts from the villages. How does one rejoin a weapon of evil with its family and hamlet? What kind of forgiveness and reconciliation would be necessary? Paul called just after noon to see how Abby was feeling and asked if she wanted him to bring her a plate of turkey for dinner.

"Yes, I would. I have a present for you," she said in a suggestive voice.

"Maybe I'll leave early then." He laughed. "We need to call Mose and Sally, too."

The Archer family had opened presents on Christmas eve, knowing Christmas day would be too busy to settle back with eggnog and unwrap gifts. Paul gave Abby a necklace with a Victorian antique key, one he had found at a thrift shop near the soup kitchen. He also bought her a pair of hoop earrings like the ones she used to wear in Boulder. She gave him a book about Cambodia before the Indochina War and an outdoor basketball. Abby's parents gave them a new 35mm Nikon camera to replace Abby's old Kodak Instamatic. Reverend and Mrs. Archer were thrilled to have their daughter and Paul home—and away from the refugee conditions.

"An Asian family came in for dinner today. They reminded me of some of our families in Malaysia and Indonesia," said Paul.

"Not so much Thailand?" asked Abby.

"Maybe more like the Vietnamese refugees than the Cambodians. Happier, more emotions."

"Did you talk with them?"

"No. Didn't want to interfere by bringing up their past on Christmas day. I did wonder if they were celebrating as Christians or were just in for the food. Very neat and clean, again, more like the refugees on Galang."

Paul and Mrs. Archer brought home enough food for a nice dinner for the entire family, as three of Abby's siblings were also there for the holidays. Abby transferred the food from the metal tubs to the "nice dishes" and supper was served around 7:00. It was bitter cold in Chicago with the traditional winds off Lake Michigan, but Abby's father thanked the Lord for the comforts He had afforded them. Reverend Archer also thanked the Lord for bringing his daughter and her husband home safely and for allowing them to work with the refugees in Asia. It was obvious that Abby's parents were proud of her and Paul for traveling to the underdeveloped world to serve the less fortunate and desperate, but relieved Abby could recover in more sanitary conditions. Not long afterwards, Reverend and Mrs. Archer said goodnight. The kids washed the dishes, and after a few minutes of catching up, Abby and Paul retired to her childhood bedroom.

Wearing only her new key necklace and loop earrings, Abby climbed on top of Paul in the small bed and put him inside her. After a few slight movements and squeezes, she sat up on her knees keeping him inside her. She took his hand and placed it on her belly. "This is my yellow." She smiled tenderly. "I don't know where that came from, something about chakras or Reiki, but I have always called it that.

Now, it's an oven." She smiled again, leaned in and kissed Paul softly on his lips. "I'm pregnant."

Paul smiled carefully, a smile Abby interpreted as joy and uncertainty. "So soon? How do you know?"

"I missed a period. I've done that before, but this time, I just know. I wouldn't tell you if I wasn't sure." Abby teared up and swallowed hard. "Thank you, Paul Garrity."

Paul's eyes followed suit. He learned forward and kissed his wife delicately as if trying not to break a soap bubble. "I love you, Abby Archer."

"Garrity. Abby Garrity."

On the morning of January 1, 1980, Abby answered the phone. It was Martin Gray in Bangkok. "It's 9:00 here and our little New Year's party is over. Time to get back to work." Gray even laughed with a British accent. "How are you feeling, Abby? Ready to come back?"

"Good and no, Martin. My doctor wants me to give it a little more time. Let me get Paul." Abby put down the phone, went into the bedroom, and told Paul that Martin was waiting impatiently to coerce him back to Thailand.

"Martin. Have you solved all the refugee problems along the border?" Paul eased himself onto a kitchen stool next to the counter and motioned for Abby to pour him a cup of coffee.

"Let me get right to the point, Paul. I need you back here now. That lifeline into the Cambodian border camps that we talked about while you were here is up and running, but we've hit a few snags. It just got shut down by the KR warlords. All the relief agencies are carving out their own little fiefdoms which just slows down the rice we're trying to send across the border. And there's the Vietnamese army. I imagine you heard about their little raid against the Thai soldiers here."

Paul interrupted. "Martin, all those problems existed before I left. Those are conflicts that you and the ambassador and the warlords need to settle. I'm just the guy who builds shelters and bulldozes roads. Remember?"

"You know as well as I do, Paul, that as soon as someone has a title or position affixed to his name that he becomes a target. You have a clean reputation, and for some unknown reason, all these angry people listen to you. Will just yells, and I'm the head of the UNHCR, the agency that all other groups seem to think is too bureaucratic and slow. No, if this Land Bridge to the other side of the border is going to be successful, we need you right now." Paul started to respond, but Martin continued. "Listen, I know Abby needs time to recover, but you can leave her there and come over for a few months. Talk with her and I'll get back to you." With that, he hung up from Bangkok.

Paul placed the receiver back into the wall unit but remained quiet. He shook his head to himself and then turned to Abby. "That was weird."

"You want to go, don't you?"

"I'm not going without you, and you can't go now."

Abby stepped into Paul's body, and they hugged. "I'll be all right for a couple of weeks, and anyway, you're bored here."

"No, I'm not going. I wouldn't make any difference anyway. Case closed."

⌘

The next day, Paul and Abby rode the "L" to the upper North Side of Chicago. The Red Line let them off on Argyle in a neighborhood that was obviously Asian, but Abby and Paul were looking specifically for signs of Vietnam and Cambodia. Grocery stores and restaurants seemed to predominate, and the couple ate lunch at one of the small diners.

"I think these refugees came after we lost the war in '73 and then again in '75," said Paul. "Not sure if any of the Boat People have made it here yet. Some will, of course."

"My dad said this was one of the seedier areas of the city before the Vietnamese began arriving. Lots of prostitution and homeless. My parents thought about opening a soup kitchen here but couldn't get enough start-up funding. They still think about it, although conditions appear to be improving without much outside help."

"That first group of refugees were upper class or upper middle class. The Boat People are much poorer. If they had any money, they probably were Chinese-Vietnamese." Paul thanked the server for refilling his water glass. "Lots of different genes in that one," he said in a whisper to Abby.

"Black GI?" asked Abby.

"Probably. *Bui doi*. That word translates as 'the dust of life.' The most heavily discriminated against in Vietnam, children of American soldiers and Vietnamese women, often prostitutes. Discriminated against over here too."

"He seems happy," said Abby.

"This is a family business. Safe. Not so much in school I would guess. I hope I'm wrong."

After lunch, Paul and Abby strolled Argyle holding hands, looking in store windows, and people watching. "What are you looking for?" asked Abby.

They sat on a bench near a tiny park. "Confirmation maybe. When the U.S. left Vietnam seven years ago, five if you start from the fall of Saigon, America was a mess. We lost a war to a third-rate power, we were divided, our economy was terrible; now, we seem to have forgotten that. I'm not sure I know what I'm looking for."

Abby listened while her husband rambled. Finally, she stopped him by putting her hand on his forearm. "Remember that first summer we were together in Oxnard? I said that my whole adult life was tied to Vietnam. Yours has been too. If America recovers, it won't be because of the politicians who messed up. It will be because of those who faced the problems and persevered, people like you and Ray and Will. Veterans."

"I'm not trying to save America; I've got enough to do with just me."

"And me." Abby smiled and patted her belly. "And this one."

An old man walked by, stopped, and turned to Paul and Abby. In imperfect English, he asked, "Were you a soldier in my country?"

Paul nodded but said nothing.

"I want to thank you." The old man paused. "And thank you for coming here." He smiled and walked away before either Paul or Abby could respond.

∾

Again, the next morning, the phone in the Archer home rang. Abby's father answered and passed the receiver to Paul. He took the phone expecting it to be Martin Gray.

"Still no, Martin," said Paul without a greeting.

"It's Will, Paul. I understand Martin called and offered you a raise. He's lying. Nobody gets a raise over here."

Paul laughed aloud. Abby walked into the kitchen and Paul pointed to the phone and mouthed silently, "Will." "What are you doing near a phone, Will? Shouldn't you be in a truck somewhere instead of a desk?"

"Remember what we talked about before you bugged out on me? The Land Bridge into the border camps? It's a brilliant idea. Well, it's up and running, but not smoothly. Every volunteer agency wants credit, and we seem to be stepping on a lot of toes."

"Who's we, Will?" asked Paul.

"The State Department and UNHCR,"

"In other words, you and Martin then." Paul smiled on his end in Chicago. "What you're saying is that your charming personality doesn't lend itself to diplomacy? Hard to imagine that."

"Well, yeah, I can be a bit abrasive. I hired a fellow Green Beret, and he can't seem to tolerate bureaucracy either. That's why we need you, someone with experience dealing with the KR and the Vietnamese."

Paul shook his head no, but Will couldn't see it. "Being a POW isn't experience, Will."

"Paul, you can talk a dog off a meat wagon, and we have so many dogs here at the border."

"Those dogs you're referencing are carrying M-16s," said Paul.

"Look, Paul. You and Mario have a massive amount of respect after driving into Nong Samet by yourselves to rescue those two dumb-ass volunteers. That took balls, and the warlords respected that."

"Where's Mario?" asked Paul.

"I'm working on him too."

⤝

Will and Camille met Paul at the Bangkok airport on Sunday evening and treated him to dinner. Chicago to Los Angeles to

Honolulu to Manila to Bangkok. "I'm really looking forward to the three-hour drive to the border tomorrow," said Paul sarcastically.

"Oh, didn't Will tell you?" said Camille. "Mario's flying in tomorrow morning, and, weather permitting, then I'll be flying us all over to Aran to save time." She laughed. "I promised you a scenic tour last month. Remember?"

"How's Abby?" asked Will, and Camille leaned in.

"Recovering nicely. She had a little bit of a bout with infection early on, but we got that taken care of. She's mostly back to being her old self. Says to tell you all hi and would have loved to have come with me. Working with her parents at their soup kitchen on a limited schedule." He rubbed his eyes with the palms of his hands and asked the waiter for a cup of coffee. "So, what's the situation?"

"All those rumors about the mass murders throughout Cambodia that we couldn't believe even though we were seeing evidence of it before," said Will. "They're true. Actually, much worse than that. And now, we're facing a humanitarian crisis of epic proportions. Imminent famine unless we can get the Land Bridge functioning smoothly. Ashford's been the man, but he needs support. Shit, he's younger than you."

Camille took a drag from her cigarette and swore. "It's a fucking nightmare, Paul. Every damned agency wants a piece of the pie, which is good, but none of them want to cooperate. Your country still hates Vietnam and supports the Khmer Rouge, which complicates everything."

"It's the same old story, Paul. Everyone over here knows who's been murdering, or should I say slaughtering, the Cambodians, but the US position never changes. Every volunteer agency and the European nations that want to help are suspicious of America's motives," said Will. His voice, always on the verge of yelling, was straddling that line.

"You're State Department, Will. I can't do your job for you."

"I know. I've been back to Washington twice since you left. I meet weekly with our ambassador. He hates to see me come through his door. The official position is that we have to support our anti-Vietnam allies . . ."

Paul interrupted with a curse word. "Resistance forces, I know.

It's not me you need over here, it's the Congress and all of Carter's advisors. Make them cross over the border and see what's left of these people."

"From half a world away, the KR are noble," added Camille. "From feet and inches away, they're the most despicable group on the face of the earth at this moment."

Will ordered a round of shots. "Paul, if this is going to succeed, this is what needs to be done. Up to two million Cambodians are on the verge of starvation. Our country will provide over half the food for their survival, but we've got to get it moving better. That's not your job; that's mine. Your job will be at the border itself. Not the Thai side, but inside Cambodia. I won't kid you; it's fucking dangerous."

Rain forced the trip to Aran to be made in a UN van, which became a working three-hour journey. Will chaired. "As you know, there are dozens of small camps where the Cambodians have clustered. Sa Kaeo and KID have stabilized, more or less, but the Thais aren't letting any more refugees across the border. The Khmer Rouge communists have mostly settled in two camps south of Aran and are stealing supplies to feed their troops. Periodically, fighting breaks out between them and the Vietnamese army. Don't go there. Our efforts, where you two will focus your efforts, are in the camps north of Route 33." He looked up. "Where you went to secure the release of the two volunteers."

Mario smiled. "That was a fun trip."

Will continued. "Nong Samet has maybe 60,000 refugees on a semi-permanent basis. Too big to set up the receiving base, so we're using Nong Chan. It's run by forces loyal to the old leader Prince Sihanouk. Non-communists. Americans don't know the difference."

"Is he still in China?" asked Paul.

Will nodded. "Nong Chan is closest to the main roads and has large open spaces where the refugees can come in and congregate, park their carts or bicycles and get in the lines. We're unloading thousands of tons of rice there."

Camille turned her head to the conversation. "Last week, the damned warlords stopped the flow of supplies, because we're interfering with their black-market operations. We knew some of that was going on, but it seems the new effort is cutting into their profits, so they closed us down."

Will stabbed his finger on the map where the warlords mostly stayed. "Mak Mun's the most squalid of all the camps. They're communists. Cambodians have somehow found money to buy rice, money they had hidden in their clothes or shoes or buried in the forest. Now, they're buying food and supplies to feed their families."

"We can't keep relief efforts going forever, Will. What about the Cambodians who aren't at the border? Is any rice getting to them?" asked Paul.

"Oxfam and some of the other relief agencies have begun shipping to Phnom Penh by sea, at the ports nearby. Vietnam is sending some rice even though they're harvests are poor. I'm not trying to say they're the good guys in all this, but any country that opposes the fucking Khmer Rouge has my blessing." Will's obscenity was echoed by Camille.

Mario wiped his brow and asked how much longer, like a kid asking his dad, "Are we there yet?" "Europe and the relief agencies think the US effort is mostly trying to support the anti-Vietnam forces, in other words, the KR."

"So," said Paul, "we go over to the camps and explain that we're just here to feed the starving refugees, that we aren't trying to tip the scale in favor of the KR, that our motives are pure, and that we won't interfere with the warlords' profits." He looked at Will and put his hand on Camille's shoulder. "No problem."

Will and Camille dropped Paul and Mario off at the UN quarters in Aran and immediately left to drive back to Bangkok. Martin Gray greeted Paul and Mario and escorted them to the UNHCR room where an international cadre of officials was waiting. On a chalkboard, a timeline of events leading up to the Land Bridge decision caught Paul's eye. An old date, December 12, 1979, was circled, the date the Land Bridge began.

"Paul," said Gray, "I want you to meet Bob Ashford. He's been the force behind putting this plan together and has been my mentor this past year. He'll fill you in on the details. He's been working in Southeast Asia a few years and tends to have little patience for politics. Don't let his youthful looks fool you."

"We've met briefly," said Paul. The two men shook hands, but Ashford did not begin with pleasantries. "Most of the international aid agencies are being pussies. They don't want to upset the new puppet government in Phnom Penh, Heng Samrin and his cronies. We don't know much about him, but we're sure he serves at the pleasure of the Vietnamese. They've completely closed the border, but that hasn't stopped a million Cambodians from congregating just miles away from where we are now."

Paul knew this but listened. He knew Vietnam's greatest concern was that supplies shipped to the border camps were being used to strengthen the Khmer Rouge guerrillas. Paul also understood that it was part of America's motives, and as long as the KR forces were viable, they could be used to continue America's war against the Vietnamese, a tragically long and destructive war that was lost years ago.

"Official relief efforts are supposed to go through Phnom Penh, but they won't get to the people here in western Cambodia. They'll starve. I'm sure you and your wife saw evidence of that before you bugged out last month." Ashford amended his last remark. "Understandably so. How is she doing?"

Paul nodded his head but remained silent.

"Because of the Vietnamese invasion last year, the rice harvest for this year won't happen, so we have to get other food to these people now." Ashford stopped talking, his silence revealing that he didn't have the answers to the interruption of supplies that had recently occurred.

Paul turned his head to the chalkboard and studied it for a moment. He started slowly. "What you've started is good, really good." He continued to stare at the board, his back to Ashford and Gray. Paul turned to Mario and whispered something. Then, he turned. "If all official supplies have to go through Phnom Penh, then let's use that to our advantage. If the Red Cross and UNICEF and some other agencies don't want to get involved here, then fuck 'em. We'll do this our way without bureaucratic interference. It'll mean walking a fine line with my country, but I have to believe America won't stop sending the supplies, at least as long as Carter is president. The officials will bitch and moan, but then the rice will end up here magically. Here's what I think we do. First, continue using Nong Chan as the primary distribution point. There are hundreds of thousands of starving refugees who don't live in the camps but can access Nong Chan. They're afraid of Mak Mun and some of the other camps. Flood Nong Chan with aid workers so that if the Vietnamese or the warlords threaten it, then they threaten harming the staff. International condemnation will follow if they're harmed. Second, the Cambodians want to go home and farm their own land, so don't encourage them to settle in the border camps. Don't supply them with anything that might encourage this. No more tents. Only emergency medical care. Give them sacks of rice, enough to last for weeks at a time. They pick up enough rice to last for a month, so they go back. At least they make decisions not to be permanent refugees. Third, start giving out seeds. Help them reclaim their farms. Let them be farmers again." Paul paused, turned to Mario for his support, which he got, and said, "And lastly, create your own emergency group that's headquartered in Aranyaprathet, not Bangkok, and put Will in charge." Paul looked to Mario who picked up a piece of chalk and wrote January 11, 1980, on the board. "We start today," said Paul.

❧

"You volunteered me?" Will was not happy.

"Your ass is getting too wide at that desk. Not a good look for a former Green Beret," said Paul.

"What if I refuse?"

"Oh, not only did I volunteer you, I accepted on your behalf."

Will swore on his end of the phone. "Camille and I will fly in tomorrow. I want that room on the second floor for my office. What role will you and Mario play in this new agency?"

"We'll be your troubleshooters along the border." Paul said this in a serious mode. "Mario and I are driving over to Nong Chan tomorrow to meet with some of those people whose livelihoods have been impacted by this rice supply."

"Warlords?"

"Yep."

"Watch your backs."

On the same day that Paul began his role in the Land Bridge, Abby sat on a stool at her parents' soup kitchen in Pilsen greeting each person arriving for a hot meal. She watched her parents who no longer prepared the meals; they had delegated that responsibility to others years ago and now wandered the large room comforting the guests with words and touches. Mrs. Archer always carried a water pitcher, refilling glasses as she talked, never sitting. Abby's father sat frequently with the guests, telling stories but mostly listening to the diners' tales. So unlike the activities in Thailand, thought Abby. So comfortable, so warm, so safe, the drive-by shooting in '76 notwithstanding. But, lines still formed waiting for a little bit of help.

Abby slid off her stool to help an elderly woman with a cane and heavy burlap bag over her shoulder maneuver the entrance and find a table. Abby lifted the bag from the lady's burden and placed it on the floor. At the same time, a young man set a plate of food in front of the lady. "Your usual, ma'am," he said. Abby patted the lady's shoulder and walked over to join her mother.

"I could get used to this place, Mama."

"I think you'd get antsy after a few months, my dear. This pace isn't in your metabolism."

"I guess we'll see, won't we?"

Mrs. Archer filled another glass and introduced Abby to a guest about Abby's age. They shook hands but said nothing. Abby's mom led Abby to an empty table near the kitchen entrance and sat her down. "This place has consumed my adult life, and sometimes your father and I ignored our children's problems. I'm not so much apologizing as acknowledging the fact." Abby started to interrupt but was cut off by her mother. "You all turned out well, so there's no need to apologize." She let out a small laugh. "I take no responsibility for the bank robbery though." She smiled warmly at her daughter. "What are you worried about, my dear?"

Abby leaned in and placed her head tenderly on her mother's shoulder for a moment before she sat up and spoke. "Paul. This is the first time we've really been apart, out of contact apart, and I miss him terribly."

"Is what he's doing dangerous?" asked Mrs. Archer.

"It can be, but he has this presence that disarms people, so he can diffuse tension." She paused. "Conflicts."

"You married a good man."

"Thank you, Mama. I did."

"He married a good woman."

"It took a while."

"No, you've always been good."

Abby chuckled. "You must not have been paying close attention."

Her mother smiled and took hold of Abby's hand. "College is for challenging limits, and you did. Prison was for experiencing the less fortunate. No doubt it was God's plan. Now, you and Paul are putting what you've learned to good use."

Abby leaned into her mother's shoulder again. "He didn't want to go, at least to leave me. I kind of pushed him." Mrs. Archer put one arm around Abby's head and pressed it tightly against her. "Did I tell you I miss him?" said Abby.

"Yes, my dear, you did. He'll be back soon. I'll keep you busy." They remained quiet for a few minutes, mother and daughter sharing warmth on a Chicago wintry day. "I noticed you were writing on a pad while you were greeting our guests. A letter to Paul?"

"No. Jotting down a few notes, trying to develop a plan. Trying to make sense of war, I guess."

"Good luck with that."

Abby sat up. "Specifically, I'm trying to devise a program for reuniting child soldiers with their families. When I was in Thailand, I thought all the child soldiers were boys, but I discovered that at least a third of them were girls. Right under my nose at the Center, and I missed it. Because of the widespread hunger, children didn't develop normally, so I didn't see gender in these kids and assumed all soldiers were boys. In addition to all the obvious crimes of forcing children into war, add rape to it." Abby paused. "In a culture where that is such a stigma."

Her mother nodded. "Sometimes the world can seem so discouraging, but from what I've seen, I suspect that like most difficult problems, it's a process to recovery, but recovery can be possible, especially with faith."

"I talked with Paul's friend Mose . . . you remember him. I called him and asked about how children, or more specifically teenagers, get out of gangs. He said it was very difficult, almost impossible without intervention. Depressing. I called the Cook County adoption agency about placing teenagers, finding sponsors or families for them. Same answer. Teens are the least wanted."

"Special breed, that's for sure."

"All that and more. Violent lives; no love. That's where I start."

Mrs. Archer narrowed her eyes and cocked her head. "How do boys and girls from such a peaceful culture become depraved killers? War is such a despicable monster."

Abby nodded. "Step One of the process: remove these children from the military. Get them away from their units. Really difficult. In Cambodia, they get every meal from the army. It's how they survived all that terrible killing, how they survived. It's what they know." Abby stopped there, sighed heavily, and smiled. "For another time."

"Changing the subject then," said Mrs. Archer, "how are you feeling? I heard you walking around last night downstairs in the kitchen.

"Hungry. It's nothing really. Just a little bit of pregnant."

Will returned to Aranyaprathet the next afternoon and found the office he had demanded set up and furnished with a desk and large meeting table, coffee pot, refrigerator, large wall maps of the border, and a chalkboard.

"Where's Paul and Mario?" he asked a Thai aide.

"They radioed a half-hour ago that they were on their way in. Reconnaissance mission this morning. Those two don't sleep, I guess." Camille passed Will a note. "Ashford's demanding that all the tourist-volunteers be kept away from the Land Bridge on the Cambodian side. Too dangerous."

Will read it and nodded. "You'd think that would be obvious. This is a war zone for God's sake. This is the world's worst humanitarian crisis, and those people just want to give a day of their vacation to feel good."

"You're being too harsh. Sometimes they stay for a week."

"Is Ashford coming too? That man is essential."

"I haven't heard. He was here this morning, but I haven't seen him since." Camille pulled two beers from the fridge and handed one to Will. "Have you eaten?"

"Not yet. Did Paul say he was going to talk to the warlords in Nong Chan or just look?" asked Will.

"He didn't say. Let's go down to the street and get a meal before they arrive."

Mario had parked the UN truck next to a Thai checkpoint for more security while he and Paul discussed what they had seen. Mario lit a cigarette and offered one to Paul.

"I've never smoked. Not even tried it. My pop would have killed me, and I guess he sits on my shoulder to this day."

Mario laughed. "My folks bought me a cartoon for my fifteenth birthday. Different culture, no doubt. What were you saying about this truck?"

"The UN insignia, its flag, and its prestige protects us along the border. It's seen as neutral, but I'm getting the sense that's changing for the Land Bridge. Almost like the UN has taken sides. Did you get that sense at Mak Mun?"

Mario took a deep drag and held it in. "Foster cautioned that. Sa Kaeo and KID have stabilized, but the border camps are bastions of strength for different factions. It's why Ashford chose Nong Chan. It's mostly anti-KR communists. Those bastards have entrenched themselves in the camps south of Aran."

Paul removed his baseball hat and wiped his brow. "Snowing in Chicago where Abby is." He replaced his hat. "Who's more dangerous, the KR or the warlords?"

"Depends on the day. It was the warlords who shut down the Land

Bridge. A threat to their black-market trade. That's who we're going to have to talk to in the next few days if we're going to get this thing up to full strength."

"That seems to be the only difference between the two factions. Up here, they're capitalists, not communists. Profit motive. Down south, they're Maoists of the worst kind. Crazy world, Mario." Paul pushed off the side of the truck. "Let's go. Will'll be waiting for us."

◌

Ashford spoke first. "I have twelve truckloads of rice just sitting outside the camps on our side waiting to be delivered. I can get that much every day if you can get the border open. Six thousand each day. Thailand is so abundant, and the world is ready to pay for it. We can do this, dammit, if we can just get the border open!"

"How many are we talking about, Ash?" asked Foster.

"We don't know. We can count the people at KID, but not in the border camps. It's a fluid population. Most of the refugees don't really stay in the camps; too dangerous. Best guess, a quarter of a million in or around the three northern camps." Ashford didn't care about the numbers because he knew what mattered was feeding whoever was there.

Will rapped on his desk. "This is what we got. A thriving black market that the warlords want to continue. Refugees who have traveled from throughout Cambodia to get away from the fighting, from both the KR and the Vietnamese, and they're about to starve to death. And international agencies that can't find a backbone, who don't want to upset the new government in Phnom Penh. I need suggestions, people."

Paul was leaning against the wall near the door. He pushed himself away. "The agencies want a guarantee. Won't happen. The agencies want accountability, want some assurances that the rice isn't ending up in the hands of the KR guerrillas. We can't promise that either because a lot of it will. The agencies think the US is paying for all this grain to support the KR in the epic battle to save the world from communism, from the Vietnamese. We all know that my country has turned a blind eye to the killing by the KR. I'm not proud of that. There are a hundred other reasons why this can't work." He paused and stepped over to Mario, as he had a habit of doing. "Look, everyone in this room has a job to do. Will, you have to keep the supplies and money flowing from America. Lean on the ambassador and his wife. Kiss their asses daily. Ash, move the trucks and the grain just as you did two weeks ago. Start the day after tomorrow. Act like these past two weeks didn't happen, just a time warp. Art, get enough buses to bring in every available aid worker into Nong Chan every morning. The temps can unload the rice at the parking lots. Don't allow them into the camp proper. Keep them supervised, since they'll be a little vulnerable. All of us need to avoid any appearance of being partial to one side or the other. We all have our biases, but we can't let these interfere. Mario and I will head over tomorrow bright and early to convince the warlords in Nong Chan and Mak Mun that this is going to happen." Paul turned to Camille. "Day after tomorrow, you're going to take me up in your plane, and fly me along the border to do a head count."

The room emptied except for Will, Camille, Mario, and Paul. Will opened a lower desk drawer and pulled out a bottle of bourbon, always the ever-present alcohol. Camille took four shot glasses from a shelf and placed them on Will's desk.

Camille threw her drink back and looked at Paul. "I don't get you. Will and Mario and me, we're longtime residents of Cambodia. We have a stake in the game. What's with you?"

Paul handed his shot to Will. "I don't know if I can explain it. I came over to Malaysia about a year ago to help build a small church. Strictly temp work. A volunteer. Someone from UNHCR thought I was an engineer and hired me. Nobody checked my credentials. Then, somebody decides I can help build a refugee camp at Sa Kaeo. I didn't know what the hell I was supposed to do, but they threw in a bulldozer, and I said okay. Sa Kaeo didn't need an engineer, it needed a sanitation expert. I sort of dropped the ball on that one, but now, I guess, I'm a sanitarian. I'm the guy who sorts out shit." He laughed. "Back in college . . . that seems like an eternity now . . . I used to write letters to the Secretary of Defense, questioning him about the Vietnam War. Then, I ended up being a part of the whole mess. My time as a POW is just a fog. I think maybe this is still my way of trying to help correct that wrong." Paul looked down at the floor and uttered to himself, "I don't know."

Will laughed out loud. "I'll bet that bastard never wrote back, did he?"

Camille stepped into Paul, placed her fingers on his chin, and raised his head. "Such a naïve boy but thank you for caring." In typical European fashion, she kissed him on both cheeks.

Mario, Paul, and a secondary interpreter left Aran at sunup to drive the short distance to Nong Chan. Mario had secured a Red Cross Land Rover rather than a UN Toyota on the premise that the warlords would see the Red Cross as less partial, more neutral. The three men carried papers identifying themselves as representatives of the Kampuchean Emergency Group rather than UN aid workers. Paul's papers identified him as Canadian. They were waived through the Thai checkpoint quickly and turned toward Nong Chan. As always, the short distance to the camp was filled with refugees on oxcarts, on bicycles, on foot; refugees sitting in family groups looking like they had never had a happy day in their entire lives. For the children, that was most likely the case.

The secondary interpreter, who was Cambodian, remained silent while Mario and Paul talked. Mario slowed the truck as they passed a burned-out hospital, a casualty of the recent attack on Nong Chan by the forces from Mak Mun. "So far, so good. Kong Sileah said he'd meet us at 8:30," said Mario. He turned slightly to the interpreter. "No matter what they tell you personally, you stay by my side. I know you already know that, but I just want to reinforce that. The warlord won't challenge you, but some of his lieutenants could." Mario returned his eyes to the road.

Paul nodded, a sign that the soldiers ahead were Sileah's men. *Security forces.* "Here we go," he said. "Did you bring that bottle of bourbon?"

The young soldiers surrounded the truck like bullies on a junior high playground. Paul spoke softly to the interpreter. "Don't look them in the eye. Keep your eyes on me or Mario. Don't' challenge them in any way."

Mario put his arm out the window and waved them away with an Italian scowl. He inched the truck forward. One soldier lowered his face to window level and ordered Mario to stop, but Mario just yelled out the warlord's name "Kong Sileah" and continued. The soldier stood and stepped back. "How did Will set this up?"

"I'm not sure it was Will. My guess is it was one of Ashford's contacts. Will said Sileah may be the rare Cambodian soldier with a bit of integrity. Let's hope."

Mario again turned his head slightly to address the interpreter. "We're about to make a deal that we can't brag about back in camp, with the least unacceptable of the Khmer units in the area. Humanitarian gains over political desires."

The interpreter nodded. "Faustian deal, huh. I understand."

The soldiers walked the truck to its destination, waving and pushing refugees off the road so the truck could pass. In a few minutes, it came to a thatched structure with only three walls. Kong Sileah sat at a card table surrounded by a handful of older soldiers. Only when Mario stopped the truck did Sileah look up. Paul noticed that Sileah's eyes did not display any sign of integrity or compassion. The three aid workers stepped out of the truck and formed together on the curb. And waited.

Sileah finally stood, issued an order to a lieutenant, and walked slowly toward the truck. Mario held out the bottle of bourbon. Sileah took it and inspected the label. "Last time you gave my subordinate scotch. I see you remembered this time. That's good." Sileah spoke in Khmer and the interpreter translated. Mario understood too. Paul had asked both to add comments about Sileah's gestures and tones as they understood Cambodian culture.

"He seems in a good frame of mind. He accepted your gift without suspicion."

Paul spoke to Sileah directly, his eyes locked onto the warlord's eyes, allowing his words to be passed on by the interpreter. "Your reputation among the aid workers is well established. It's said you're tough but fair, that you are a Cambodian first, so I come to you first. If you and I can reach an agreement this morning on the resumption of rice deliveries, I'll need to travel to Mak Mun to speak with another soldier who may not be a Cambodian first."

Without taking his eyes off Paul, Kong Sileah handed the bottle to an aide. A moment passed between the two men. "I understand that not every nation supports this new effort to transport and distribute rice to my people." He let that statement hang in the air, allowed Mario and Paul to consider their response. Sileah then continued. "Many of those nations want only for rice to be distributed from the government in the capital. Do you know what that means?" Sileah was testing Paul.

Paul nodded ever so slightly. "I do. It means that the people in western Cambodia will starve. Those shipments will never make their way to these camps and to the thousands who live around these camps."

Sileah continued. "If we accept this grain, if we allow distribution from Nong Chan, we risk another attack from Mak Mun. Worse, we face the wrath of the Vietnamese army. They will say the rice strengthens our ability to fight them."

"Both of those things are true. You're facing a difficult decision. What I know is that you have faced other difficult decisions over the past five years with courage. I also know that there may not be another Cambodian who can make this decision except you."

Sileah considered Paul's words. He understood that the foreigner was playing to his ego, but he saw something else, and he was trying to unwrap what he saw. He turned slightly to an aide, commanding him to get the aid workers identifications. The soldier spoke to the interpreter. Mario produced the IDs, and Sileah inspected them. He handed them back to Mario and looked to Paul again. "Canadian?"

Mario tensed, but Paul did not flinch. His eyes stayed fixed on Sileah's as he spoke. "No. American. I use this phony ID to open doors. I know why you might hate my country, why you might not trust me. I will tell you this. I was once a soldier in Vietnam, but I was captured by Cambodians across that border. I spent over a year in the Highlands. I was a prisoner, but I worked as a farmer. Every day I heard the bombers fly into your country." Paul paused. "And return. Empty planes make a slightly different sound than full planes."

"First, it was your country. After that, it was my country that killed my people. Now, it is the Vietnamese. And still my own people are at war with ourselves. The country of my youth no longer exists, and this evil war continues. Do you really expect me to think you understand?"

The interpreter felt what Kong Sileah felt.

Paul blinked. "I can never truly understand or make amends."

"I don't understand America. It makes war and it sends food. Can you help me with this?" asked the warlord.

"Somehow . . . after World War II, we lost our way. My government thought we had to fight communism everywhere. Vietnam bloodied our nose, embarrassed us, and now my government refuses to accept that outcome. But many in America are good people. My country has provided aid for every famine or natural disaster in this century. Every one, everywhere in the world. If it had been up to me, I would have flooded eastern Cambodia with food instead of explosives, but my government has stopped listening to its people."

Sileah stood silent and then sneered. "Touching. Tell that to my people who no longer live to hug their children or to the children who no longer live." His eyes bore in on Paul with an anger that Paul had seldom seen before. Small arms fire erupted in the background, but neither man flinched. It was outside the camp, and they were in no danger. Sileah controlled his breathing, a soldier who had great discipline and terrible experiences. "I will tell you this, Mr. Garrity, if I allow this Land Bridge, as it is called, to restart, we will be attacked again, maybe not this week or this month, but we will come under fire from those who have no trust. I understand that. What Cambodian can trust anyone?"

"Sir, if you don't allow the Land Bridge to continue, over a million Cambodians will starve before another harvest. Don't allow that to happen."

"And can you promise me that this Land Bridge will continue after this season and the next and the next? What then?"

"It will not. Along with the rice, we will give seeds and farming equipment. The refugees will take sacks of rice and the means to go back to their land and become farmers again. It's not a perfect solution, but it gives you and your people a chance. The Land Bridge is a chance, and you hold that future in your hands."

"How do I tell my soldiers to be generous?"

"We will not hold a strict accounting of where the rice goes. Some of it will end up on the black market, as it always does, but we will supply so much that enough finds its way to civilians. Our only goal here is to avert the coming famine. You need to act now. Today. The agencies are ready to roll the trucks that are already stacked with rice tomorrow. Let the word go out that food will be distributed from Nong Chan."

Kong Sileah nodded. "Going to Mak Mun is futile. My counterpart there will not accept this and will see me as weak if he hears it from you. I will send a soldier to tell him what will be done and that we will fight him if he tries to stop us. We will not be surprised again. I will inform him that a truckload of grain will be his every morning."

∾

The Cessna 310 twin engine plane left the Aran airfield early; Camille wanting to take advantage of the cooler air to get airborne. Mario had begged off, citing fear of flying in any size plane. Camille flew east-northeast to remain in Thailand to acclimate Paul, soaring over the Khao-I-Dang mountains near the refugee camp. She climbed to a few thousand feet and did slow turns allowing Paul different perspectives of the camp. She watched him and was pleased that he showed no fear.

"Two months ago, there was nothing here except a few farms," said Paul. "Today, there is a city of nearly a hundred thousand. Something isn't and then it is. Someday, it won't be again. But for now, . . . "

"This plane has a history, Paul. Care to hear about it?" she asked.

"I would. Seems like everything about you has a history."

"Evidently, a Vietnamese pilot with the Republic of Vietnam's Air Force flew it out of Tan Son Nhut with his family in April of '75. Saigon was about to fall and the NVA was shelling all the airfields. I don't have to remind you about all that. Several Vietnamese pilots commandeered planes and helicopters and flew their families to safety. This particular pilot wanted to land in Bangkok but ran low of fuel and put it down in Aran. He unloaded his family and was never heard from again. I bought it cheap and had it repainted red and white. I traded a Cub for this Cessna, so this was quite a step up. Besides better speeds and stability and safety, it's still a good bush plane, doesn't need a long runway to land."

"It never occurred to me where all those planes went. I just assumed they were either destroyed or captured by the NVA. Hmm."

Camille turned east toward the Cambodian border but well north of the Nong Samet, Mak Mun, and Nong Chan camps. "There are dozens of smaller camps, unofficial camps all along the border. Since the border isn't marked, no one is sure whether all these camps are in Cambodia, Thailand, or both. The Thais patrol the border, as you know, but in some places, it's so wild that anything goes. We'll straddle the border on this pass and pretend we're over Thailand."

"Have you flown into Cambodia before?" asked Paul.

"No. Too dangerous." She laughed. "What's the worst that can happen? If you see anyone shooting at us, let me know, and I'll climb higher." Again, Camille laughed.

"How old is this plane?"

"I've had it about five years, but it's pushing twenty or so. It's a good one. Your country took good care of it when it was theirs. No bullet holes."

"Why red and white?"

"No particular reason. My favorite French wines? Maybe today the Khmer Rouge will think we're with the Red Cross and hold their fire." Camille accelerated as she decreased the plane's elevation. "Let me know if you want to see anything closer or off to one side or the other."

What Paul saw over the next dozen minutes saddened him. Thousands of refugees existed outside of the camps in both small and large groups. All of them were in tatters. Many did not even look up as the plane passed overhead. Paul saw soldiers beneath them wearing their black KR pajamas, but equally ragged. An entire nation on the move trying to find safety, trying to survive a hell on earth, trying to find another meal.

"God damn," Paul uttered softly and slowly. "Ashford said there could be 100,000 or more. I didn't believe him when he said that number could exceed 400,000. From what I see, even that number could be low."

Camille could only shake her head. She thought Ashford would need to double the number of trucks he was scheduling for Nong Chan to even come close to feeding this horde. "Where to next, Captain?"

"I know what I'd like to see, but I don't want to put you in danger."

Camille pulled back on the controls and her plane responded quickly. She banked toward Aran as the plane passed over Nong Chan. "I've got plenty of gas. What do you want?"

Paul blew out heavily. "You can nix this if you're uncomfortable, but I'd like to head north like we did the first time and then come in about twenty or twenty-five miles farther east. I want to see how far this extends." Paul paused as Camille continued into Thailand, Aran to her left. "Those people look more desperate than what shows up in the camps. Will and Ashford have to make this work if they're to have any chance."

Camille banked to the north again, ten miles into Thailand. "One pass. Top speed. Low level. The Vietnamese won't have any compunction about shooting at us. Pray that they think we're Red Cross." She shook her head and looked severely at her passenger. "I'm going to go farther north this time. Take a different flight path so that those people we passed over last time won't see us this time." She leaned into the dashboard and patted her plane in an attempt to comfort it like she might a pet dog, or as Paul thought, in an attempt to coax it into top performance. "You'll owe me when we get back to Aran."

Paul reached over and squeezed Camille's arm. "You wouldn't do this if you didn't love this country, would you?"

"There is no country any longer, just its people, and they need us to do this foolish thing. We'll come to a small river soon. Tell me when you see it. At 200 miles an hour, you get ten minutes in and fifteen minutes straight south. That should put us east of Poipet and the main highway from Phnom Phen to Aran and Bangkok. We'll follow that back. Keep your eyes open because I'm not doing this twice."

In just a few minutes, Paul pointed to the river. "You can abort this, Camille."

"Hang on, Cowboy. Low and fast. See it all because I won't. I'll be looking for tall trees or short soldiers." Camille leaned into her plane as it picked up speed. "Nine minutes in. Here we go."

The Cessna probably thought it was on a military mission in Vietnam from a decade ago, and except for the Vietnam part, it was. Camille wasn't kidding about the tops of trees, but it wasn't all forest, and when the forest ended, the fields began, and it offered no cover. Families grouped together around their oxcarts or crude shelters as they had on the earlier pass, and Paul saw an equal number of Cambodians in the same condition as on the first pass. "Nine minutes," she said and turned her plane south toward Poipet. "This will take about fifteen minutes. If I see the highway sooner, we head in. I'm not going south of Route 33."

The bushes, the trees, the people, the soldiers passed by at 200 miles an hour, but Paul saw everyone, took it all in. In his concentrated state, he stopped sensing danger. He tried to estimate numbers but couldn't. He was interrupted twice when Camille turned sharply, because she thought she saw units of Vietnamese soldiers on the horizon. Neither time did the soldiers fire their weapons or shoot rockets. Camille swore to herself in French a handful of times. *La vache, merde, fils de pute*, and *putain* being the cuss words she most used. Fifteen minutes exactly and the highway to Poipet came into view.

All the way back, oxcarts filled the paved road. Two trucks of Vietnamese soldiers waved at the plane, but another truck scrambled its soldiers who jumped out and pointed their weapons at the Cessna. Whether or not they fired, Camille could not tell. She flew directly over Poipet and into Thailand. "That's the biggest black market operating along the border. Amazing how people with nothing can find money to trade for things they've been deprived of for years."

"Especially adequate food," added Paul.

Minutes later, Camille landed in Aran. Waiting for them was the contingent of Ashford, Will, Foster, Gray, and Mario. Camille taxied to a stop near her tie-down, and she and Paul climbed out. Before Paul could say anything, Will pinned him against the plane, his forearm choking Paul.

"You son of a bitch! You said you were only going to fly along the border. We saw you come around the first time. You were gone way too long to just travel the border again. You could have gotten Camille killed!" The four other men pulled Will off and shoved him away from Paul, trying to calm him down. Only when Camille grabbed Will did he walk away.

"You okay?" asked Mario.

"Yeah." Paul turned to Ashford. "It's worse than you estimated. The whole population of Cambodia is out there waiting for help."

After spending two hours-plus with Ashford and Gray going over details for the resumption of the Land Bridge, Paul used the phone in the UNHCR office to call Abby. The long-distance time limit was seven minutes. From there, he went to the aid workers' cafeteria for a late lunch, finding Mario already seated at a table enjoying another rice dish. The two men finished, scraped their metal plates into the trash bin, and headed past the clock tower to a warehouse. That was where Will found Paul and Mario around 7:30, loading 60-pound rice sacks onto converted Thai army trucks for transportation to Nong Chan in the morning. Will watched the two men work side-by-side lifting the heavy bags to other volunteers.

"Need another hand?" asked Will after about five minutes of spectating.

Paul smiled. "Nah. We don't allow management to mess with union chores."

"I need to apologize," said Will offering his hand.

Paul shook it. "No need. I understand. Thanks for not hitting me. I kind of deserved it."

Will smiled slightly and nodded. "Guess I got a little bit protective. Forgot that Camille has a will of her own. She knew what she was doing."

"You know whatever it is you're paying her, it isn't enough."

"She doesn't work for me. She doesn't work for any agency. She does all this strictly as a volunteer." Will nodded at Mario. "Camille was raised near Verdun in France, her family lost their house in WWI, lived through the Nazi occupation in WWII, so she knows a little about war and suffering. She's been in Cambodia for over fifteen years. Loves this country. She does everything on her own."

Paul called two tourist volunteers who were standing with their arms folded by the warehouse's open end to come over and take his and Mario's place in the line. "C'mon. Let's go get a beer."

Aran had numerous bars frequented by the aid workers. Mario chose a tiny spot run by an Italian couple from Milan. They greeted the three men in Italian and ushered them to a relatively quiet table behind a paper barrier. Mario had been here before. Frequently.

"It's a little bit of home for me here," said Mario. "Nice to hear the native tongue and catch up on the peaceful chaos of Italian politics every now and then. Nice to hear opera music and drink cold beer."

"Abby says hi to everyone. Says she misses this. Don't know if I told you, but she's pregnant."

Mario lifted his beer glass in a toast. "Conceived in Thailand! Answers our questions as to why she didn't come back with you this time."

Will maneuvered a fourth chair to the table with his foot, so he could put his legs up. "You two have put in quite the work week in these last four days. I appreciate it."

Paul and Mario lifted their glasses as a response. "Between the travel and the operation, we haven't slept much. When you told me Mario was coming, I had assumed he was in Italy."

Mario smiled. "I was vacationing in India."

"Some vacation. Working with UNICEF along the Ganges," said Paul.

"Had a few extra days," said Mario.

Paul turned to Will. "What do you need us to do tomorrow? I was thinking about heading home now that all the hard work is done?"

"The hard work is just starting. I figure the two of you can drive the trucks now; it's the only job you haven't done yet." Will signaled the owner for another round, then pulled a folded piece of paper from his shirt-pocket. "This is a list of thirteen aid agencies most involved in this effort. There's more, but these are the ones I need to talk with in the coming days to see if they'll continue their help. Care to help?"

Both Mario and Paul shook their heads. "No thanks, boss. We'll drive trucks," said Paul. "I suspect you're heading back to Bangkok then?"

"Early tomorrow. Back to the desk job."

∾

The following morning, Paul rode the bus to the Thai side of Nong Chan, transferred to a rice truck going to the parking lot where rice was already being distributed, and then walked to the same office where he had met with Sileah two mornings earlier. Sileah was clad in a blue leisure suit, black jacket that seemed three sizes too small, and a gaucho-looking cowboy hat. His long, wavy, black hair seemed to be held in place with hair spray, but Paul doubted that was the case. Sileah looked relaxed, unlike he had been 48 hours ago. For a man in his mid-forties with the weight of his country on his shoulders, he appeared like a giddy teenager about to go out on a date with the prom queen. Sileah sported two pistols on his waist and was still surrounded by his heavily armed bodyguards. Maybe he wasn't going to the prom.

"Ahh, Mr. Garrity, care to join me? I'm headed out to see if your rice is getting to these wretched hordes of my people." Sileah smiled broadly as if he had made a joke and punched his interpreter in the arm.

Within minutes, Paul found himself engulfed in a sea of refugees, some heading east, their carts or bicycles loaded with bags of rice, some heading west into Nong Chan to get that rice. Babies, small children, old men, and lots of women walking both ways for the promise of rice. Sileah's soldiers, those who rejected the communist Khmer Rouge, who pledged loyalty to the exiled Prince Sihanouk, directed traffic on the muddy, sloppy road. Watching all these people get rice, Paul understood why Sileah had been smiling earlier.

∾

"Where's Garrity?" asked Martin Gray as he and Bob Ashford spoke with Mario two evenings later in Aran.

Mario shook his head. "Haven't seen him since I shared beers with him and Will. Have you checked up at KID?"

"We've called all over, and no one seems to know where he is," said Gray.

"If I see him, and I probably will tomorrow since we're scheduled to work on some fliers with Foster, I'll tell him you're looking for him."

❧

Paul sat cross-legged on the ground listening to a language he couldn't understand but tonight felt. Bits and pieces. This would be his second night sleeping on the ground with a Cambodian soldier. Tonight, they shared a ragged tent with an old uncle and three other men of undetermined age. Cooking fires from before had mostly died out and the sky filled with stars. It was quiet, and it wasn't. No machinery, but the hum of a thousand hushed conversations, fearful conversations that Paul sensed were about living and dying. Not like the conversations he and Mose and Sally and Jonas had in college a decade ago, but those also were about war. Not like the hushed conversations he and Abby had in bed after making love in Oxnard or Chicago or Bidong or Aran. No, not like those at all; these were nothing like those. The other men smoked.

Two mornings ago, Paul walked with Sileah for an hour, then shook his hand and turned east into Cambodia. Moments later, one of Sileah's men jogged up next to Paul. He said nothing, just walked with Paul. The soldier had been Paul's companion since. They didn't talk except for a few French phrases. This soldier did not order anyone around, made no demands. He simply walked next to Paul with a weapon, wearing his camouflage uniform. Last night, they slept under an oxcart covered with a blue UN tarp. Earlier today, Paul caught himself humming "Walking Man," by James Taylor. Paul laughed to himself. There was no frost on any pumpkin in this sad land, but another line in the song stayed with him. "Most everybody's got seed to sow." That's the goal, Paul thought to himself.

Tomorrow, Paul planned to walk back to Thailand. Will might put his elbow in his throat again. Martin would be frustrated that Paul hadn't given him a heads-up. Mario would understand though. So would Abby, but she would worry. Mario wouldn't.

Paul thought about Pilsen, the soup kitchen where hungry people came to get fed by a small group of Chicago volunteers who cared about the conditions of their fellow humans. Along the Thai-Cambodian border, hundreds of thousands hung by a thread, a thread being strengthened by the efforts of volunteers with the same cares. A dangerous land under the control of vicious men with no principles, and yet, these refugees refused to give in. They too were walking men—or walking women and walking children. Paul nodded his head. There is great dignity in walking—and along this border. Their lives would be changed, hopefully given back to them. Paul understood that his life had also been changed forever.

SEGMENT III
TRANSFER
1982-1984

11

After cleaning herself, Abby returned to the bedroom with a warm washcloth to clean Paul. "I'm never sure if my parents hear us, but at least Baby Moses didn't wake up." Rituals. She smiled to herself. "I checked in on him." She wadded up the cloth, stood, and turned. "I'll be right back."

When she returned, she snuggled into his body, and Paul said, "My guess is your parents hear you. Every morning after you've been loud, when I walk into the kitchen, your dad pats me on the back. On other mornings, he doesn't." They both giggled. "Your parents have been so good to us. Each time we return from a sojourn with the United Nations to help refugees, they have our room ready for us."

"And put us right back to work in Pilsen. I think they think we're going to take over the soup kitchen at some point. I know they would like us to." She paused. "We're going to have to make some important decisions about our work and our family. We both want another child."

"Or two," said Paul. "So many of our colleagues live two lives, a family in their home nation and their work lives overseas, but it seems like the work life takes precedence. They fly off to spend a week with their wives and kids but then hurry back to the refugee camp. This work consumes them. At the camps, so many of them live, I don't know, single lives. Lots of bars."

Abby let his thoughts hang in the air for a moment before she responded. "I'm not sure I can go down to Mexico right now with you. I know Jules wants us both again, but you're the one he most needs immediately."

Paul kissed Abby on the forehead. "That big picture thing. It's wrong, you know. The UN may want me, but the Guatemalan people need you. You're the one who nurtures, not me."

Abby lifted her head and looked into Paul's eyes. "I love you so much. My worst fear in prison was that I wouldn't make a difference. You gave my life purpose." Paul started to speak, but Abby shushed him gently. She knew that he would try to deflect his importance; he always tried to do that, but she believed her words. "I want to go with you, at least to make sure the structure is in place. I don't have to stay long; maybe two weeks."

"Your mom probably wouldn't do irreparable damage to Moses if you were gone."

"Your sarcasm is noted, smartass." She went quiet for a moment. "The question is, can I be away from Moses for two weeks? I'd miss him from the moment I stepped onto the plane."

"After I was in Gaza for two months, it seemed like Moses had forgotten who I was when I returned. That was so hard. My first fact-finding trip with Jules to Guatemala was the same."

"I remember." She paused to gather time. "That was just before Christmas. These past six months have been another whirlwind." She came back to the current problem. "We could take him with us." Abby had offered this suggestion before.

Paul made a slight headshake. "When we were in Aran, maybe we could have done that. The camps were dangerous, but Aran was mostly safe. I wouldn't feel at all comfortable with Moses in Chiapas. The Guatemalan army has raided across the border and murdered a few people already, and neither the UN nor the Mexican army has been able to fully protect the refugees."

"It's why you do this, you know," said Abby.

"Why we do this." He pulled Abby into his body as tightly as possible and just held her. "Tens of thousands of Mayan Indians have already fled the terrible civil war, and we were so hopeful when the military staged the coup in April and threw out that murderous General Garcia." Paul paused. "Especially the Maya, but it looks like the new general is worse. Some of the reports are absolutely gruesome. I think you should stay home with Moses on this one until I get a clearer picture."

When Abby's father came down to breakfast, he patted Paul on the shoulder, poured a coffee for himself, and took a seat next to him at the nook. "You're up early, Paul." He tapped Paul's legal pad. "Refugees?"

Paul breathed out heavily and sat back, extending his arms backward toward the ceiling. His neck popped. "Going over my notes from the UN call yesterday." He lowered his arms and breathed out heavily again. "You sure you want to hear this?"

"General Rios Montt is a murdering thug, huh? No surprise there." Abby's dad followed current events with an interest as great as Paul's was when he was at the University of Colorado in the 1960s studying under Dr. Orr. "I made a few calls. Seems like the general is an Evangelical Protestant pastor, a friend of two of television's most famous ministers, Jerry Falwell and Pat Robertson. He studied at the School of the Americas in Panama. Did you know that?"

Paul shook his head. "Not about being friends with Falwell and Robertson. A good Christian anti-communist who seems to be slaughtering his own people. And he has the blessing of President Reagan." Paul put his face into his hands, rubbed them into the skin, and then cupped them over his nose and mouth. An act of frustration. "Why does the United States so often seem to be on the side of bloody dictators?"

Reverend Archer reached across the table and touched Paul's forearm. Held it. "If I wasn't a man of God, I'd swear, but I am, so I won't." Paul had never heard Abby's father utter an obscenity. "What new information did you get yesterday?" asked the older man.

"There are refugees all over the country and into Mexico, into Chiapas. Jules says there are at least 60 camps in Mexico, 100,000 Guatemalans. Maybe more. We knew that. What's worse are the reports of outright massacres of entire villages in the state of El Quiche. Something called Operation Sofia, at least that's what the whispers are calling it. There's a French photojournalist who seems to have access in Guatemala City."

"Is he safe?" asked Abby's father.

"She. You never know, but her sources are painting an awful picture of what's going on in the rural areas. General Rios Montt's address to his people was blunt. 'Either you're with us or against us. If you're with us, we'll feed you. If not, we'll kill you. *Fusiles o frijoles.*"

"Guns or beans. The rural farmers have no choice then, do they?"

"It's the same old story, people just trying to live and raise their children get forced into the great Cold War struggle. When the revolutionary forces are around, the farmers have to pledge allegiance to them. When the army arrives, the farmers have to support them. Only with Rios Montt's army, they don't ask. Every Mayan farmer is the enemy." Paul paused. "And all of his family."

"When are you leaving?" asked Reverend Archer.

"Next Tuesday, as it sits right now. I don't have my ticket yet."

"Will Abby be going with you this time?"

"No. I told Jules I wouldn't allow it. Just me."

"Will you be safe?"

"I'll do my best."

∿

On July 12, 1982, Paul flew from Chicago to Houston to Mexico City. The next morning, he flew on a twelve-passenger charter with six other UNHCR aid workers to San Cristobal de las Casas, Chiapas, Mexico, for his first briefing. Thousands of Guatemalans were scattered throughout Chiapas living with individual Mexican families. UNHCR had no way of knowing how many. Thousands of others had fled the central highlands of El Quiche into the Lacandon Jungle in the state of Peten, a shrinking rain forest. The leader of the Guatemalan Operation for the UN was a Thai Frenchman, Jules Beaufort, and his mood was bleak.

"No one in this room is to cross the border! Understood?" Beaufort's eyes sought absolute confirmation. "Aid workers have been shot, and our presence in Guatemala has not reduced the risk to the native Mayas. Our mission this week is to get as much information as we can on the refugees already in Mexico and to see if there are ways to transport those people from the refugee camps in Guatemala to safer areas. We are getting no cooperation from the Guatemalan government. Additionally, Mexico has no official refugee policy. The people in Chiapas have been mostly welcoming to the Guatemalans, for several reasons, but lately, the sheer numbers seem to be undermining that welcome. I don't have to tell you that Mexico's economy is in the tank, so some see the Maya as a threat to their livelihood." Beaufort called on a woman in the group to provide a bit more information.

"In the past, Guatemalans have crossed their northern border into Mexico to work and then returned home, but with this ongoing civil war, and especially in the last five years, they tend to stay because they're safe. The refugees inside Guatemala are in terrible health, nearly as bad as what we saw in Cambodia. I'd hate to compare the Guatemalan army to the Khmer Rouge, but if the stories the refugees who make it across the border are to be believed, another genocide is beginning. Like Cambodia, information is difficult to come by."

Paul raised his hand. "Can I take a quick flight to the capital to get a sense of the official government position?"

Beaufort nodded. "I'll let you go while the rest of us visit the border camps on the Mexican side."

"Can I get the name of the English teacher working with the language skills of the Guatemalan army?" The group laughed, knowing that Paul was referencing a Green Beret soldier who was providing tactical training to the Guatemalan army on counterinsurgency. "Also, will I get thrown out of the country if I speak with the U.S. ambassador?"

Beaufort knew of Paul's aggressive lines of questions. "Will you promise me not to deliberately antagonize the man?" Paul shook his head. "I'll get you out tomorrow. Three days in the capital, and then I'll see you back here."

❧

Paul discussed his findings with Beaufort by phone three days later. "The ambassador wants me to get with the program. Same line as always with these Central American governments. Front line in the fight against Cuban-directed communism. It's as if Fidel Castro is in the mountains in El Quiche directing the war against our allies. He says he can't guarantee our safety."

"No shit!" responded Beaufort. "What else?"

"Nobody in the capital talks. Everyone's afraid. News isn't getting out. Like Cambodia between '75 and '78. We need the press down here." The two men spoke for several more minutes exchanging observations about the conditions of the people of Guatemala and how best to serve them. Good options were not available. Finally, Paul added, "I've chartered a plane for this afternoon. I'm heading up to Nebaj and Chajul in central Guatemala. I need to see for myself."

"That's a negative, Garrity." Beaufort's directive was too late. Paul had already hung up the phone.

☙

Abby flew to Geneva to present her plan for reuniting child soldiers to the UNHCR committee on children along with UNICEF for four days leaving Moses with her parents. She hadn't spoken with Paul since he left Guatemala City for the camps. While in Switzerland, she had dinner with Martin Gray and several aid workers from Thailand/ Cambodia. All of them expressed great concern for the refugees in Guatemala, and they were pessimistic about the outcome of that mission.

"Your husband has confirmed that we're servicing about 35,000 refugees who have made their way across the border, but that's a drop in the bucket. We're having a difficult time reaching the other 200,000," said Gray. "Jules and his crew are doing the best they can, but the terrain is nearly impossible to traverse, and communication is worse. Hand delivered messages are the norm, although we've been able to use walkie-talkies for short distances." Martin wondered if Abby knew that Paul had flown off on his own into the most dangerous region of Guatemala but didn't bring it up.

"Are we seeing many child soldiers among the civil patrols in Guatemala?" asked Abby.

"Again, Beaufort's information is weak. Certainly, the bulk of the civil patrols are from eighteen to 30, but there are some reports of soldiers a bit younger. We aren't seeing any girls in the civil patrols, but we'll have to wait to get better information."

"Is it as bad as these new reports are indicating?" asked Abby.

"Worse." The United Nations executive stood and walked to a window. To Abby, he looked exceedingly tired. In time he turned back to Abby. "When your husband gets back, I want to send him to the Middle East. Israel has invaded Lebanon, again under the guise of rooting out the PLO, but as always, civilians bear the brunt of these attacks, and the refugee camps there have come under attack. It's not our department's charge, and we won't be able to get into southern Lebanon, but I'd like to send Paul to Gaza to meet with the mayor of Gaza City, maybe to reassure him that the United Nations hasn't forgotten them."

Abby felt the anger, the desperation, and fatigue in the room. The Palestinian refugee situation was under the auspices of the UNRWA and had been ongoing for three decades with no end in sight. As long as the United States gave unconditional support to Israeli expansion, the refugee camps in the region were at risk. Still, Abby worried about Paul. "Don't you think you're spreading Paul a little thin?"

Martin turned back to Abby. "You and your husband bleed for the refugees of any land. I remember a conversation we had in Thailand when we were all exhausted after a particularly difficult day at KID. We were talking about our reasons for getting into this business, and Paul spoke eloquently, and philosophically, about his fascination with borders and particularly with those in the Middle East. Imaginary lines. Imaginary lines drawn by past generations or by men in elegant rooms like the Palace of Versailles that must be protected from crossing, even by the very people who live on those lines."

Abby remembered, and she knew Paul would choose to go. She would go with him.

∾

As the plane approached Nebaj in central Guatemala, Paul observed the people running into the forest. He had already seen scorched cornfields and two burned-out villages. "This is not good," said the pilot as he prepared to set the plane down on the dirt runway. The only person remaining was a Catholic priest who stood near what appeared to be the airport's terminal, a one-room adobe house painted blue and yellow. He ran toward the plane as it taxied to a stop.

"You cannot stay here," yelled the priest in English as Paul and the pilot began to climb down. "You must get back in your plane and return to Guatemala City or fly to Mexico. The army has already killed many of my congregation this week. You cannot help us now." The priest kept looking over his shoulder into the forest. "Go!"

"Come with us, Father," said Paul.

"No! I will not leave my people or my home. Go!"

Gunfire erupted in the forest, and screams could be heard. Paul and the pilot jumped into the plane, and in seconds, it was racing down the runway. Paul looked back and saw the priest running toward the firefight, saw him crumble to the ground but get up. Paul lost sight of him as the plane left the dirt and rose into the cloudy sky.

"I'm not sure going back to Guatemala City is the best idea," said the pilot. "The army down below will radio ahead and tell them that we witnessed what just happened."

"Do you have enough fuel to get to Tapachula?"

"Probably not."

Paul thought for a moment. "Turn north and we'll make a run for the camps just across the border in the Lacandon Jungle. If I remember, there's a small airstrip there."

"Hang on. I'm going to gain as much altitude as I can to get around this mountain." The pilot turned the plane sharply to his left and then accelerated to the Cessna's full speed. Paul remembered another Cessna he had flown in across another border.

"Does this plane have a name?" asked Paul.

"No, sir, but maybe we'll call it Lucky and hope it lives up to that name." The pilot did not smile. He was an American, last name Fillian, who had flown helicopters in Nam, loved flying, and taken a job as a bush pilot in Guatemala for whoever paid, mostly the U.S. military and trekkers. "Sonofabitch!" he said. "We've got company."

Coming from the east, from the direction of Chajul, a Huey helicopter rose from out of the trees on the top of a hill. It was still several thousand feet away from the plane but closing fast.

"Can you outrun him?" asked Paul.

"I can—if I can first elude him right now. We'll have to assume he's not here to talk." Fillian banked sharply and down to gain any last bit of speed. As he maneuvered, he talked. "America isn't supposed to be supplying military gear to the Guatemalans. Carter and Congress and human rights, but now that Reagan's president, the rules are being bent." Fillian's voice seemed controlled to Paul, almost like a rehearsed speech. "It looks like this Huey is commercial, so the Guatemalans had to arm it down here. Of course, they've gotten technical support from us, but again, we may catch a break if the guns haven't been forward mounted yet."

Paul shifted his view from one side of the plane to the other to keep the Huey in sight. "Looks full of soldiers, like they're hanging out the sides."

"Keep your belt on. If we're gonna to make it to Mexico, I've gotta turn north and fly as straight as I can. If you know a prayer, say it now, because they're about to start firing at us. Glad they're not our Air Force, because we'd be in flames by now. These guys are rank amateurs."

As Fillian turned north, the plane flew in front of the Huey for a few dangerous seconds. Paul remembered being transported to various Landing Zones in Vietnam on Hueys, remembered jumping out into the colored smoke and running to tree lines. "They've opened up, but it looks like their alignment is off kilter," yelled Paul, his voice not as controlled as Fillian's had just been.

"Like I said, . . ." Fillian's voice trailed off.

As the plane flew perpendicular past the nose of the Huey, Paul watched as soldiers, whose feet hung out of the helicopter side doors, raised their weapons and fired. Haphazard since the Huey banked to chase the plane.

"How many in the Huey?" asked Fillian, more as a command than a curiosity question.

"It's packed. At least a dozen," answered Paul.

"A Huey in the right hands is a beautiful machine, but it has its limitations. Range and payload. Too heavy and it slows it down. Picking up the dead and wounded in Nam slowed us down. An empty Huey can do 120, but not this one." Just as Fillian said this, the Huey turned back toward Nebaj. "We've escaped for the moment," said Fillian.

Paul shook his head. "Good for us, not for the Maya back there."

"Remember Nam?" asked Fillian. "Free-fire zones." He went quiet for at least a minute. Then, "But the Maya don't have weapons."

For the next 40 minutes, Paul jotted notes from the fly-over. Fillian had found a river he believed to be a tributary to the Usumacinta and followed it. "I'm going to stay on this course as long as the fuel tank says we have something left. I have no desire to put down on the Guatemalan side. Good thing we have daylight left." Paul put down his pad and watched the riverbanks for any sign of a camp or town. Mostly, dense forests. As the river turned more northerly, Fillian spotted houses.

"What does that look like?" Fillian asked.

Paul had seen enough refugee camps to know. "Looks mostly secure. Do we have a choice?"

"Nope," answered Fillian. "The gauge is registering E. Do you see a landing strip?"

Paul looked out of both sides of the plane and then pointed to a short road or runway. Fillian pointed the plane down and made a bumpy landing. The plane sputtered to stop next to a white adobe house, where a handful of men emerged to greet them.

Fillian had landed at Beremerito, a refugee camp run jointly by Mexico's refugee organization, COMAR, and the UNHCR, Paul's employer. Beremerito was not the largest of the border camps in Chiapas, just one of over 70 small camps in the Lacandon Jungle, a rainforest that spread across northern Guatemala, Chiapas, and parts of the Yucatan Peninsula. These camps were the most important refuges for the Maya if they could make it across the border. The jungle itself had been the heart of the great Mayan civilization of previous centuries.

Paul found a phone and called Jules Beaufort in San Cristobal. "Piece of cake. I had no success with the ambassador. He's maintaining the lie that the revolutionary army is committing most of the atrocities against the rural population. The official U.S. position is that the targeted assassinations of a couple of prominent landowners in El Quiche justifies the actions of the Guatemalan government to pacify that region. We flew over some of those villages that are being pacified.

Several of them have been burned to the ground, Martin, and my fear is that the Guatemalan army is murdering these farmers and their families. Rumors without authentication, but substantial. I'm going to stick around here for a couple of days and talk with the refugees."

Beaufort had heard similar reports. "Our biggest problem is getting food and medical treatment to the refugees in that region. No roads. We have to fly in everything."

Paul shook his head to himself. "No, Jules. That may be your biggest problem, but the biggest problem is that the Guatemalan people are being slaughtered. They need safety. The UN's efforts here will go for nothing unless we can find a way to move those people into Mexico and beyond. You're also going to have to find safer camps. The Guatemalan army is targeting these jungle camps. I'll get more information tomorrow and in the next few days, but they're not secure." Paul paused. "By the way, if you need a good pilot, I've got one for you. Former U.S. Air Force."

"One more thing, Paul. Call your wife. She's worried about you."

⚬

"It's so good to hear your voice! Where are you?" asked Abby.

"One of the small refugee camps in Chiapas." Abby knew the geography of the region well. "I'm going to stay here for a few days, but the best work is being done by Catholic Services. The Mayan people are so spread out, the ones who've gotten out. This isn't going to turn out well."

Abby felt the discouragement in his voice, a tone that was seldom present. "While I was in Geneva, I heard that the new Guatemalan government was organizing civil patrols. Is that true?"

"Yeah. Led by army officers. Brutal. Surreal. The rural farmers are trapped inside their own country. They can't escape."

Abby heard Paul breathe out heavily. "In what universe," she asked, "do cultures torture and mutilate their children?"

"So, some of these atrocity reports are getting out to the world. I wonder if our government will read them?" With his off hand, Paul leaned into the wall, holding the receiver in his other hand. "I don't think it would matter if they did." At a tiny refugee camp in Chiapas,

Mexico, Paul laid his forehead against a wall in a small adobe office. "I fear this story won't get out, that a silent tragedy is unfolding, and there's not a damn thing I can do about it."

∾

Abby flew to Mexico four days later, meeting Paul in Tapachula, a city on the southern coast of Chiapas. He had been staying in the various camps along the northern border of El Quiche, in tents with the refugees themselves. The UNHCR was nominally in charge of these camps, but since the Mayas crossing the border were not given refugee status, certain protections and provisions could not be provided. Fillian flew Paul from Beremerito to San Cristobal and then to Tapachula on the morning Abby arrived, and Paul introduced him to Martin before heading off to meet Abby. She arrived on a twelve-seater from Mexico City.

"You didn't tell me about your adventure," said Abby. "You introduce me to a bush pilot who casually mentions that his plane was shot at, that he flew out of a village that had been burned to the ground just hours earlier, that a priest was gunned down as you lifted off?"

Paul smiled. "He left out the part where he landed the plane without any fuel. Pretty cool. He glided in."

"Not funny, my dear." She gave him a glare and then leaned in for a tight hug. "God, I miss you when you're gone," she whispered into his ear. "Moses does too." They spent the next half-hour talking about their son.

∾

"Tapachula is quite the little city," said Abby over an afternoon meal on the patio of a neighborhood cafe. "I thought San Cristobal was the center of this state."

"Geographically, it is, but the future is here with the commerce. Lots of Guatemalans too. Many of them illegally, but lots of others just cross the border on a regular pattern to do business. Americans only think of Mexico's northern border with the U.S., but movement across their southern border, especially with the wars in Central America, creates a national emergency. This city is housing refugees from El

Salvador, Honduras, and Nicaragua too."

"Nicer than Aran," said Abby. "Can't the UN work out of here?"

"We have an office, but I don't see a successful . . ." Paul paused to search for a word. Finally, he said, "path." He paused again. "Chiapas is the first place of refuge for the Guatemalans, for all of Central America for that matter, but it's so poor and so remote. Up north where I was, there really are no roads to speak of. Fillian flew me over these camps so I could see. The refugees were walking across the border, trying to get across rivers completely on their own. The aid agencies have an impossible task in accessing these camps. It's easier for the Guatemalan army to get at them than for us to help them." Paul paused again. "Guatemala is at war with itself, just like Vietnam and Cambodia, and the US is on the wrong side. All of Central America. And we see the ordinary people as the enemy, communists, so we put pressure on Mexico not to be an active ally to these refugees. When I spoke with our ambassador, he basically threw me out of his office saying I just didn't understand. He told me that Chiapas is fertile ground for a communist insurgency in Mexico, and that we can't allow that. To him and all those right-wing dictators America supports with military supplies, every refugee from Central America is a likely communist sympathizer ready to help Cuba further rebellion in the Western hemisphere."

In college Paul might have given the benefit of the doubt to America's official position, that the Cold War struggle against communism took precedence over human rights. He was nineteen then, early twenties, but as a 35-year-old refugee worker with first-hand knowledge of brutal atrocities against local populations, hundreds of thousands of poor farmers, he knew that the United States, his country, was assisting military dictatorships in a massacre. Abby never had given her government the benefit of the doubt. It was why she had earned the moniker "Explosive" for her opposition to the Vietnam War. And now, Paul's angry frustration set her off.

"Refugee agencies work to clean up the ashes with contributions from congregations and concerned citizens, but we can't stop the war machines fueled by tax dollars. Will said as much in Cambodia. A former Green Beret who fought in that misguided war and then worked to clean up that mess. He knew that the trauma inflicted on those people would take a generation or more to recover, and maybe never recover." Abby swore. "Now, it's happening in Central America!"

It hadn't happened often in the years Abby had been out of prison, once or twice to Paul in Oxnard over her stupidity in robbing a bank, once on Pilau Bidong when she couldn't get her supervisor to provide extra security for teen girls, and once in Thailand over the unsanitary conditions at Sa Kaeo. Abby seethed. Her body trembled, her eyes narrowed, and she clenched her fists. On this afternoon, she locked her eyes on Paul as if only he could control her, but at the same time, like she wanted no part of control. Paul leaned into the table taking hold of Abby's fists and intertwining his fingers in hers.

"Time to fight," he said in a low voice, in a tone that was both a statement and a question to his wife if she wanted to answer it.

She breathed deeply and nodded once. Finally, she blinked. "I just know there has to be more I can do other than return to the camps and work eighteen-hour days."

Paul leaned in even further. "You've spent the last decade chastising yourself for one stupid deed; holding your anger at injustice in, but it's time you stop beating yourself up for that bank job. You've paid your penance. You've earned your anger back."

"I won't give up my work with my girls, with those angry boys who were ripped from their families, with the babies!" she said defiantly. For a moment Abby's tone changed. "I can't adopt every child who tugs at my heart; I can't send them to my parents or friends. I need to keep the mission at the forefront, that we are trying to keep families and cultures together."

Paul sensed another line of travel in his wife. "We talked about adoption. Don't beat yourself up for leaving Moses with your parents occasionally. We've seen the love and value of extended families, something that maybe America needs to get back to. It's not like we dump him off with them; we live in the same house, a house filled with love."

A waitress of undetermined age refilled their water glasses and took away the empty tray of corn tortillas. She looked confused, wondering if she could get their attention to ask if they wanted another cerveza to finish their fish tacos. Abby released her left hand from Paul's grip, held up two fingers, and said, "Dos, gracias." She regripped Paul's hands and eyes.

"You can't. They need you. But here's what I've been thinking about. It's part of our mission with UNHCR to help return refugees to their homes, but these people can't go back. They'll be killed, no question about it. They've got no other option than to stay out of Guatemala. Mexico's welcome won't last forever, especially near the borders. Somehow, we need to convince anyone who'll listen to move the Maya people into Campeche and into the Yucatan. For years to come, until the world regains its sanity."

The waitress returned with two beers, set them down, and turned away.

Abby released Paul's hands, took both beers and examined them, handed one to Paul, and raised hers. "We'll do more than that, my dear. We'll help move Guatemalans into the United States," she paused in the middle of her thought. "We'll help move them into our country legally and illegally. If my government doesn't want to give them asylum, at least my country can provide them sanctuary." She lowered her glass to her lips, smiled coyly, and then took a big drink. "Along the Thai-Cambodian border, Camille knew she couldn't save all the refugees. She knew her limitations, so she set out to save one at a time. That's my plan. One at a time."

After a few moments of introspection, after drinking half a glass of cerveza, Paul asked an obvious question, "You have a plan on where to start?"

"Yeah. The churches. We need to figure out how to get the refugees across the border into Arizona and then get the churches in Tucson to scatter them into cities."

Paul nodded. "A conduit. My guess is you've talked with your parents?"

Abby nodded. "They're all in and will convince some of their Chicago friends to help. I called Father Thomas in Oxnard, and he's in on the condition we convert to Catholicism." She smiled. "You know as well as I do that the Catholic Relief Services is as committed as any relief agency." She ran her finger over the rim of her beer glass. "And I may have a contact near the border in Arizona, an old guy and a woman who hide migrants in a small town in western Arizona. He's a bit of an anarchist, and she has an anger over for-profit cross-border adoptions."

"Remember that house you wanted in the suburbs? Looks like that'll never happen. Your plan is a lifetime commitment." Paul stared at Abby with probing eyes. "So, we continue working with UNHCR and spend our America time working with churches to place illegals?"

"Not really, my dear, I fully intend to work with refugees in camps. We just need to help where we can with the sanctuary movement. It's not a new concept, and there are already groups doing just this sort of thing. I'm not smart enough to think of this on my own. I just want more Americans to be healers instead of soldiers."

"Have you spoken with Sally and Mose?" asked Paul.

"Sally's the one who got me in touch with Father Thomas."

12

The next morning Paul flew with Fillian from Tapachula to survey border camps on the Mexico side. He took two cameras, one still and one movie, to document his visual sightings. Fillian told Paul that he would fly him into Guatemala if he so desired, but Paul waivered on the offer. "Let's see what we see on this side of the border."

Abby met with UNHCR aid workers along with the International Red Cross and Catholic Relief Services. All were intensely frustrated over their inability to access the dispossessed inside Guatemala and with Mexico's reluctance to get crosswise with the United States. Paul had purchased a colorful scarf for her from a Mayan street-cart in Guatemala City. She wore it as she visited the refugees in Tapachula, a sign of respect to the women and a reassurance to the small children in aid shelters. Through interpreters, she listened to the horrifying stories the refugees told. What she heard over and over was that for every Mayan who had escaped into Chiapas, Mexico, ten others were trapped inside Guatemala. A million Mayans walking to flee the violence of their villages, walking to find safety in the next valley, the next forest, but finding no refuge. So much like the tragedy of Cambodia, a silent genocide being perpetrated against the most defenseless in society.

"We try to give these people a measure of dignity in our shelters here and along the border, but they are so desperate," said one Red Cross aid worker. "Guatemala refuses to allow us into their country, so we are unable to serve the neediest."

Abby knew this. The United Nations could not get any of its relief organizations into Guatemala either. Unless people could find a way across the border on their own, there was no international aid available. Abby rode to another camp closer to the border in the after-noon, a camp in name only. A few adobe structures crammed with migrants. She walked the main street holding hands with two Maya teenage girls while she listened to the tales of torture happening just across the border. Abby had nothing to give these refugees except her ear. She listened and nodded, frequently hugging a child or mother. Like children elsewhere in Third World countries who suffered from hunger related diseases, these children were small, weak, tired, and fragile, but these Maya had walked a hundred miles to survive. Abby tried to give them a sense that their trek would not be in vain.

"Tell them," she said through the interpreter, "that they will not be sent back until their country is safe for that return." It was part of the UNHCR creed to return refugees to their homeland, if possible, but for these refugees, that was not an option at this time. Abby sensed it wouldn't be possible for years to come. In one shelter she sat with a refugee who spoke English.

"We are people without a home," said the man. "We have lived in Guatemala for all the generations of my family, but now, that has been taken from us. We are not wanted here in Mexico. What is to become of us?" He looked over to a woman holding a baby and nodded. The short woman stepped to Abby and gently handed the baby to Abby. She held it as carefully as she held Moses back in Chicago and imme-diately felt the differences. Boney. Desperate eyes.

The real world, thought Abby. How do I tell them that I can't promise them the next day, much less the next year? The rigid ideol-ogy of old men was more important than protecting the lives of babies. She had no words for the man. She kissed the child on her forehead—Abby assumed all babies were girls until she found out differently—and handed her back to her mother. Abby leaned forward and did what she had done for the past two years. She took hold of the man's hands and captured his eyes. She would not cry, would not show tears; she would project hope and concern. She would pass on her own determination. At the same time, she would allow his heart to flow back into hers. Always, her message was that she would do what she could, that she cared.

∾

When Paul returned to Tapachula, he found Abby sitting on the cement floor of a makeshift cafeteria, cross-legged, holding the hands of a teenage girl who had been raped and beaten by Guatemalan soldiers just a week earlier, but had somehow survived and walked into Mexico. Abby still wore the Mayan scarf. The two women were taking softly, a little bit of Spanish, a little bit of English, but somehow communicating. Another aid worker handed Paul a coffee and then returned to a table where several aid workers were handing out tortillas and beans to refugees. The UNHCR couldn't do much, but it would do what it could. Abby didn't notice Paul. He shook his head slightly and moved to the table and began dishing beans onto paper plates to the continuous line of hungry people that stretched from Malaysia to Thailand to Pilsen to Tapachula, Mexico. An unending line. The never-ending line.

On September 6, 1982, just weeks after returning to Chicago from Mexico, Abby and Paul flew to Geneva on Swissair flight 111, the "UN Shuttle" as this flight was called. New York to Geneva daily, ferrying United Nations workers between the two cities. For two days, Abby met with aid workers specifically trained to meet the needs of refugee children. She met with the head of the task force on children, a French woman named Marie. Paul learned all he could about the work of the Relief and Works Agency, the group formed three decades earlier to deal directly with the homeless crisis created by the Arab-Israeli War of 1948. While Paul had been working with Central American refugees flooding into Mexico, Israel invaded southern Lebanon in June, hoping to defeat the PLO and Yasser Arafat. Paul learned he would not be allowed to visit camps in Lebanon or the West Bank because of the war, so he would be traveling to Israel and then taken to the Gaza Strip to meet with Palestinian leaders there. He also learned that funds for supplies for the UNRWA were dwindling, that international support for the Palestinian refugees was drying up, specifically from U.S. donors who viewed the PLO as a terrorist organization.

From Geneva Paul and Abby flew to Lod Airport just outside Tel Aviv, amid high security. They were met by a UNRWA field administrator, Rory McMahan from Ireland. They were taken to the Gaza Strip in an Israeli taxi, where they switched taxis to one driven by an Arab, entering the Palestinian territory at the Erez Crossing at the northern end of the Strip.

"You will be staying at Mama House in Gaza City. It's the only place in the city suitable for visitors," said Mac, the name Paul and

Abby would come to refer to this man who loved golf and hard work. "The attitudes of the Palestinians, not just the refugees in the camps but of those who have always lived in Gaza, are hardening. No one sees any progress in the negotiations to send the refugees back to their homes. Negotiations regarding the two-state solution have ground to a halt. Palestinians in Gaza are the pawns used by both Arabs and Israel."

From her backseat, Abby nudged Paul and pointed to the numerous guard towers along the way. Paul nodded and addressed Mac. "The Israeli cab driver who left us off at the border made an interesting comment. He said he was originally from Philadelphia but emigrated a decade ago. He said that America had slavery, and Israel has the Palestinians, and that neither country has been able to handle its lies and overcome the past. In America the cab driver had been a history teacher."

"And Ireland has England," said Mac. "Catholics and Protestants, Muslims and Jews, Blacks and Whites. Always someone to hate."

"In Geneva your bosses told me you were having money problems. How are you keeping up?" asked Paul.

"A branch of the Muslim Brotherhood, a group calling itself Mujama, is helping out. Tomorrow, I'll introduce you to its leader. Israel sees this group as less political and certainly less strident than the PLO, so it encourages them to do charity work. They've been very helpful in rebuilding homes and schools that have been damaged in previous wars. They have focused on social and humanitarian work, but even this group can't avoid seeing the intransigence of the Israelis over the years."

Abby leaned forward to address Mac in the front seat. "Paul dated a Jewish girl in college who emigrated to Israel to help in the '67 war and stayed."

Mac gave directions to the cab driver in Arabic and then turned back to Paul. "When was that? Have you kept in touch with her?"

A rusted van slammed into the taxi striking it on the passenger side near the rear door where Paul was sitting.

∾

The sheikh sat in his wheelchair in the parlor at Mama House, an aide helping him smoke his cigarette. Next to him on an elaborate couch sat the recently deposed mayor of Gaza, Rashad al-Shawwa, also smoking and sipping coffee. While they waited for their guests, they spoke with sadness about the one-sided war in southern Lebanon. Neither man cared much for Yasser Arafat, but they knew that hundreds of innocent Palestinians would die as Israeli forces shelled the towns and camps between Israel and Beirut.

"Refugees always pay the price," said al-Shawwa. "It will be no different this time. I'm already hearing reports that the Lebanese Christians have surrounded the camps near Beirut."

"No one cares for Palestinian refugees. We are pawns in a greater chess match. We are always the first ones sacrificed," said the sheikh.

The conversation was interrupted when Mac, Paul, and Abby were escorted into the parlor, Abby on the arm of Mama. Abby had a bandage on her chin and walked with a slight limp. Mac had a bandage on his forehead. Paul had no visible injuries from the previous day's accident.

Mayor al-Shawwa stood and made a slight bow. Mama made the introductions, at the same time kidding the sheikh for not standing when he was introduced to Abby. "Where are your manners?" she asked him. "Mr. and Mrs. Garrity, this is Sheikh Yassin, the founder of Mujama al-Islamiya. He will use his wheelchair and poor eyesight to gain your sympathy, so be aware of his charm." Mama coaxed everyone to sit while her workers served cakes, a citrus drink, and coffee.

"I am so glad your accident wasn't serious," said Yassin through his interpreter. "A few stitches but no broken bones, I'm told. Mr. Garrity, I see you allowed your wife to protect you during the crash."

Abby spoke. "My husband never seems to sustain any injuries on his sojourns. A charmed life."

Paul smiled. "We apologize for our elaborate arrival. We had hoped for something less spectacular, less of a crowd. How is the driver of the van? I understand he's still in the hospital."

"He will be fine in a few weeks," said Mayor al-Shawwa. "The price he has to pay for driving recklessly. We will use him as a test case in our new hospital that the sheikh's organization is building for us. The taxi driver will be fine in a few days also."

Mac steered the conversation to the cooperation between his organization, the United Nations Relief and Works Agency, and Sheikh Yassin's young movement, Mujama. Abby noted the general tendency of the two Palestinians to talk past her, to direct most of their words to Mac and Paul. The ex-mayor spoke of his influence in the Gaza, that the Israelis had forced his removal for his opposition to their occupation. Israel called the occupation necessary while negotiations were underway for a permanent treaty. "Security concerns." Abby shook her head sensing that the discussion was more about politics than children.

"We all know the Zionists will not negotiate directly with the Palestinians. Orthodox Jews want all of the West Bank, what they call Judea and Samaria, and the northern segment of Gaza, since it is within Judea." The ex-mayor paused. "It is not just Orthodox Jews, but a small segment of their population who steal our houses and erect settlements on our land. Is it any wonder why Gazans are angry? There will be an awakening."

Sheikh Yassin blew out a smoke ring. "The Zionist state tries to de-humanize us, but we are strong. The 24-hour surveillance, the police brutality, the separation of fathers from their families, the restrictions on travel even within our own lands are all designed to humiliate us. Their defense forces cultivate informants within our midst to gather information, part of their devious plan to control us and ultimately to deport us."

Paul listened to this one-sided account. For all his life even as he started work as a refugee worker, he had held a strong bias in support of Israel. He understood the gravity of the Holocaust and the Jewish promise to never again allow it to happen. In his work with his university professor, Dr. Orr, he began to unravel the complexities of the Middle East, in particular, the Holy Land. He learned of the struggle of the Arabs in the region over the centuries too. It never was a land without a people, waiting for a people without a land. Putting faces on the suffering here just as he experienced in other refugee camps reaffirmed his belief that there are people caught in the middle whose lives are precious and valuable. He leaned in closer to the two men whose people were caught in one of these middles trying to find something to take back to Geneva that might ease the suffering of the Palestinians.

"Mr. McMahon tells us that the two of you have seen many refugee camps in the past few years," said ex-Mayor al-Shawwa. "Today, we will take you to see a couple of ours. They won't be made up of tents like those camps in Southeast Asia or Central America. No, our camps may surprise you in their construction, but look into the eyes of the refugees."

Imam Yassin finally turned to Abby. She had been told that he was blind, but she realized that he had some vision. "And you, Mrs. Garrity, your specialty is children and young soldiers, I'm told. You will find lots of both here in Palestine, often in the same body. The Zionists' policies make every child a potential soldier. Our soldiers throw stones sometimes, but we have few guns. In every battle we are at a great disadvantage, but we will never surrender." He paused, and his white eyes seemed to Abby to glisten, as if he knew the future.

"The fighting in Lebanon continues," said Paul. "When my wife and I were given instructions to come here, we expected to be stationed in Beirut, and we planned to bring our two sons and live in an apartment there. Our sons remain in Chicago with their grandparents. Abby's father is also a minister, and he and her mother run a soup kitchen for the poor there. Mac tells us that your organization is providing similar aid here in Gaza, and you have received the permission of the Israeli authorities."

The mayor politely interrupted. "My friend's organization did not seek the *permission* of the police to provide the services they provide. No one should ever need *permission* to provide food and medical care for the needy. I understand that the United Nations tries not to, how do you say, ruffle the feathers of the occupying forces, but sometimes in life, those feathers not only need to be ruffled, but they also need to be plucked."

❧

That afternoon at Jabala, a refugee camp in the heart of Gaza City, Paul walked slowly alongside Imam Yassin who was being pushed in his wheelchair. Refugees stepped forward to speak to the Mujama leader, to touch him and offer support. Yassin acknowledged each person and at the same time, maintained a dialogue with Paul through the interpreter. "We need to help ourselves; it is obvious the world has forgotten us. My people have become disillusioned, and our young people have little hope for a better life. When their grandparents tell them of the life they once lived, our children hear a fairy tale. These camps suffer many of the same deficiencies as refugee camps around the world: overcrowded, poor sanitation, high unemployment, poor health facilities."

"These conditions, maintained over decades, can only lead to volatile futures," said Paul. "Do you see that in your future?"

"The Zionists have cut new roads through our farms and citrus orchards. They make it difficult to travel from north to south. Families are cut off from family members. Without hope, there will be an uprising. Right now, we are tolerated as an alternative to the more militant branches of my people, but we will move in that direction if conditions continue to spiral downward. My people are not blind like I am. They see the events in Lebanon and know it will happen to them soon. When you go back to America, you might tell your nation the truth about what is going on here." The imam was interrupted several times before he spoke again. Then, "Your wife sees and hurts for my children. She doesn't differentiate. She sees only the pain and wants to heal."

Abby watched her husband stare out the second-floor window of Mama House at the city below, at Gaza City. He had visited six refugee camps spread over 22 miles of the Gaza Strip from north to south. He arrived back at Mama House dusty and tired. He had barely touched his dinner, barely spoken with Mac, and excused himself to return to this room. He asked about Abby's day in a perfunctory manner, but she wasn't sure he heard much of what she said. She had seen this before: along the Cambodia-Thai border and after he had returned from Guatemala. It was how he processed and then recharged, but somehow tonight was different.

"It was good for the mayor and the imam to talk to you, you know," said Abby from bed. "You're a good listener."

Without turning away from the window yet, he hmphed. He lowered his head and took in an enormous breath, letting it out slowly through his mouth. He turned and looked at his wife. "My strength, I guess. It was a one-sided conversation." He walked to the bed and sat next to Abby, taking hold of her hand and then looking at it.

"What are you thinking?" she asked and then waited.

Paul took his time to answer. Finally, after staring at her hand for a couple of moments, he lifted his eyes to hers. "Today was a day where a lifetime of beliefs was severely challenged. Intellectually, I understood that Israel's treatment of the Palestinians was defective, was cruel." He paused again. "But I've always given them a pass because of the Holocaust and their absolute need for a place of their own. It matters, and I fully support the need for a Jewish nation, but it wasn't the Palestinians who perpetrated that horrific crime against the Jews. An answer needs to be found soon. Time is rapidly evaporating . . . if it hasn't eroded altogether. The time to fix this was immediately after The Great War, 60 years ago. It's a late-Twentieth Century remnant of British colonialism." He lowered his eyes again and put his other hand on top of Abby's hand that he was already holding. "I also know that another generation of soldiers is being created by Mujama. Child soldiers today, but tomorrow . . . As we both know, child soldiers have no conscience; they're the most brutal of all, and they grow up to be brutal men. Mujama will become indistinguishable from the PLO. Tonight, it seems as if this land is the best example that several things can be true at the same time, but neither side hears the other's truth."

Abby felt his heart struggling to match his respect for the Jewish struggle to survive after World War II and their current treatment of the Palestinians. He was a refugee worker now, not a diplomat redrawing boundaries, and this day had revealed inhumane conditions. She had faith that he would figure it out, but tonight he would ache. Tears filled her eyes. She wanted to sit up and hug this gentle man who had been forced to be tough and demanding so many times. She worried about his soul. "Paul . . ."

He looked back with pain in his eyes. "What am I here for? This isn't like those other places where I felt like we could make a difference."

He stopped himself.

"We did make a difference in those places."

Paul's thumb massaged the back of Abby's hand. "This place, and I imagine those in southern Lebanon and the West Bank, will not get better anytime soon. All the negotiations for a two-state solution are just talk. I saw it in the eyes of the Israeli soldiers, and it's reflected in the eyes of the Palestinians. Hatred towards each other." He breathed out heavily. "They're both just creating new excuses for the next great Middle East war. The cycle of hurt . . ." He stopped again and Abby sensed a change of purpose. Paul breathed deeply. "In another generation, Mujama will be no different from the PLO, devoid of any humanitarian goals to improve the lives of the people they claim to represent. It will morph into a violent wing. We must distinguish the terror groups from everyday people, from those caught in the crossfire."

Abby scooted up, withdrew her hand from Paul's, and hugged him, his head falling onto her shoulder. "We aren't politicians. We don't get to decide. We're refugee workers employed by the United Nations. While we're in the camps, we'll do all we can. That's what we do."

"Becoming a refugee," Paul paused. "Becoming a refugee lessens one in the eyes of the world, like you're not as good as . . . a real person. We've seen that. The good intentions of so many get swept away by the zealots who profess to know the truth . . . with a capital T. Back in Oxnard, we both worried about how incarceration had changed us, but we had a place."

Abby nodded. "What I saw today reminded me of my jail. Restrictions on everything, threats of violence for misbehavior. It hangs over one's head all the time." Abby went back in time to her incarceration. After a moment she returned. "Some of my fellow prisoners never escaped because they had lived their entire lives that way. I had a path, and I had support."

Paul had traveled that same path, but tonight wasn't about his journey. "I have this horrible, horrible dread that something terrible is about to happen," he whispered.

∾

A week later, on September 16-17, 1982, hundreds of Palestinian refugees living in the Sabra and Shatila refugee camps in Beirut, Lebanon, were slaughtered by Phalangist Christians while the Israeli Defense Forces watched just outside the boundaries of the camps.

On September 20, Abby and Paul Garrity returned to Geneva to give their findings on the Gaza camps. The next day, they returned to Chicago, to the soup kitchen in Pilsen.

Hamby and McNabb. Abby thought it was funny. Her parents' lawyers. Attorneys at Law. What else could they be? Veterinarians? Plumbers? Harold Hamby and Jefferson McNabb were working pro bono to defend Abby's parents against the federal government. Reverend and Mrs. Archer had been arrested at their food kitchen in Chicago for alien smuggling, as were religious leaders in Arizona and Texas. The Immigration and Naturalization Service claimed that immigrants from Central America were fleeing economic conditions rather than escaping life-threatening environments. The Archers, through Hamby and McNabb, said the indictments were against people of conscience, against people who stood for the Constitution and the Gospels. If the Government couldn't round up all the "illegals," they would go after those who were facilitating the "migrants" with food and shelter. In the summer of 1984, two years after Paul and the UNHCR had first witnessed the murderous atrocities of the Guatemalan regime against their own people, the INS was arresting Americans for harboring Central American refugees.

On the other end of the phone in Chiapas, Mexico, Paul listened and wondered about the treatment of this conscientious couple. "Were they handcuffed?" he asked.

"Yep. We demonstrated in front of the INS building yesterday, and I suspect my parents will be released today. Hamby and McNabb have people ready to post bail for them. But still, two nights in jail at their age. They said they were doing fine." Abby paused to say something to her sister who was at their parents' home during the crisis. "What are you hearing?" she asked Paul.

"Fillian . . . by the way, he's going by the name Redbone now . . .

compared all this to the book Nineteen Eighty-Four, since we're in that year Orwell predicted totalitarianism would have taken over. He was drinking at the time. When he leaves here, he thinks he'll be hired by the UN to fly aid workers in the Great Lakes region of Africa. Anyway, as you probably know, almost none of the refugees from Central America are getting asylum. Reagan still insists the Guatemalans are merely crossing into Mexico to harvest coffee like they've done for decades. Seasonal migration, you know."

Abby didn't respond immediately, but Paul waited. After a few moments, "When are you coming home? We want you here for Father's Day. That's on Sunday."

"Redbone is flying me to Mexico City in two days, so I'll be home on Saturday. Mexico has started moving the people in the camps up north into Campeche. Most of them don't want to go, but they're forcing them to. Some have run away back into Guatemala. It's good and it's bad, but I've seen what I need to make my report. I got a call from Jules in Geneva; they want me to go back to Lebanon and Syria to check on the Palestinian camps there. I told him I wouldn't commit without talking to you." He paused. "You could come and bring the two boys."

∽

The next afternoon, when Paul and Redbone returned to Tapachula from a flight along the border to observe the camps once more, Mexican authorities arrested them. Paul tried to determine if the interrogator was sympathetic to the refugees or frustrated that outside agencies like the UNHCR were meddling in issues that were Mexican affairs. In a small office at the local police station, a captain leaned against the wall smoking a cigarette and staring at Paul. Eventually, he pushed himself off, snuffed out his smoke between his thumb and index finger, placed the stub behind his ear, and asked Paul his first question.

"Did you get permission to fly into Guatemala this time?"

Redbone's flight plan covered the area along the border up to the state of Peten and back with no variances into Guatemala. The Mexican officials would not have granted permission to fly across the border. "Did we deviate off course a little?" replied Paul.

The captain hmphed, nodded, pulled out the second chair at the table where Paul was sitting, and put his foot on it. "A deviation is a few miles. A deliberate infraction is a few hundred miles. Baja Verapaz is in the center of Guatemala. Were you and your pilot looking for fishing spots there?"

"When I was first here in '82, they were just starting to fill the dam there along the Chixoy River. Curious to see how the reservoir was coming along."

"It's pretty much full now. Needed hydroelectric power for that part of Guatemala." The captain leaned over the leg that he had lifted onto the chair. "But you knew that." He waited for Paul's response.

"I briefly met a Catholic priest in that area a few years back. Just wondered how he was doing." Paul knew what had happened to that priest. "Guatemala must have had to move several people when the reservoir flooded their villages. Several thousand, I would imagine."

"I'm sure that was the case. Unfortunate, but it happens around the world. Progress. Your country moves entire neighborhoods to build baseball stadiums. But what does all that have to do with you and your pilot violating Guatemala's airspace? They have filed a complaint, and that strains relations between our two countries even more."

From the reservoir, Redbone had flown due north, a course similar to the one he had taken two years earlier when he was fired upon by a Guatemalan helicopter. Conditions had improved slightly from the reports the UNHCR heard from refugees fleeing the violence in their native land. Improved, but not completely ended. Mayan people were still being persecuted as counterinsurgency guerrillas, even killed for no reason other than being in the wrong place when government troops came. "You must have a direct line to the Guatemalan government to get such a report so quickly," said Paul.

"Mr. Garrity, I'm just a local police captain doing what he is ordered. You and your United Nations organization operate in my country with our gracious permission. Thousands of Guatemalans are living in my country without permission, taking jobs away from my neighbors. We know that terrible things have occurred in Guatemala as they struggle to put down a communist revolution, a revolution that tends to spill over into Mexico these days. When you and your pilot fly into the heart of that revolution, you spit in Mexico's face; you show only disrespect to your host." The captain removed his foot from the chair and walked behind Paul. "I know you people look down upon me and my country."

"Quite the contrary, sir. Since the summer of 1982, I've made nine trips down here to see what could be done for the Mayan refugees. They are a forgotten people, victims of some of the most terrible crimes one can imagine. About the only nation that cares even a little about their plight is Mexico. I understand what a strain it's put upon your economy, how difficult it is for the people of your town and your home state of Chiapas, and I'm thankful for your generosity." Paul did not turn around. He stared straight ahead to where the captain once stood.

"Two years ago, my family hosted a Guatemalan family running from that violence. The world does not understand what Chiapas has done for them," said the captain.

"No, it doesn't," said Paul. "My organization serves about 50,000 refugees in 100 camps. They are poorly housed and supplied. Your state of Chiapas, your town of Tapachula is taking care of ten times that many, providing sanctuary for them. Your country walks a fine line in this region trying to maintain relations with Guatemala and El Salvador, but more importantly with my country. I understand more than you might realize."

The captain stayed silent for a moment. In time, he walked around to face Paul. "You and your pilot are in trouble for your actions. You will be flown to Mexico City today to face possible charges and jail time. Mexico jails are not pleasant. Your pilot's plane is now Mexico's plane, and he will not be getting it back. Maybe that will be enough to satisfy the authorities who matter in Mexico City. Because you seem to care a little about my town, I will let you call your organization to let them know where you are. Maybe they can influence my government to send you home. If I may give you a bit of advice, don't play games with the authorities in Mexico City. Apologize and then remain silent. Do not lecture them on my country's behavior in this sordid episode."

Ironically, Paul and Redbone were passengers on Fillian's plane, now Mexico's plane. They were handcuffed to their seats and flown the 550 miles from Tapachula to the capital that afternoon, just as the captain had told Paul they would be. Upon arrival at Benito Juarez International Airport, they were met by a senior U.S. State Department official, a representative from UNHCR, and two Mexican federales, who escorted them down the terminal to a Delta gate for a flight to Los Angeles.

∾

Father's Day, June 17, 1984, Chicago, Illinois. There were no secrets between Abby and Paul. She knew how close he had come to being jailed in Mexico for his journey into the heart of the Guatemalan genocide. She knew that he had been chastised by the UNHCR for his reckless act, even though the information he gleaned substantiated the accounts of the refugees. Upon his arrival in Los Angeles, he had briefed both the State Department and the UNHCR about the continued atrocities in Guatemala, accounts that he shared with Abby when he arrived in Chicago. The mission of the UNHCR in all refugee situations, after protection, was to return the refugees to their homeland as quickly as possible. Repatriation. But for the Maya of Central America, especially Guatemala, they wouldn't be going home soon, and Paul put part of the blame on his homeland for this tragedy. Abby and Paul would not be allowed to continue their work in Chiapas, Mexico, and that fact made them feel dispirited.

Abby's parents were home, out of jail, and not likely to be returned, so Father's Day was joyous. Paul, the father, held his two boys throughout the day whenever possible. Moses and his little brother Sal. Corny, but meaningful names. They were the reason Abby did not accompany Paul on extended missions as she had to Malaysia and Thailand, but she continued to fly to Geneva to meet with Marie to establish guidelines for aid workers in refugee childcare and family reunification. And the healing of child soldiers. In three days, on Wednesday, she was heading back to Switzerland to meet with UNHCR officials to discuss operations in Africa. Paul would be the stay-at-home parent for a while.

That night in bed, Abby traced the new lines around her husband's eyes. "Guatemala was different, wasn't it?"

"Yeah," Paul answered. "Two years and we mostly failed."

"I never appreciated the importance of the media in getting the news out to the world about refugees, about how much pressure the press can bring to bear on these situations." Abby kissed Paul again and pulled his face into her neck. "Do you ever miss Oxnard?" She felt Paul's head gently nod.

He pulled back slightly. "When we were having dinner this afternoon with your parents and brother and sister and their kids, I thought how normal this all was, except for the fact that we don't have a home of our own, but the laughter and all. Our two boys. It was great. Your dad is so understanding. He takes it all in, but your mom makes it all possible, I think. I see so much of you in her." He paused. "Or is it her in you? Anyway, they complement one another so well. I hope you always feel that I am nothing without you because I'm not. You are my rock."

Abby smiled and kissed him on the lips, a kiss that started out as a gentle thank you but turned into a passionate request. His body responded immediately; he rolled on top of her, and they forgot about Guatemala and Oxnard for the moment.

"God, I love making love to you!" said Abby. "Our bodies just fit together."

"Your dad is going to pat me on the shoulder at breakfast tomorrow, you know."

In Geneva Abby again met with several United Nations agencies, including the Relief and Works Agency that had been assigned most of the relief responsibilities to the Palestinians in the Middle East. Over 50 refugee camps dotted the region giving varying qualities of aid to Palestinians who had been removed from their homes over the previous three-plus decades. While many Palestinians were acclimating well in Jordan, those who lived in Lebanon, Syria, and on the West Bank fared less well. The worst situation continued to be along a narrow strip of land along the Mediterranean Sea. Gaza. The Western World played the charade that Gaza and the West Bank would become the new Palestine in a Two-State Solution with Israel, but with each passing year, each passing war, that plan became less of a reality. The task of providing for the Palestinian refugees fell more and more into the lap of the UNRWA.

Abby also met with UN officials who were frantically searching for money and workers to stem the terrible famine occurring in Ethiopia. A continuing drought in the region and a civil war had already caused 100,000 deaths, and the situation was not improving. It was a crisis that showed no signs of abatement, no signs for optimism, a crisis that if left unchecked could spread to the other countries along the Horn of Africa and the Great Lakes region in central Africa. Undernourished families were leaving their homes in search of food, and governments faced the multiple problems of housing and caring for this stream of refugees.

Abby had become one of the United Nations' principal authorities on the treatment of child refugees. While Paul had evolved into one of the UN's leading trouble-shooters, Abby's reputation for handling any situation involving children grew. She cut through the bureaucracy and red tape to deal directly with the crisis on the ground. UNHCR pamphlets showed a photo of her administering to a starving boy while carrying another child on her hip. Abby was tough but understanding of the special needs of society's most vulnerable. In Thailand, a Khmer Rouge guerrilla soldier had said Abby possessed the biggest heart of any relief worker, but it was cloaked in armor. Only with Paul did she shed tears over those children.

∾

Abby returned to Chicago after ten days in Europe. Her trip had been extended by four days, but her time had been productive. New guidelines were put into place for the treatment of children in war-torn areas, not so much new as refined, especially in the area of psycho-social integration. The United Nations also encouraged her to resume her full-time work, going so far as to assign her a new position as Director of Operations in her specialty. They wanted her in Geneva. Abby also carried a letter from the UN to Paul. She smiled.

"Technician?" said Paul not really as a question. "Your new job title would be Senior Specialist: Child Protection, and I would be a technician? If this job comes with a desk, I don't want it. I just want a tent and an interpreter."

"You would be a Field Officer on Special Assignment. Jules said Technician sounded more professional than Fix-It Guy." She paused. "It would mean we wouldn't work together very often."

Paul nodded slightly and then continued to read the letter. "He wants me to go to Nicaragua. Did he talk to you about this?"

Abby stepped to Paul and took the letter from his hands. "I told him it would be your decision, but I was against it. You have a reputation in Central America, and it isn't one that sits well with the current governments in that region. You've been shot at in camps by Guatemalan soldiers and civilian forces. You and Redbone were shot at in his plane which they later confiscated. The US ambassador threw you out of his office. You've been shoved, threatened, and warned to stay away because you put the refugees ahead of government policy. You have this crazy habit of going off by yourself to get first-hand information. Now, he wants you to go to Nicaragua to check on the Miskito Indians. I'm not sure I want you to go back to that region."

Paul wrapped his arms around his wife but stayed silent. He knew what she said was true, but what he most was thinking was that he missed working alongside Abby like they did in Malaysia, Indonesia, and along the Thai-Cambodian border. They had left Oxnard to work as volunteers for the Catholic Relief Services, and now they were salaried by the United Nations and being assigned tasks they never dreamed of six years ago.

Without removing her face from Paul's shoulder, Abby said, "Somewhere around 50 Miskito villages have been burned to the ground over the past two years. Many of them have aligned themselves with the Contras against Daniel Ortega's Sandinistas. This is totally screwed up; I don't know which side we should be on in this situation. What Jules wants you to do is fly down to Managua and speak directly with President Ortega." Abby paused. "You already know about this, don't you?"

"Yeah. It's so messed up, just like every other armed indigenous struggle. The locals get caught up in a larger global struggle and are forced to take sides. It never turns out well. The world sees Ortega and the Sandinistas as standing up to the big, bad United States and can't see them doing anything bad, but in this case, it appears as if the Sandinistas bombed and burned and gunned down the local Miskito just like the right-wing dictators did in El Salvador and Guatemala." Paul swore in a whisper.

"You need to go," said Abby.

"I don't know. I'll call Jules tomorrow after I give it some thought. I wonder if I can talk Redbone into another adventure."

Paul grew up in a white neighborhood, attended suburban schools, and saw color only on television. As an adult, especially beginning with his stint in the Army, he worked around and served persons of color. Persons of color. What a term! He and Abby discussed the UN request for three days before deciding he would go to Nicaragua, would meet with Daniel Ortega to discuss the treatment of the

Miskito Indians there. Paul would also meet with those Miskito who were living in refugee camps across the border in Honduras, and, if it could be arranged, with the leaders of the Indians who had aligned themselves with the Contras to oppose the Sandinistas. Paul would leave Chicago on June 30, fly to Houston and then on to Managua where he would meet up with Redbone.

In the week they were together before Paul left, Abby mused frequently about their next journey. She liked the offer to move to Geneva because it offered a bit of permanency, something they had never experienced in their marriage. Despite the cost of living in Switzerland, with two incomes above what they had ever earned as aid workers, she thought they could get an apartment big enough for a family of four. "Of course, we'd have to improve our French, but the boys would grow up bilingual." With job titles, both Paul and Abby could choose assignments.

"It would mean giving up this one room apartment here at your parents' house, you know," said Paul. He knew that they had rapidly achieved a measure of respect within the UN, despite their relatively short tenure and on again off again employment with the international aid organization. "It would mean raising Moses and Sal outside the United States, but it would give them a chance to have us home with them more often. We've talked about how our jobs sort of make them orphans. We're gone so much."

"As much as I rail against America, I still love most of what we are. I want our boys to be Americans at heart. I don't see us staying in Geneva forever, but this opportunity seems to fit us just now."

Paul agreed, and he liked the idea of continuing their path of working with the world's refugees. The alternative was getting an apartment in Chicago and gradually taking over the food kitchen as Abby's parents aged, which provided stability for the boys, but didn't scratch the itch that both Abby and Paul felt. Meaningful in so many ways, but maybe too stable. "And," said Paul frequently, "once it became our kitchen, we would probably stay in Chicago forever."

A couple of days before Paul left, they told Abby's parents about their decision. Abby's mother laughed at her daughter's apprehension about revealing the plan. "Of course, you'll accept the UN offer. We knew you would. The kitchen will go on, the church will continue to provide for our poor brothers and sisters, and your father and I will be fine. We'd love for you to stay here, but we know that's not your destiny. The kitchen is for adults, and your calling is with children." She looked at Paul. "And you need your adrenaline rushes to feed your insatiable spirit to help the world's homeless. You both have talents needed by larger organizations than our little church." She reached across the table and took her daughter's hand, and then looked to her husband.

"In a sense we're relieved," said Abby's father. "We thought you might take jobs with Catholic Relief where you started and convert." He smiled broadly, and they all began laughing at his joke.

"No, Dad. I'm a U-U, and Paul is still an Episcopalian in remission."

Paul nodded. "If only the Vatican would offer employment at a higher salary."

∾

Daniel Ortega surprised Paul. The leader of the Nicaraguan Revolution was courteous and introspective, even though he promised Paul just ten minutes of his time. In the midst of an election campaign to become the first elected president of the new Nicaragua, Ortega's first question to Paul centered on why the UN would send an American to discuss human rights, especially someone without a title.

"We are at war with America," he said. "Your country funds the Contras, the mercenaries who kill my people."

Paul nodded, but before he could answer, Ortega offered him a seat and a drink. Paul took the chair but waved off the drink. "I'm not here as a representative of the United States State Department. They don't even know I'm here, as far as I know." Paul studied the revolutionary. He presented himself as a soldier, the uniform and the trappings of his office, but he seemed to want to be more, maybe a soldier in transition to statesman. Before Paul got on the plane in Chicago, he had been given a photo of Ortega in a suit speaking in New York. Clean.

Ortega took a seat behind his desk. "I find it difficult to believe your government doesn't know you are here."

"I ran a bit crosswise with my government a couple of years back."

Paul paused. "In Guatemala. The ambassador threw me out of his office, and then Mexico escorted me out of their country."

Ortega rubbed his hands together in front of his face. "Then you're on our side in this little war of ours? Or should I say in this little corner or the world where capitalism and communism battle for the souls of poor farmers?"

"I'm on the side of the poor farmers. In the countries where I've worked, they seem to be pawns of the powerful who claim to represent their best future. You and the Sandinistas have a positive reputation among many around the world, certainly among the nations in Europe, but rumors abound about your treatment of certain indigenous groups in your own country."

Ortega challenged Paul with his eyes but remained silent for a moment. Then, "Your country is hardly a model for its treatment of indigenous people."

Paul nodded. "Not many large countries are, but I'm not here to either defend or prosecute my country's history. America struggles with many problems, and as a child of my country, I take responsibility for its sins."

"So rather than staying home and working on your country's problems, you come here to Nicaragua to lecture me?"

Paul tried to look past Ortega's large glasses and into his eyes. The soldier had a full head of hair and the revolutionary mustache and scruffy beard. Ortega had been on the front lines, been shot at, met with Castro, challenged the CIA and the Contras, stood up to others in his own movement, but on the issue of the Miskito, Ortega and the Sandinistas had—were—persecuting them violently. "No lecture, just a plea. Thousands of Miskito have fled your country into refugee camps in Honduras. You know that, and you know that the UNHCR cares for them. Thousands of others, a lesser number, but a substantial number have allied themselves with the Contras. Many, and I don't have precise numbers, have been murdered by your soldiers."

Ortega interrupted. "Very few, and that was early on."

"Hundreds, if not a thousand, but even a few is too many. The Miskito are still being persecuted by your government. It appears likely that you will become Nicaragua's first elected president in decades. I

come to ask you to end the killing of some of your own people, to
live up to the platform you have publicly espoused, to be that model
you say you are for Central America, and to own up to your movement's transgressions. As you stated, my country has this history and
hasn't done a very good job of owning up to it. It continues to haunt
America."

Behind those glasses, Ortega considered.

Seeing his reflection in Ortega's glasses, Paul reconsidered.

❧

Paul flew commercial from Managua to Tegucigalpa, Honduras,
after his meeting with Daniel Ortega, and met with Miskito leaders
and refugees there. They assured Paul that some of the killing had
stopped, but since they had been forced to join either the Sandinistas
or take up weapons against them, they had been labeled, classified as
the enemy, and as such, guerrillas who needed to be defeated. The
Miskito and other, smaller indigenous groups wanted to remain in
Nicaragua but were afraid to return for fear of Sandinista abuse. Both
the Contras and Sandinista forces were recruiting the young men in
the camps to serve as soldiers, leaving the majority of the farm work
to be done by women. Paul assured the Miskito leaders that he would
talk to the UNHCR about sending additional officials to document
the treatment and protect the refugees.

Redbone secured another airplane. Smaller, older, and less reliable,
but nevertheless, as he said when he met Paul for dinner, less of a target
and fully paid for. "It will get you to the camps in a couple of hours.
When are we leaving?"

"The three most important camps are in the Mocoron area,
about 25 miles north of the Nicaraguan border on the Atlantic side.
Together, they house about 15,000 refugees." Paul had been briefed
but had not been to any of these camps. "What are you hearing, Red?"

"Lots of activity at the Mocoron airfield. U.S. military personnel,
U.S. helicopters and military supplies are being unloaded there. It's
a CIA/Contra staging area. There's an American colonel strutting
around directing activities. Recruitment by the Contras of Miskito
men is unrestricted. We won't be welcomed with open arms."

Paul shrugged. "You'd think an American colonel would be happy to see two ex-servicemen, especially one with special skills."

"I assume you mean your POW survival skills." Redbone laughed. "By the way, my new plane has a name. *Bonnie Raitt*, because of its color. Red with a white slash on one wing. Catchy, huh?"

"My wife and I saw her at a concert in Los Angeles once. One of our favorites."

∾

"What about safety at the camps?" asked Paul as Redbone pulled back on the wheel and *Bonnie Raitt* lifted off.

"It's a lot safer than those camps in Mexico that supposedly protected the Guatemalan Maya. Remember those days?" asked Redbone with a grin as if it had occurred several decades earlier.

After an hour in the air, Redbone banked slightly south to follow the Rio Coco which formed a large part of the border between Honduras and Nicaragua. The land leveled off and a vast expanse of rain forest developed. La Mosquitia. "It's a land nobody controlled for centuries, a hard land to navigate. River travel mostly. Roads that go nowhere and connect to nothing. A good land to get lost in," said Redbone. "I've been shuttling a few scientists into Puerto Lempira. Mocoron is west of there and twenty or so miles north of a little village called Leimus. You see lots of military there."

"Ours or Sandinistas?" asked Paul.

"Ours and Contras. The Sandinistas stay clear. "You make me laugh, Garrity. I tell you all this stuff and find out later you already know everything about these areas. A walking encyclopedia."

"Just double-checking my sources. Your perspective is always unique. What can you tell me about the US military in the area?"

"Good and bad for you. They don't want us snooping around, but mostly tolerate the UN workers, and they keep the camps safer. No raids by the Sandinistas. That colonel, North, I think his name is, is all soldier with carte blanche orders to get the job done."

"I wonder where he's getting the money to fund all of this. America isn't supposed to be militarily involved," said Paul.

Redbone shook his head. "There's always an open cash drawer for the military somewhere, and right now the CIA seems to be funneling money to our Central American allies. Seems like you and I have had this discussion before." He pointed to a small airstrip across the Rio Coco from a small village. "Leimus. We'll set down here. There's a little café I like, and they speak English like lots of folks in the region. And they have plenty of beer since the US soldiers arrived. Bad history there of late."

While Redbone ate, Paul walked the dirt main street and made small talk with the people. Not all were Hondurans. Several were Miskito Nicaraguans who had crossed the river but chose not to go to the UNHCR camps 25 miles to the north. His organization's policy was not to work in war zones, so these people did not show up on the refugee tally sheets. Paul talked with a couple who called themselves Sumo, not Miskito, and discovered that several indigenous groups were fleeing Sandinista persecution. His discussions confirmed what he had been briefed about, that Nicaraguan refugees had to walk through the rain forest to get to the Mocoron camps, a trek of about 25 miles. Paul wished Abby was here. Her ability to connect with desperate families exceeded his; she obtained information from refugees easily.

Redbone found Paul in a small grocery store talking with the proprietor who was happy since business had improved with the migration of Nicaraguans and the presence of American soldiers. Leimus was the only crossing of the Rio Coco in the area, so refugees stocked up at his store. Paul bought cigarettes and candy to give to the migrants, enticements to open up about their recent lives.

"Let's beat the rain. I'll drop you off and head out for a few days. How long will you be staying at the camp?" asked Redbone.

"My plan is three nights, one night at each camp. That should give me a pretty good feel for what needs to be done. I'm just an observer this time, no real work to do. My bosses want recommendations as to staffing."

∾

Abby drove her two boys to Little Saigon, the section of Chicago that she and Paul visited a few years earlier. They were too young to appreciate the vibrancy of the area, but she wanted to begin the process of exposing her boys to the life she and Paul had chosen, because she was sure they would become a part of it soon. Moses walked alongside his mother, while Sal rode in a stroller. Abby greeted the neighborhood residents in their native language. She spoke courtesy Vietnamese, not conversational Vietnamese, but she could tell her attempts were appreciated. Not all the people in the neighborhood were Vietnamese; a few were from other Southeast Asian nations who fled during the late-Seventies and early-Eighties. The immigration flow had not ended.

At noon Abby stopped at a small café for lunch, a noodle dish agreeable with Moses. The café, no larger than 150 square feet, was run by a Cambodian family, and the young girl who brought out the water seemed about nine or ten. She set the glasses down, but abruptly stopped and stared at Abby. Then, she turned and scurried back into the kitchen. She returned holding the hand of her mother, a frail-looking lady. The little girl pointed at Abby.

"She's the one, Mama," the girl said in Khmer. The mother smiled broadly, leaned into Abby, and bowed. Abby looked at the girl over the mother's shoulder, her eyes asking, What?. In English the girl said, "You found my mother for me. You were at Khao-I-Dang. I remember you."

From the kitchen an old man appeared along with two teen girls. The little girl waved them to the table and introduced them to Abby. They were the girl's grandfather and two sisters. Her father and a brother died in Cambodia.

Abby lifted Sal from his booster seat and handed him to the girl. "This is Sal, and this is Moses. My husband is away right now working with other refugees in another part of the world."

∾

The rain came down in torrents as if a brigade of firefighters was throwing buckets of water on his tent. When Redbone dropped him off, Paul met with US Army officers. When these soldiers discovered that Paul had been a soldier and a POW, their attitudes softened, and they answered his questions about the covert war in Nicaragua. From this brief meeting, Paul met with five UNHCR officials and walked around the camp, a camp similar to so many others where he had worked, blue tarps and red and blue plastic buckets, shirtless men and boys. Paul ate dinner with a handful of Miskito men.

"The Sandinistas came to our villages and told us we would have to leave, that we would have to move inland. Their revolution was the most important thing; it is a revolution of the poor. Even though we were happy and prosperous, we did not support Somoza. We refused to leave. They sent in their soldiers and burned many of our villages."

Paul took it all in. The reports indicated that around 50 villages disappeared. He also knew that reports from the refugees were closer to the truth than the reports of the governments in war-torn nations.

The Miskito man continued. "The planes came and dropped bombs. They hanged our friends, and when we ran, they gunned us down. We were not Contras. We were not helping the Contras, but when the Sandinistas did this, many of us became allies with the Contras."

"Tell me about Jinotega and Leimus," said Paul.

The man deferred to an older man. "Somoza, Ortega, it doesn't matter. We simply want to be left alone. We are far from Managua and of no importance to them or to the rest of the world. We are our own world. When the Sandinistas finally overthrew Somoza, we were glad, but that quickly changed. They demanded our loyalty five years ago, in 1979. We said we were not interested, so they began to send troops. Together with the Sumu and Rama, who we have not always gotten along with, we formed an alliance."

Paul said, "MISURA, correct?"

"Yes. We didn't want to fight the new government, but we had no choice. They wanted to move us off our lands to make us more pliant. As Esteban has said, we were not Contras in the beginning, but now maybe we are." He wiped his face with his hand in the manner of a man with a sad memory. "Just before Christmas, just across the river in Leimus, many were killed. I want to believe it was Miskito men protecting their families, but I have heard contrary reports, that maybe some Miskito men who have taken up with the Contras and your soldiers started the shooting. We may never know the truth, but after the shooting ended, bodies floated down the river. Throughout the department of Jinotega, peasants have been killed. In the mountains some peasants were shot by American soldiers." He wiped his face again. "We are not puppets of Cuba. We are not communists. We are Miskito and want only to live our lives."

The table went silent while Paul processed the information. The rain eased slightly. Finally, he spoke. "You want to go home?"

The men nodded.

"And the people in the other camps too?" asked Paul.

The men nodded again.

"My organization, the United Nations High Commissioner for Refugees, desires to help you return to Nicaragua and live safely without fear. In two more days, I will go back to Tegucigalpa with your message. I will try in the months ahead to help you and your families return to your lands. Tomorrow, I will speak with the main American officer here to urge him to use restraint when fighting in this area."

The next morning Paul contacted Redbone and asked him to pick him up in two days.

∾

"I think I should stay another day or two," said Paul to Redbone when he arrived at Mocoron. "I'd like to speak with the Rama too. Nobody seems to care about them, since there are so few of them."

Redbone was on no particular schedule, just whatever popped up with tourists. "Suit yourself. I'll fly up to Puerto Lempira and see if anyone needs a ride back to Tegucigalpa. I'll swing back by tomorrow. I can earn a few dollars by taking a couple of soldiers with me on the way." Redbone stood and stretched. "I think there are several Rama here in Mocoron working with the CIA. They threw in with the Contras almost immediately and have been pretty good soldiers. No fans of the Sandinistas from what I hear." He saluted Paul on his way out.

Paul added a few thoughts to his notes and then walked out to watch Redbone take off. For two years, whenever Paul was in Central America, Redbone had been his pilot and companion. Another Vietnam veteran conflicted by that war's outcome and legacy, who couldn't put it aside and return to normal work in postwar-America, a good man with that unscratchable itch. Bonnie Raitt lifted off and banked north. An American soldier, an officer, approached Paul and offered a cigarette. Paul refused and asked where the man was from.

"Army brat, so all over. Military runs in the family. You?"

"Colorado. At least I grew up there," answered Paul.

"Colonel North says to be careful around you. Said you aren't on our side."

"What side is that?"

"Helping the Contras fight communism and Cuban interference in the rest of Central America."

"Unlike you, America doesn't pay my salary, so my job has a different description. This war uproots lots of families that don't want to be a part of the fighting. My job is to see they get some protection. If you've been here long enough, you understand that our politics don't have a lot of importance to the natives, except when the fighting starts. Then, they choose sides based on survival."

"So, you don't try to influence them either for us or against us?"

"No. I'm not smart enough to know the long-term answer. I try to stay in the moment." Paul knew that wasn't entirely true, but this wasn't the time to examine the politics of the Reagan Era. Before Reagan, it had been Johnson and Nixon.

"Tell your pilot friend to be careful too." The soldier nodded and walked away, leaving Paul alone at the side of the airstrip. At that moment, he wished he was back in Chicago. He missed Abby terribly and just wanted to hug her and his boys. Paul was tired and didn't have any answers.

⌀

The bright red puddle jumper, nicknamed Bonnie Raitt, went down at dusk in a heavily forested region just across the border under uncertain causes: maybe adverse weather since it was raining, possibly mechanical failure, hopefully not groundfire. Abby did not find out about the crash until early the next morning when a United Nations coworker called from Geneva. Paul was thought to be on the plane, but the bodies had not yet been recovered and identified.

〜

"He thinks he's bulletproofed," said Abby softly to her parents. Her father held Moses on his lap, and his mother held Sal. "I remember him jumping into the water off a rocky cliff in Bidong to pull a boy out of the sea. Do you know that he was afraid of swimming in the ocean? He couldn't swim that well." Abby wiped her nose with the back of her wrist and then sniffled hard. "We don't know for sure yet, do we?"

Mrs. Archer reached out and touched her daughter's shoulder. "No, we don't. We can only pray."

Abby held her hands in front of her mouth, breathing out of it instead of her nose, almost panting. "It was Fillian's plane, and he loved working with Fillian. Paul always called him by his nickname. 'Redbone.' Evidently, Fillian hunted in the woods back here in the States and could sniff out the dangerous animals, sort of like a hound dog." Abby paused. "Maybe Paul should have a nickname like that." She had not slept in the 24 hours since she received the call. "I hated those small planes. This was not supposed to be a risky trip. This wasn't Cambodia or Guatemala!" She stood and walked to the kitchen window that looked out over the backyard, her back to her children and parents. And cried. Her parents watched her shoulders shake. Moses climbed down from his grandfather's lap and went to his mother. Without saying anything, he hugged her. Abby bent over and picked him up. Moses tucked his head into her neck and held his mother tightly.

〜

The men in the dugout canoe had heard about the crash along the Honduran bank of the Rio Coco almost as soon as it occurred. News of tragedies passes along quickly in dangerous times. These men had in the previous months taken their families inland from the Caribbean/Atlantic Coast, the Mosquito Coast as it was generally referred to, for safety during the revolution. They were Sumu, a small indigenous group who lived on both sides of the river, and who tried to avoid participation in the Nicaraguan civil war. Knowing recovery of the plane's passengers would be extremely difficult, these Sumu men decided to float the river to the closest spot and walk to the crash site, to do what they could in the recovery. Two days earlier, an American had walked into their camp with a guide to learn about their plight. He did not hide the fact that he was American, even though his country was a participant in the on-going war that disrupted their lives. He didn't take sides; he listened, asked questions, ate with them, gave them cigarettes, and slept in a tent on the ground.

A Sumu woman asked about his family and his eyes lit up. His wife and children were in Chicago, a city with more people than what lived in all of Nicaragua or Honduras. She was there with her parents, religious leaders in their community. His own parents lived in Denver near the Rocky Mountains. He told the group that his boys were named after two great friends who had helped him recover from wounds he incurred when he was at war. He laughed when a man asked if he knew Elvis.

"How did you become a refugee worker?" asked one man.

"I could always work with my hands, fix things, so I worked with a Catholic church in California doing small jobs." The Sumu nodded; they knew the Catholic Church. "My wife also did volunteer work for them, and an opportunity arose to help repair a church in Mexico and then help refugees from another war on the other side of the world, so we went. My wife does incredible work with children and teenagers. Once she gets to a village or camp where children have been harmed or damaged, she wraps her arms around them and protects them from being hurt anymore."

The woman stood and left the room where the discussion was being held but returned quickly. She handed a woven scarf to the American, telling him it was a gift for his wife. He examined it closely and thanked the woman. "Scarfs are her favorite."

In the morning, the American shot baskets with three boys on a makeshift hoop with no net. The American promised that he would send a couple of new basketballs and nets when he returned to Chicago. "And some soccer balls too," said one of the boys. After breakfast the American walked out of the camp with his guide.

∾

On the second day, Abby did not want the phone to ring. She wanted only silence. She believed if she didn't hear anything, Paul would still be alive. Since the plane hadn't burned, the bodies would be identifiable, and then the U.N. would call her with the bad news. So, when the phone rang just after noon, she let it ring six times before she lifted the receiver off its base. She didn't speak; she just held the receiver to her ear, steeling herself for the shock she had so far delayed.

"Abby."

"Oh God!" she whispered.

"I just returned from a Sumu village and heard about the crash. They thought I was on board and were surprised to see me. You must have been told two days ago. I'm sorry to have put you through this."

"You weren't on the plane?"

"No. It was Redbone's plane and he died along with two anthropologists from the University of Chicago. Somebody saw a Chicago identification badge and assumed it was me."

"I'm so sorry about Fillian."

Paul breathed hard on his end of the phone. "Yeah. A good man."

Abby bit her lip. She was torn between ecstasy that her husband was alive, that he would be coming home to his children, and the death of a trusted colleague who had become a close friend. "Paul." Her voice brought him back. "Do they know what happened?"

"No," said Paul softly. "I can't believe it was a mechanical failure or pilot error; he was too careful about that." There was a silence on both ends, both Paul and Abby considering another possibility. "If . . . we'll never know, because if it wasn't accidental, the official cause will say it was mechanical."

"I want you home this instant, but I know that's not possible, so get here when you can."

"I'll take Redbone's body back home. Arkansas. I need to talk at him on the way home and then with his family. I don't think he was still married, but he had a couple of children who live with his ex."

"I understand."

"He was going to be a career soldier before he became disillusioned with Vietnam, at least that's what he told me. He expected so much more from us, believed the United States was in a unique position to do good for so many people, but . . . kept saying we were on the wrong side of every conflict in Central America." Paul paused. "A soldier at the air base near our refugee camps warned me to warn him to be careful. He didn't elaborate, just told me to tell him to be careful."

Abby could tell that Paul was both angry and hurting. She waited, wanting only to hold him, to hold him and never let him go.

SEGMENT IV
REPOSE
1985

Geneva held little sway for either Abby or Paul. They were field workers, volunteers at heart, their hearts pumping blood directly into the veins of refugees desperately in need of transfusions. Neither had slept in a tent for seven months except for the ones constructed from couch cushions and bedsheets for Moses and Sal. Paul traveled monthly to camps around the world to inspect and consult, to gather data or pass information along. Indeed, "the fix-it guy," but now, a "VIP fix-it-guy." Abby had a desk and wore dresses. She brought her work home with her to be with the boys. Moses had taken on some characteristics of his namesake, quiet and musically inclined. His papa procured an upright piano, small enough to fit into the apartment. Sal imitated his parents' adventurous persona, exploring as soon as he was able to walk.

"I miss America," said Paul one quiet evening after the kids had been put to bed. "And Mose and Sal miss their grandparents." He paused. "My mom's not doing well either."

Abby smiled, leaned into his body, and kissed his cheek. "You know, we could do all these things back in Chicago, and I'll bet Jules will still assign you a few new places to visit."

They stayed quiet for a while, nestled in each other's arms. Paul's latest assignment had been Africa, where a famine was devastating Ethiopia. In a land of desperation, the famine had hit harder and lasted longer, according to Paul and other UN experts, than it should have. A decade-long civil war and a world with problems of its own exacerbated the suffering. Once again, Paul had been expelled from the country when he publicly blamed Ethiopia's government for misleading the world about food shortages in the northern region and for implying that it was the policy of the government to starve those in the opposition. Paul's car was riddled with bullets late in the evening on December 31, prompting him to say, "Goodbye, 1984. Don't let the door hit you in the ass as you leave us." Fortunately, just one UN aid worker was injured, and it was only a flesh wound, but the message had been sent, and Paul was ordered out of the rebel-held regions of Ethiopia.

He had also returned to Gaza, spent a week in Jordan, and spoken with Palestinian leaders in southern Lebanon too. He was sitting in the back seat of another taxi when it swerved to miss a young girl on a narrow street in Beirut and crashed, but again, he was uninjured while the other passengers were. His account to Abby, who was in Paris at that time speaking to a group of Catholic aid workers, "The taxi hit a building, but I'm fine."

Abby's work had been along the lines of her Paris visit. Consulting work, conferences, sharing her expertise about refugee children and young soldiers forced to kill to survive, and writing guidelines for United Nations volunteers. She even made a trip to Bangkok to meet with Will and Camille, a follow-up to the Cambodian refugee crisis. They were busy, but Abby could take the boys with her on some of her trips. However, Abby and Paul seldom traveled together, and they missed that.

Paul finally broke the silence. "Israel is withdrawing from Lebanon."

"Not all of it, I hear. Going to keep a force in southern Lebanon as a buffer zone."

"Not a surprise. I have a meeting with Javier on Thursday," said Paul.

Abby sat up and turned her face into Paul's. "As in Javier Perez de Cuellar, the Secretary General of our employer?"

"The big cheese."

"Wow! Is he going to reprimand you or reward you?"

"I have no idea. Jules just came down to the office and told me."

Abby smiled. She kissed him. "Big shot!"

Paul shook his head. "I've never been a big shot. Just a grunt."

"Ten years of being my big shot."

∾

The Secretary General of the United Nations asked Paul to become a special envoy of the UN to Rwanda, to make himself available for special operations in the Great Lakes region of Africa. Paul turned him down, seeing the offer as becoming a policy director, a bureaucrat, and he resigned from all positions at the United Nations. He had wanted to go to Rwanda as a field worker, not as a suit-wearing official, and he knew he made the correct decision. The first children he and Abby needed to take care of were their own. Later, at the apartment in Geneva, he sat on the piano bench with Moses listening to an original composition. Magical. Abby had taken Sal to the market, fresh vegetables for a special dinner. The Garritys were going home, returning to Chicago to manage the soup kitchen, to begin that normal life they talked about so often. They would play with the kids and attend their elementary school activities. They would wake together, work together again, eat meals together, go to bed together, make love frequently with energy rather than being too tired.

After dinner, Abby showed pictures of her parents to the boys and talked about their grandparents. Moses remembered, but it was difficult to tell how much Sal did. Paul read to them as they fell asleep. Shortly afterwards, Abby called her parents to tell them to get her bedroom tidy again. Then, Paul called his parents. Finally, they called Mose and Sally to warn them, as Paul said.

"I can't believe you guys will be giving up your careers?" said Sally.

"For now, just a hiatus," answered Abby. "Instead of yelling at bureaucratic refugee directors, I can rant at political corruption in Chicago, and Paul can walk the neighborhoods on the Southside to get a sense of the housing crisis there.

"Seriously," chimed in Mose, "are you ready for a routine life?'

"We are," said Paul. "Down the road we'll get back into this. Our bosses said we could return at any time; just call. Geneva is too comfortable, too removed from the real deal. So today, it's time to put a priority on our kids. Besides, Abby's parents are ready to step back a little, but they don't want to close the kitchen, so we'll start to take that over and organize a new leadership group. There're also trials for the sanctuary people in Arizona beginning later this year that I want to follow."

"So, do they have any strawberry fields in Chicago for you?" asked Mose sarcastically.

～

In October Paul and Abby flew from Chicago to Arizona to spend a week with fellow travelers they had met a few years earlier when they were involved in getting a dozen Guatemalan dissidents to the US for asylum. The Sanctuary Trial was to begin October 23 in Phoenix, a battle pitting "The Government" against the "alien smugglers." Paul and Abby rented a car and drove into the Sonoran Desert, to the road-side town of Why where a handful of old codgers were hiding and transporting a few of the most vulnerable Central American refugees to safe cities farther north. Smitty, an MIT graduate from the Forties, and Julie, a middle-aged curmudgeon, hosted a dinner at the only bar in the town of 35 eccentrics. Seated at the table were four others with "behavioral problems."

"Do they have any chance?" asked Abby.

"Innocent until proven guilty," said Smitty. He laughed. "No, not much of one. The judge will deny any defense motions that might allow them to present information about the atrocities occurring in Central America by those right-wing military governments. Our government knows that when these refugees are deported, they are being sent back to the very same authorities who want to kill them. The case will be decided on the law, and conscience be damned."

Julie took a drink of her beer. "All of us at this table could be on trial. Maybe we all are."

Abby, remembering the trial of Patty Hearst, took a hold of Paul's forearm. "I think our government is on trial in the long run. Asylum is a human right and legal, and our country should acknowledge that fact. It's the government that's breaking the law, not the religious lead-ers leading the sanctuary movement. Why is it so easy to turn our fears onto strangers? Why do we hate the poorest and those least capable of defending themselves?" It was mostly a rhetorical question.

The table went silent for a moment. Then, a scraggly old man spoke. "Because we've turned away from God and Jesus's teachings."

Smitty patted him on the shoulder. "Well, yeah, that, and we need scapegoats for our other problems. Many in America believe these people who've walked months to get some sort of safety for their children came to steal jobs or live off welfare."

"And most believe they're all Mexicans. They don't realize that so many of these refugees are fleeing the violence in Central America," said Julie. She shook her head. "We're not protecting any Mexicans; our work is entirely aimed at Central Americans."

Again, the table went quiet, all of them wrapped up in their own thoughts about refugees and immigrants.

"How long are you staying?" asked Julie.

"Paul's planning to stay for a week of the trial, but I'll fly back on Monday. I need to be with the kids and run the soup kitchen," said Abby. She looked at her husband, whose jaw was tight. "What?"

"Just a throwback thought." Paul pointed to a map on the wall over the bar. "Alaska. What? Six times larger than Arizona. Two, three times bigger than Texas? Maybe we could transport every poor refugee up there to start new lives."

An old man in a wheelchair spoke for the first time. "Pretty sure my old friends in the last frontier wouldn't want them either."

Smitty laughed like someone who had heard a preposterous statement. "You mean every refugee in America? Every illegal? How you gonna get them there?"

Paul shook his head slowly. "No. I mean every refugee everywhere in the world. I know that's impossible, but my point is that there has to be imaginative, empathetic people in our government, in governments around the world. Refugees can't be relocated forever, and countries can't keep sheltering them." Paul paused to settle himself. 'There are lines of refugees around the world calling for a chance in life, people who've been denied all those things we take for granted. And those lines just keep getting longer. Refugees aren't criminals; they're not demons. They're just," he paused.

Abby finished his thought. "Unwanted."

The table went quiet for a few minutes, pondering thoughts each person had considered often in the past. It was Paul who finally spoke, almost as if wrapping up the conversation. "We've all looked back on our experiences and know the answers now, but we didn't see those solutions back then. We've lived through so many conflicts and seen that war serves no purpose for the farmer or the fisherman and their families. It serves only the purpose of the men in power and those who have invested money in the arms machine." Abby gently slid her hand into her husband's.

As the gathering started to break up, the scraggly codger cleared his voice and instructed the table to seat themselves again. Joining hands, the "criminals" said a prayer, which seemed to be equal parts grace, entreaty, and confession.

∾

Abby flew home on Monday morning, two days before the Sanctuary Trial was to begin. After dropping her off at the Phoenix airport, Paul drove two hours to Tucson to attend a prayer service for the defendants at a Presbyterian church. In attendance were church officials from a dozen different faiths. They spoke of The Constitution commingling with The Gospels. From there, he drove to Nogales, to the border crossing between the United States and Mexico, where he sat with a cola in the late afternoon to watch the lines of people, cars, and trucks waiting to enter America. He wondered how many of those people were legal in their movements. He wondered how many were Mexican, how many were Guatemalan, how many were from other Central American countries. He didn't know, never would, but he felt a sense of pride that some people in his country still welcomed, for the most part, desperate people even if his government did not. Seven pre-teen girls in school uniforms passed him on their way to the gate leading back into Mexico, presumably from a Catholic school in Nogales, Arizona. Two young boys ran after the uniformed girls. He missed running after his two young boys, Moses and Sal. He shivered. It was time to go home.

∾

Paul arrived at his motel in Phoenix at 8:00, 10:00 p.m. Chicago time. His boys would be asleep in bed, but Abby would be awaiting his call. He dialed, knowing she would answer the phone at her parents' home.

"Hey," she said in her soft, tender voice. "I miss you already."

"Hey back. I changed my plane reservation to Wednesday night. This trial will go on without me, but the soup kitchen needs me to make all those mashed potatoes."

"Uh-huh. What else?"

"I miss my boys. I'd hate to miss another day walking Moses to school or chasing down Sal."

"And?"

"There's this beautiful woman who has my heart, and I'd like to be with her."

"Ohhh, I think I know that woman. I don't know if she's beautiful, but she does have your heart, and she wants you next to her. So, I'll make sure she picks you up at the airport on Wednesday night."

They talked for several minutes, each asking about the other's day, each wanting more details than initially provided. Abby told Paul of her sister's desire to become more involved with the soup kitchen and of a report in the *Chicago Tribune* about the rising rate of violent crime in South Chicago, just a few blocks south of the kitchen. She suggested Paul walk these neighborhoods and set up a tent to get a true feel for the situation. They both laughed.

"Real funny, but I was thinking maybe we ought to move out of your parents' house and get a place of our own. Maybe," he drew out his words, "if we're going to be the managers of the soup kitchen for a while, we ought to live in that neighborhood and send our kids to schools in Pilsen." He waited for his wife's response, knowing she was considering the ramifications.

"A place of our own with a yard filled with roses . . . in the neighborhood where we work . . . among the people we serve. A place to walk in the evenings." Abby made a sound like a chuckle, but a warm chuckle. "Rent or own?"

"Rent probably. Your sister will eventually take over the kitchen, and we'll head off to Africa or the Middle East. It's kind of in our blood, our DNA."

Abby laughed aloud. "Speaking of heading off, Will called. He wondered, his word, if we would be interested in going to Sudan."

Paul shook his head from 1400 miles away. "No. For now, we'll tend to the lines of people outside the kitchen and to our boys. And to each other."

Abby smiled gently, hoping her husband could feel it through the wires. "Yeah," she said softly. "For now." She knew full well that there would be more tents in their future, but for now a rose bush would do.

EPILOGUE

On September 2, 1998, Swissair Flight 111, the "UN Shuttle" crashed into the Atlantic Ocean off the coast of Nova Scotia killing all 229 passengers and crew members. The flight departed New York City bound for Geneva, Switzerland. Ten of the passengers were United Nations officials, including Pierce Gerety. (See his obituary in the *New York Times*, September 4, 1998.)

Mr. Gerety's life was the inspiration for my first novel, *The Hill, '67*, which has nothing to do with refugee workers around the world, and for this book, *Refugees Among the Lines*, which has much to do with the amazing work done by refugee workers everywhere who place their own lives at risk to help the least fortunate in their desperate struggles to survive.

Pierce Gerety's wife, Marie de la Soudiere, continues to devote her life to helping the destitute and the homeless, to repatriating child soldiers, and to children on every continent who seem to have no future. She and her co-workers provide them with one.

It is in Pierce Gerety's memory and to Marie de la Soudiere and to the UNHCR agency, Refugees International, the IRC, the CRS, to No More Deaths, and other refugee organizations and volunteers that this book is dedicated, humbly and with great admiration. These people are the true bridge builders.

Roger

The End